Thomas Pelham Dale, Helen Pelham Dale

The Life and Letters of Thomas Pelham Dale

Vol. I.

Thomas Pelham Dale, Helen Pelham Dale

The Life and Letters of Thomas Pelham Dale
Vol. I.

ISBN/EAN: 9783337020538

Printed in Europe, USA, Canada, Australia, Japan

Cover: Foto ©Raphael Reischuk / pixelio.de

More available books at **www.hansebooks.com**

THE LIFE AND LETTERS

OF

THOMAS PELHAM DALE.

VOL. I.

THE LIFE AND LETTERS

OF

THOMAS PELHAM DALE

SOMETIME RECTOR OF ST. VEDAST'S
FOSTER LANE, CITY, LONDON

EDITED BY HIS DAUGHTER

HELEN PELHAM DALE

WITH PORTRAITS, COLOURED PLATES FROM MR. DALE'S SKETCHES

FACSIMILES OF LETTERS FROM JOHN WESLEY

AND OTHER ILLUSTRATIONS

IN TWO VOLUMES

VOLUME I.

LONDON

GEORGE ALLEN, 156, CHARING CROSS ROAD

AND SUNNYSIDE, ORPINGTON

1894

CONTENTS.

LIST OF ILLUSTRATIONS.

LIFE AND LETTERS

OF

THOMAS PELHAM DALE.

CHAPTER I.

THE DALE FAMILY, AND JOHN WESLEY'S LETTERS TO MISS PEGGY.

LIKE all histories, that of ecclesiastical reform repeats itself. There is a constant ebbing and flowing of fervour and belief. A great truth, which yet is but a part of the whole, takes firm hold of some earnest mind, and is explained and dwelt upon with two results—the bitter enmity of those who cannot and those who will not receive it, and the exclusive devotion of those who accept the revelation and close their eyes to all else. So a fresh wave of thought, consequent often on the other, rises in its turn with more or less strength, according to its own purity and the purity of those it carries with it, "if it be of God or if it be of man." In one sense the world never grows older. Gamaliel's advice is repeated and neglected generation after generation. The descendants of a persecuted sect read their call to persecute in their time of power as clearly as any fanatic of old, or—equally dangerous opponent—as those who found it expedient for the preservation of their personal welfare.

To simplify matters which time has somewhat entangled, we are apt to accept only our own martyrs, and to refuse to acknowledge that those others had more than their deserts.

And yet in our hearts we know that they suffered and died with the same elation, the same support, as those we reverence.

And herein lies the strength of the English Church, that she can acknowledge her errors of government and the weakness of her humanity even while she claims that her mission is divine and her gifts those of the Holy Spirit.

Cruel and shortsighted as the interpretations of her rulers have often been, they are not final, they are confessed as errors, not admired as virtues: they are the earthly stains on her heavenly robe, that may be washed by repentance and atonement. They are, in short, interpretations, more or less faulty, that may conceal but cannot destroy the divinity of her life.

It is in this breadth and tolerance that her strength lies —in that power of accepting the good and refusing the evil, of atoning in her hours of calmness for the errors of her moments of agitation. But the constant confession that her dogmas are divine and her actions human, while it gives her the power of clinging to the one and reforming the other, does not ensure future perfection of action, and what has happened may happen again with the same consolation, that no wrong is irretrievable.

It was the intention of this work, as originally planned, to trace the effect of the waves of thought that broke the stagnation of religious life during this last century, to prove that the eighteenth-century revivalists gave birth to evangelicalism, and that ritualism is the logical outcome of evangelical training. But, alas! the scholar's mind and pen are gone from the partnership of the proposed work, and only the collection of facts are left to be recounted. That being the case, the value of the work no longer lies in the definition and origin of the various phases of thought, but in the truthful picture of the thinker, in his own life and its influence on others. It was the intention of Mr. Pelham Dale to trace this thought from

his early training and his father's life to his own opinions
on Church doctrine. The present writer was to tell the
facts, to "nothing extenuate or aught set down in malice."
To explain or teach was beyond her capabilities. Now
left to herself, she offers only the simple story of honest
conviction, and a picture which, if it is unintentionally
coloured by affection, is faithful in all its outlines, of a
priest of the English Church who suffered abuse and imprisonment rather than sin against his conscience. The
form of the book is retained, but the lesson must be drawn
by the reader; the writer has neither the largeness of heart
nor the experience of life to enable her to appreciate views
she does not entertain, and is moreover blinded to the
possible virtues of the persecutors by her devotion to the
persecuted.

But of one thing the reader may be assured: there is
no important fact stated in the following pages that cannot
be proved, and no personal imputation made on any one.
As far as possible, actions shall speak for themselves without
comment or possibly unjust interpretation.

The history of the controversy that led to the passing of
the Public Worship Regulation Act, if told in its fulness,
must, of course, include what is called "The Oxford Movement." But that has been already related fully and power-
fully either by the pens or in the biographies of the leaders
of that movement. This, as a personal history, is an
appendix to that; it shows many of the same characteristics
—the active hatred on the one side, the passive suffering
on the other. But it is but a personal history, a part of the
whole; and the whole, the history of religious life, will go
on so long as the world lasts, in the same constant movement, with, God be thanked, the same consolatory conclusion—the triumph of faith, and the deep gratitude of those
souls who, through their leader, have found a light in the
darkness.

It has been the fashion of late years to talk very learnedly about heredity. But the world has lasted some time, and every generation must be a greater mixture of traits and characteristics than the former (though even Cain and Abel, with their limited ancestry, were sufficiently dissimilar in character), and the difficulty of tracing this or that gift or virtue becomes more complicated. The Dales came from Northumberland; the elder branch of the family still remains there. Only one or two rose above the level of local distinction and obtained a wider fame. One was Peter Dale, a celebrated borderer and cattle-lifter, who is alluded to in Sir Walter Scott's "Rokeby." Then, later on, Dr. Dale, an ambassador in the reign of Queen Elizabeth, who was constantly in hot water with regard to the mismanagement of her Majesty's matrimonial affairs. In the reign of Queen Anne, Captain Dale, serving under Lord Rodney, was knighted after a naval engagement. He carried off his wife from a convent in Spain or Portugal, and was married to her on board his own ship and in presence of his crew. Report says that Dame Judith was very proud of her title, and out-dressed the ladies of her husband's family on the strength of it.

In all these stories one finds nothing to stamp the race with any particular characteristic, certainly no religious one. It might be the old borderer's instinct prompted the sailor to carry off his bride, but the descent is not necessary to the action. William Dale came to London somewhere about 1780, but all the descriptions of his actions and his movements are very shadowy. Of himself there is an excellent portrait, as far as painting goes; of the likeness no one can say. He was a clever man; he mixed with the artistic and literary society of the day; but he was a Bohemian, a rolling stone, unstable; in brief, a scamp, especially from a domestic point of view. He took life cheerfully and his responsibilities lightly, and, as is usual in such cases, he caused a good deal of trouble to inoffensive people. He married and was left a widower with four young children. Then he sailed for the West Indies, and was heard of no more. He went to found a newspaper and make a fortune, and for his family the rest of his history is a blank. In those days the world was so much larger, and there was more room to escape from one's responsibilities.

It is this that makes all that is known of him so indefinite. His wife's mother, with whom the children were left, was naturally not fond of him, more especially when he repudiated his responsibilities so effectually. The children could not remember him, and were not told about him. There was a silence and cloud about his memory. They knew his portrait, with its humorous, satirical expression, not a favourite humour with children. That and pastel portraits of two of the children, Thomas and Anne, and a packet of letters, were all that he left them. The letters convey a description of a very different character from his own. They had belonged to Miss Peggy Dale, or, as she was the eldest of three sisters, Miss Dale, according to the direction of the letters. She and Molly and Ann lived near Newcastle, under the guardianship of Miss Lewen, probably their aunt. There, at Newcastle, they heard John Wesley preach, and Miss Lewen was evidently anxious to bring the girls under his influence. So in 1765 Peggy sought an interview and told him all her temptations and trials, all her faults and failings, and the correspondence between Wesley and her began. He wrote every month when they did not meet to her and to Miss Lewen, and, later on, to Molly.

To a history such as this the letters of the great revivalist preacher add an additional interest. They were written more than a hundred years ago, when the world in many respects was a very different world from this that we are in

in 1893; before railways had scarred it or telegraph wires
encircled it, when a light was struck with flint and steel,
and the glare of gas was unknown. It was not a pleasanter
world for every one. The list of convictions and punish-
ments in a newspaper of that date are simply horrible in
their curtness and severity. Here are a few, taken at ran-
dom from a paper of rather later date. For stealing four
pairs of shoes and a pair of boots, one John Cochrane was
tried, and, after an account of the witness and circumstances,
the paragraph finishes—Guilty, Death. The whole column,
which includes an account of an outhouse set on fire by a
girl of fifteen, a man stealing five pints of cider, and another
a £5 note, ends with the same curt intimation. Crime
was never more rampant, society never more lax. But for
Peggy Dale, in her quiet home, all this roughness and
wickedness were outside her knowledge. Her life, in its
peace and simplicity, was evidently a pleasant subject of
contemplation to John Wesley.

He was at this date, 1765, sixty-two years old. He had
lived a hard life—austerity and self-denial at college, missionary work in the American colonies, travels abroad and
at home, and then a long ministry of preaching from place
to place, and ruling those numerous converts that followed
his teaching. His religion was full of excitement; there
were strange conversions, wrestlings with Satan, trances,
and cries. Yet in spite of all this, and of the fact that
twice he had considered himself on the point of death,
there were still years of vitality and work before him. He
died in 1791, in his eighty-eighth year. He had been
married, but his wife had not yet left him. According
to Southey, she suffered agonies of jealousy over letters
written by him to women. She had torn out his hair in
these paroxysms, and finally carried off some of his papers
and letters, and left him, never to return. He did not ask
her to do so, and wrote his letters in peace for the future.

Anne Pate

Sister of Thomas Pate

Castlebarn
June 1. 1765

My Dear Miss Peggy

Certainly you not only need not sin,
but you need not doubt any more. Christ is yours:
All is yours. You can give Him all your Heart. And
will he not freely give you all things? But you can only
retain what He has given, by continually receiving
more. You have reason to bless Him who has cast ÿ
lot in a fair ground. Even in this world, He does not
withhold from you any manner of thing ÿ is
good. Let ÿ Heart be always open, to receive
his whole Blessing!

How far do you find Power over your Thoughts?
Does not your Imagination sometimes wander? Do
those Imaginations continue for any time? Or have
you power to check them immediately? Do
you find continually the Spirit of Prayer? And are you
always happy? I trust, you will be happier every
day: And that you will not forget.

My Dear Sister
Your Affectionate Brother
J Wesley—

The letters in this packet have been very carefully preserved, and are numbered, but of the original thirty there
are but fourteen. Probably they have been given away to
some of the many admirers of the great preacher. William
Dale would no doubt have parted with them cheerfully
enough, unless he had any great affection for Peggy's
memory. But if she did not outlive twenty-three, he could
have known little or nothing of her except by hearsay.

The first letter of all is missing. The packet begins with
number two, but this is so much more formal than those
that follow, that the first was probably even stiffer, and
began "Dear Madam," a commencement that in one of the
letters has been scratched out and altered to "Dear Peggy."
It is directed to Miss Dale, at the Orphanage, Newcastle-
upon-Tyne. The Orphanage was a centre for the meetings
of Wesley's followers, and they called here for his letters,
or received them when they came together.

The postmark of the letter is Castlebar. It is written in
a clear, delicate handwriting. The spelling and punctuation
of the original are preserved.

PORTPATRICK, *June 1st*, 1765.

MY DEAR MISS PEGGY,—Certainly you not only
need not sin, but you need not doubt any more. Christ
is Yours: All is Yours. You can give Him all your
Heart: and will he not freely give you all things? But
you can only retain what He has given, by continually
receiving more. You have reason to bless Him who
has cast y^r lot in a fair ground. Even in this world,
He does not withhold from you any manner of thing
y^t is good. Let y^r Heart be always open, to receive
his whole Blessing!

How far do you find Power over your Thoughts?
Does not your Imagination sometimes wander? Do

those Imaginations continue for any time? And have
you power to check them immediately? Do you continually find the Spirit of Prayer? And are you always
happy? I trust you will be happier every day: and
that you will not forget, my Dear Sister, your Affectionate Brother   J. WESLEY.

This method of asking questions respecting the soul's
health was a very favourite one. Peggy evidently answered
them with much careful consideration, and found she was
guilty of Wandering Thoughts. She is more comforted
and exhorted than rebuked; indeed, Peggy's confessions
are never treated with sternness. She is more praised than
could have been quite wholesome for that Simplicity of
Heart mentioned by her guide. She must have been pretty,
with a fair youthful prettiness that accentuated her simplicity and sweetness; a plain and awkward girl is not
praised for the same virtues as a pretty one, and Wesley
was at an age when her gentle innocent fairness would most
appeal to his own wayworn experience.

He alludes often to the perfection of her lot, which gave
her no worldly anxieties, but, thanks perhaps to Miss Lewen's
care, offered no temptations of gaiety or wealth.

July 5th, 1765, Wesley was still in Ireland, a tempestuous
mission.

Number three is written from Kilkenny.

MY DEAR SISTER,—Altho it is certain the kind of
Wandering Thoughts wch you mention, are consistent
wth pure Love, yet it is highly desirable to be delivered
from y^{m}, because (as you observe) they hinder profitable Thoughts. And why shou'd not you be delivered?
Indeed in what manner this will be done we do not

know. Sometimes it pleases our Lord to work a great Deliverance, even of this kind, in a moment. Sometimes he gives the Victory by degrees. And I believe this is more common. Expect this & every Good Gift from Him. How wise & gracious are all his Ways!

Do you commonly find in yourself the Witness That you are saved from Sin? And is it usually clear? Or do you frequently lose it? I do not know, why you sh^d ever lose any Good Gift. For is not He the same yesterday, to-day & for ever? And yet you have known but a little of Him. You are to sink a thousand times deeper into Him:

> "That Sea of Light & Love unknown,
> Without a Bottom or a Shore."

I hope Miss Lewen & you speak to each other, not only without Disguise but without Reserve. How is your lot cast in a fair ground! How well are you situated, for making the best of a short Life?

> "Secluded from the World & all its Care,
> Hast Thou to joy or grieve, to hope or fear?"

That is with regard to present things? No: GOD has given you a nobler Portion. You have nothing to care for, but how you may most entirely and effectually present yourself a living Sacrifice to GOD.

When I reflect upon your Earnest Desire to do this, & upon your Simplicity of Heart, it gives an unspeakable pleasure to, my Dear Sister, your affectionate Brother   J. WESLEY.

I expect to be at Dublin till the End of this Month. I send Miss Lewen's Letter by Portpatrick to try, wch comes soonest.

The next two letters—numbers four and five—are missing, and number six is dated from London, November 6th, 1765.

Probably Wesley has been to Newcastle since his return to England, as there is a month in which there has been no letter. The letter also is freer and more intimate. He knows Peggy better, and has been told of her conviction that she will not live beyond three-and-twenty. There was probably some delicacy of constitution in Peggy and her sisters, for one of them, Ann, died the next year. It is very evident that Wesley has a belief in the fulfilment of her conviction that adds to his tender regard for the girl.

MY DEAR SISTER,—By our intercourse with a beloved Friend, it often pleases GOD to enlighten our understanding. But this is only the second point : To warm the Heart is a greater Blessing than Light itself. And this effect I frequently find from your Letters. The Lord repay it sevenfold into your own bosom ! Do you still remain in the persuasion, That you shall not live beyond Three and twenty ? Do you remember, when or how it began ? Does it continue the same, whether your Health is worse or better ? What a mercy is it, that Death has lost it's sting ! Will this hinder any real or substantial Happiness ? Will it prevent our loving one another ?

> Can Death's interposing tide
> Spirits one in Christ Divide?

Surely no! Whatever comes from Him is eternal as Himself. My Dear Sister, Adieu.

In her answer Peggy evidently asserted the strength of her conviction, for the subject is continued in the next letter.

This letter has been sealed and enclosed in another; it has only the date for its heading, December 31st.

MY DEAR PEGGY,—Whether that persuasion was
from nature or from GOD, a little time will shew. It
will be matter of great Joy to me, if GOD gives you
many years, to glorify Him in y^r Body, before He
removes you to ye World of Spirits. The comfort
is, that Life or Death, all is Yours, seeing *You* are
Christ's : All is good, All is Blessing ! You have only
to rest upon Him, with the whole weight of your soul.

Temptations to Pride you may have, or to anything :
But these do not sully y^r soul. Amidst a thousand
Temptations you may retain unspotted Purity. Abide
in Him by simple Faith, this moment ! Live, walk in
Love ! The Lord increase it in you a thousand fold !
Take out of his Fulness, grace upon grace. Tell me
from time (to time ?) just what you feel. I cannot tell
you, how tenderly I am, my Dear Sister, your affectionate Brother,   J. WESLEY.

Letter number eight is missing, and number nine is not
written until April 1766 from Manchester. They have
probably met in the interval. Meanwhile, Peggy has been
confronted with some of the puzzles of life, and faith has
for a moment failed her. In answer to this confession of
hers Wesley writes in a strain of loving exhortation.

MY DEAR PEGGY,—I perceived, that about the time
when you wrote before, your treadings had well-nigh
slipped. You was within a little of casting away your
confidence, & giving up what GOD had wrought. But
his eye pitied you & his hand held you up, & set your
feet again upon the rock. Now, my Dear Maid, abide
simple before GOD ! And if the thought comes, (as it
may do a thousand times) "*How* do you *reconcile* this

or this with pure Love?" Do not *reason* but look unto
Jesus: And tell him earnestly, & without delay, "Thou
shalt answer for me, O Lord, my GOD!" Continue to
love & pray for, my Dear Sister, your affectionate
Brother   J. WESLEY.

The next two letters are lost, but it would seem that
some restlessness and dissatisfaction had been roused and
was not easily allayed. She began to long for a fuller life,
a fresh interchange of thought; she wished, and it was a
natural wish for a girl under any circumstances, to see
something of the world outside that home that Wesley
thought the perfection of peace and comfort. But the
letter numbered twelve is a curious revelation of his feelings
towards her. It is incoherent and agitated. The thought
of this lamb of his flock being sullied by contact with the
world is inexpressibly painful to him. That she should fall
under another influence than his he dreads also. The
letter is undated, and runs as follows:—

MY DEAR PEGGY,—Is *our* intercourse drawing towards a period? Let it be so, if that be best for *you*.
But I have another doubt: I am afraid, if you go to
Laton-Stone you will give up Perfection: I mean by
placing it so high, as I fear none will ev^r attain. I
know *not one* in London, that has largely conversed
with Sally Ryan, who has not given it up, that is, with
regard to their own Experience. Now this, I think,
wou'd do you no good at all. Nay, I judge, it wou'd
do you much hurt: it would be a substantial Loss.
But I do not see how you *cou'd* possibly avoid that
loss, without a free Intercourse with me, both in
Writing & Speaking. Otherwise I know and feel, I

My Dear Peggy

Is our intercourse drawing toward
a period? Let it be so, if that be best for you. But
I have another doubt: I am afraid, if you go to
Eaton Stone, you will give up Perfection: I mean,
by placing it so high, as I fear none will i'll attain.
I know not one in London, that has largely conversed with Sally Ryan, who has not given it
up, that is, with regard to their own experience.
Now this, I think, would do you no good at all. Nay,
I judge, it would do you much hurt: it would be
a substantial loss. But I do not see, how you can
possibly avoid that loss, without a free Intercourse
with me, both in Writing & Speaking. Otherwise
I know & feel, I can give you up, tho' you are
exceeding near & dear to me. But if you was to
be moved from your Stedfastness, that w'd give
me pain indeed.   You will write immediately
to, My Dear Peggy,
                 Your Affectionate Brother
                          J Wesley

can give you up, tho you are exceeding near & dear to
me. But if you was to be moved from your Stedfastness that w^d give me pain indeed. You will write
immediately to, my Dear Peggy, your Affectionate
Brother   J. WESLEY.

The Sally Ryan mentioned in this letter was at one time
housekeeper to the school at Kingswood. It was of her
that Mrs. Wesley was so jealous. A note in Southey's
"Life of Wesley" says of Mrs. Ryan: "Her account of
herself, which is printed in the second volume of the
Arminian Magazine, is highly enthusiastic, and shows her
to have been a woman of heated fancy and strong natural
talents. It appears, however, incidentally in Wesley's letter,
that though she professed to have a 'direct witness' of
being saved from sin, she afterwards 'fell from that salvation.' And in another place he notices her 'littleness of
understanding.'"

The next two letters are missing, but it is evident that
Peggy submitted her judgment to John Wesley's, and stayed
at home. How much influence Ann Dale's illness and
death may have had on her decision we cannot tell. Number fifteen is dated London, November 7th, 1766.

MY DEAR PEGGY,—How happy it is to sit loose to
all below! Just now I find a paper on wch is wrote
(in Miss Lewen's hand) " March 24. 1762. Margaret
Dale, Ann Dale, Margaret Lewen wonder in what
state of Life they will be in the year 1766." How
little did any of you think at that time That She wou'd
then be in Eternity! But She now wonders at nothing,
& grieves at nothing:

> Extinct is the Animal Flame,
> And Passion is vanishd away!

You say " Do not forget me till that time!" I think
there is no Danger. I remember your Determination
to be all for GOD: Your childlike Confidence in Him:
Your Tenderness to your Friends: Your honest, artless Simplicity! O give all the Glory to Him, for
every gracious Thought or Word, that brings you
nearer Heaven! A few days remain for you & me:
Let us husband them to the uttermost. I long for you
to burn with the flame of the Seraphim, to love wth
Love like theirs! O press forward! Wrestle & fight
& pray!

And sure neither Life nor Death shall separate you
from, my Dear Sister, your Affectionate Brother

                                    J. WESLEY.

The great difference of age between them—he was sixty-
four—would, from the wording of the letter, show that Peggy
clung to her conviction that she would not live beyond
twenty-three. The death of her sister probably strengthened
this belief, which Wesley seems to have adopted. This
halo of an early death doubtless increased the impression
of childlike innocence that she made upon him. The
poetical quotations in this and other letters seem deficient
in poetical feeling, but no doubt they are from hymns much
in use among the Methodists of the period—the one quoted
for a second time in the next letter may still be found in
old-fashioned Church hymn-books.

Peggy had accepted her affliction with gentle submissive-
ness. She would say, "Thy will be done," but yet had
a certain shrinking from the pain and sorrow which Ann
and she had suffered. Wesley answers her thus in his
sixteenth letter, Dec. 19th, 1766.

My Dear Peggy,—Indeed it is an unspeakable
Blessing to be convinced, That GOD does all things
well! But what wonder is it, that such poor, shortsighted Creatures as we are, cannot *explain* the Reasons
of his acting? Many times these are among y\ᵉ Secrets
of his Government, wch we shall not understand, till
Death opens our eyes. O What a Scene will then be
unfolded, when we shall *see*, what we now *believe?*
Do you find Faith's abiding impression, realizing things
to come? Do you feel no Decay of Love? Is the eye
of your Soul always fixt, & always unclouded?
And yet what a Depth of Blessing remains for you?
It is indeed

> "A Sea of Life and Love unknown
> Without a Bottom or a Shore!"

It comforts me to think, that you are sinking deeper
& deeper into this, & receiving more & more of Him
that loves you. I hope you are not weary of visiting
the poor & sick. Abound more & more in yᵉ work
of the Lord! And still love and pray for, my Dear
Sister, your Affectionate Brother,   J. Wesley.

Wesley went to Ireland, and Peggy followed the in-
junctions given her in his letter, and worked and visited
among the poor and those "converted" persons who met
together at the Orphanage. Again a letter is missing. On
March 29th, 1767, he writes from Portpatrick. As that
makes a month without a letter, he had probably visited
Newcastle before his departure for Ireland.

My Dear Peggy,—Those you mention are Israel-
ites indeed, to whom you will do well to speak with all

freedom. A few more in Newcastle are of the same spirit: Altho they are but few in whom y⁰ Gold is free from dross. I wish you c⁴ help poor Molly Stralliger. I am often afraid for her lest she sh⁴ be ignorant of Satan's Devices, & lose all that GOD had wrought in her. Do you still find a Witness in yourself, That GOD has purified your heart from Sin? Do you never feel any return of Pride, or Anger, or Self-will, or foolish Desire? Do you stiddily endure, seeing Him that is invisible? Are you always sensible of his loving Presence? Are you constantly happy in Him? Does He keep you sleeping & waking, and make your very Dreams devout? O stand fast in glorious Liberty! And be sure to remember daily, my Dear Sister, your Affectionate Brother,   J. WESLEY.

As usual, Peggy examined herself carefully in answer to these questions, and found herself guilty of anger. She related the sin and the occasion of it in all penitence, so that in return she is comforted rather than rebuked. Wesley writes from Castlebar, May 17th, 1767:—

MY DEAR SISTER,—Concerning that Displeasure one may doubt, whether it was any other than the Concern you ought to have felt on the occasion: Or at least, whether it was any more than Temptation to Sin? But if it was, what w⁴ it prove? Not that y⁴ Heart *had not been* cleansed, but that being off your guard, you suffer'd a degree of Evil to re-enter. Was it so? Then (if it be not done already) the Lord cleanse you from it this moment! Woman, Be it unto thee even as thou wilt! Believe & feel the Blessing! Certainly the more vigorously you follow after Him

the clearer will that Unction be, without wch it is
not possible on some occasions to distinguish between
Temptation & Sins. But you take yᵉ right way:
Without perplexing your mind about anything else.
Now give yourself up to GOD. This is all you have
to do. And even while you are doing it, Light will
Spring up. I feel it does me Good to converse with
you even at a distance: O never diminish either your
Love or your Prayers for, my Dear Peggy, your
Affectionate Brother   J. WESLEY.

This letter is certainly the most priestly in tone of any
in the packet. He wrote to her once again before he
returned to England—a letter that is missing—and then
they met once more at Newcastle. It must have been
a subject of great rejoicing and excitement when the
leader of the party was known to be coming amongst
them. Newcastle was the first place he had preached at
in the North of England when he began his revivalist
mission. He had there crowds larger and more excitable
than in any other place, but he wrote, "The grace of God
flows here with a wider stream than it did at first, either
in Bristol or Kingswood: but it does not sink so deep
as it did then." Of this other visit many years afterwards he writes thus to Peggy from Witney, August 27,
1765:—

MY DEAR PEGGY,—I thought it was hardly possible
for me to love you better than I did before I came last
to Newcastle. But your artless, simple, undisguised
Affection, exceedingly increased mine. At the same
time it increased my Confidence in you, so that I feel
you are unspeakably near & dear to me. O what a

Cordial is this, wch is given to quicken us in our way! Surely

> An Earnest of our great Reward
> On Earth our Master pays!

We have all reason, to give ourselves up to Him without reserve, & to glorify Him with our Bodies and with our Spirits!

If you cleave to Him with simplicity of heart, certainly you need not feel Sin any more. Indeed you will feel Temptations of various kinds & sometimes closing you in on every side. But still your soul may stand fast, believing on the Lord. By Faith you will overcome—All! "Believe, while saved from sin's remains! Believe yourself to Heaven." I am, my Dear Peggy, your Affectionate Brother

> J. WESLEY.

Dont forget what you have learnt in Music.

This letter seems to give us a peep into Wesley's mind and memories. We can imagine him wearied with travelling, worn with the tension of those excited crowds that, whether hostile or whether falling with cries and shouts in those throes that were a sign of conversion, kept him in a responsive excitement; we can imagine him, no longer young, coming back to the restful home at Newcastle. How peaceful and innocent must the life and faces of Peggy and Molly Dale with Miss Lewen have looked as they surrounded him with tender care and admiring attention, hanging on his words with that whole-hearted adoration that fires none but these simple women. His words are complete, final, to them. They listen to him with reverence and awe and affection, and he can lean back and call smiles to their faces by his playful tenderness, or see

their solemn sympathetic glances as he tells them of the
"experiences" of the sinners he has convinced. Their
little troubles and temptations are listened to and advised
upon; and then, perhaps, Peggy showed what she had
learnt in music, and blushed at his praises.

Wesley was always inclined to be jealous for the supremacy of his influence. The next letter he wrote, dated
from Bristol on September 29, 1767, does not give
Mr. Whitefield such unqualified praise as it might have
done had he been anxious to recommend him to Peggy.
But doubtless the constant disputes and threatened divi-
sions between the Wesleys and Whitefield had left a lasting
soreness between them. All such religious revivals, de-
pending upon appeals to emotion and excitement, become
too personal to allow of confidence and unity among the
preachers, and these letters show plainly enough the thirst
of influence and power it aroused in the minds of the
leaders. They needed for unity a more definite dogma
and doctrine than were ever insisted upon by either Wesley
or Whitefield. Lady Maxwell, mentioned in the following
letter, had provided the money for the building of the school
at Kingswood in 1748. Wesley's theories for the management of the school proved very disastrous, and in 1766 he
handed the institution over to trustees. It was many years
after this first gift that she formally joined the Methodists.
She lived to be the oldest member of the Society. Whether
she would have allowed a mere girl like Peggy Dale to speak
to her in such a way as would break down her natural and
habitual shyness is doubtful. Probably Wesley reckoned
on her being equally impressed with himself by Peggy's
purity and innocence.

MY DEAR PEGGY,—I hope Mr Whitefield was an
instrum^t of Good at Newcastle & a means of stirring
up Some. He is very affectionate, & very lively & his

word seldom falls to the ground: tho he does not frequently speak of the deep things of GOD, or the Height
of yᵉ Promises.

But you say not one word of Lady Maxwell? Did
she call at Newcastle going & coming? Did you converse with her alone? And did she break thro' her
Natural & habitual Shyness? How did you find her?
Seeking Heavenly things alone, & all athirst for
GOD? It will be a miracle of miracles if she stands,
considering the thousand snares that surround her.

I have much satisfaction when I consider, in how
different a situation you & my Dear Molly Dale are.
You have every outward Advantage for Holiness wch.
an indulgent Providence can give. And what is happier
still, you have a fixt Determination to use all those
Advantages to the uttermost. Let your Eye be steddily
fixt on the Mark! To be all-Love! All-devoted! To
have One Desire, One Work, One Happiness, One
Christ reigning alone, & filling you with his Fulness!
I am, my Dear Sister, your Affectionate Brother
                                J. WESLEY.

Of the remaining four letters two are only copies—one
bearing the endorsement of the fact that the original had
been given away by Canon Dale. One has been in a cover
which is lost, and with it its number. So though, thanks to
Wesley's invariable habit of dating his letters, they can be
put in the order in which they came, there is no trace of
the number of letters between each one. Only the last but
one, marked 29, shows that the correspondence had slackened, since only seven letters had passed between September
1767 to May 1769. According to the commencement of
the letter of April 1, 1768, this falling off was due to Peggy,

since he claims that he answers every letter within a day or two. But very probably Molly's letters would supply those missing months. This packet contains only a portion of Peggy's. In April he writes from Liverpool :—

MY DEAR PEGGY,—I do not understand what Letter you mean. I have answer'd (if I do not forget) every letter, which I have receiv'd, and I commonly answer either of you, within a day or two. In this respect, I do not love to remain in your debt. In others I must always be so, for I can never pay you the Affection I owe. Accept of what little I have to give.

Mr Law does well to insist so much on those sister graces, Lowliness, Meekness and Resignation. These one would most importunately ask of GOD: and indeed without them Love is only a name. Let your faith thus work by Love and it will make you fruitful in every good Temper & every word & work.

I hope to be at Glasgow on Wednesday the 19th instant, at Aberdeen ye 28th, at Edinburgh May 5th at Newcastle on Friday May 20th.

Peace be with your Spirit! I am, My Dear Peggy, your affectionate Brother   J. WESLEY.

The reference here is to Law's "Serious Call." William Law was one of Wesley's early teachers, and he was always an admirer of his works, though he attacked Mr. Law for some of his beliefs—an attack that was most temperately and gently answered.

On May 20th they met once again ; but Peggy is troubled with doubts of her sanctification—a term which Wesley defines and explains—probably the noisy conversion and violent throes of her fellow-sinners, made her begin to doubt if her experience was in any way similar to theirs. And this doubt continues to trouble her. The keen edge of her excitement had perhaps worn off, and she was alarmed at her supposed indifference. Not even religious emotion can be kept at fever heat always, and unless the flame of devotion be calm and peaceful it cannot burn steadily. In answer to her doubts and troubles Wesley writes as follows, on June 30th, 1768 :—

MY DEAR PEGGY,—It is a certain truth That the witness of sanctification is a Privilege wch every one that is sanctified *may claim*. Yet it is not true That everyone that is sanctified does enjoy this. Many who are really sanctified (that is *wholly devoted* to GOD) do not enjoy it as soon as that work is wrought, and many who received it do not retain it or at least not constantly. Indeed they cannot retain it in two Cases : Either if they do not continue steddily watching unto prayer, Or secondly if they give way to reasoning, if they let go any part of Love's Divine Simplicity. I am afraid this was *your* case, you did not remain Simple, you gave way to evil reasoning. But you *was* as surely sanctified as you was justified and how soon may you be so again ? The way, the new & living way is Open ! Believe & enter it ! I am, my Dear Peggy, your Affectionate Brother   J. WESLEY.

The next letter is nearly a year later. Apparently Molly's marriage was the trial Peggy had to endure. The sisters had given up the world and devoted themselves to good works, and Molly fell away—into matrimony. Peggy, who had been firmer, felt her sister's defection with perhaps an undercurrent of regret that she had always been so firm since she was now left alone. Wesley had, with one exception, or rather two, always preached the superiority of a single state, and now a bitter experience served to confirm his opinions. The two exceptions had been when he first thought of marriage for himself, an affair in which Charles Wesley interfered, with the result that the match was broken off, and his second and successful attempt, ending in his marriage with Mrs. Vizelle. He had formerly published a treatise in recommendation of celibacy, entitled, "Thoughts on a Single Life"—a fact that put him in an awkward position when he contemplated matrimony. Southey tells us " He thought it expedient to meet the single men of the Society in London, and show them ' on how many accounts it was good for those who had received that gift from God *to remain single for the kingdom of heaven's sake*, unless when a particular case might be an exception to the general rule !' To those who properly respected Mr. Wesley this must have been a painful scene : to his blind admirers, no doubt, comic as the situation was, it was an edifying one."

Two years after this letter he separated from his wife for ever, and, as he was suffering from her suspicion and jealousy, he was firmly convinced of the superiority of the single state. His jealousy of any stronger influence than his own added to the conviction. He writes, May 20, 1769 :—

The hearing from my Dear Peggy at this critical time gives me a particular satisfaction. I wanted to know, How you bore such a trial, a wound in the tenderest part. You have now a first proof, that the GOD whom you serve, is able to deliver you in every trial. You feel & yet conquer. We conquer all when we can say, " Not as I will but as thou wilt." I hope you are delivered not only from *repining* with regard to

Her but from *reasoning* with regard to yourself. You
still see the more excellent way, & are sensible of the
Advantages you enjoy. I allow *some* single women
have fewer Advantages for Eternity than they might
have in a married State. But, blessed be GOD, you
have all the Advantages weh one can well conceive.
You have affectionate, wise & pious Friends, deeply
experienced in the way of GOD. You have leisure &
opportunity for every Good Work & for Improvement
in all Holiness. O may you improve every advantage
to the uttermost! And give more and more comfort
to, my Dear Peggy, your ever Affectionate Brother

J. WESLEY.

The last letter in the packet shows us Peggy returned to
her work and prayer meetings, and reproaching herself that
she does not speak or pray with sufficient boldness. There
is no more question of doubt or reason, only a desire for
service, and Wesley encourages her to persevere. He has
had always a high opinion of Peggy's influence with others.
He writes from London, November 17, 1769 :—

MY DEAR SISTER,—If any man Lack Wisdom, let
him ask of GOD, who giveth to all men liberally &
upbraideth not. That particular Branch of Wisdom,
Readiness of Thought, He is as willing to give as
any other: Yea & ready Utterance whenever it will
be for his Glory, & the furtherance of his Kingdom.
And if you want more Courage & Boldness in his
Cause make your requests known to Him with thanksgiving. Perhaps He will first answer you, by giving
you a deeper Sense of Want, with an increase of
Desire & Resignation together. And afterwards you

shall have the petition wch you asked of him. But there is one Rule wch our Lord constantly observes, "Unto Him that hath shall be given." "Unto Him that *uses* what he hath:" Speak therefore as you can: & by & by you shall speak as you wou'd. Speak tho' with Fear: And in a little time you shall speak without Fear. Fear shall be swallowed up in Love! I am, my Dear Peggy, your Affectionate Brother

J. WESLEY.

The rest of Peggy's history is a blank. If she outlived her twenty-third year it was by very little, since it is evident that she would not have parted with these letters in her lifetime, especially to any one so religiously unsympathetic as William Dale must have been. Probably he had them from his father, her brother, not from her. But as has been explained, except that the name of William's father was Thomas, and that he was a younger son of the family in Northumberland, no particulars were known to William's son. During his childhood he was both ignorant of, and indifferent to his father's family. His love was given to his grandmother, who cared for him with a very tender affection. But when he became a man and attracted attention to himself by his talents, his kinsman in the north wrote to him and identified the relationship. They exchanged visits, and Mr. Dale resumed his family crest—a swan, with the motto *Meliora Sequor*, and he regained the position his father had flung away.

So Peggy Dale's strong Methodistical belief had very little influence on her great nephew, but the belief itself, having revived a certain similarity of tone in a body of Churchmen, certainly was the foundation of evangelicalism ; and to this party Mr. Dale belonged, but through the teaching and influence of his home life, to which his

father's family contributed nothing. These letters, however, give us an insight into Wesley's method of dealing
with souls. He is affectionate and gentle in his exhortations
mild in his rebukes, jealous for his influence. It strikes one
as curious that, excepting Miss Lewen and Lady Maxwell,
he writes of every one as Molly or Sally or Peggy. The
youth of the Dale girls is an excuse for their names being
used intimately, and the baptismal Margaret and Mary and
Sarah did no daily service in those days; but it seems an
imprudence, with a jealous wife reading his letters when
she could, to carry on the habit with the older women, as
in his mention of Mrs. Ryan. This letter-writing must have
been no small portion of his labour, for doubtless Peggy
was but one of many who hung on the lips of the great
preacher, and watched, as she did, their own impulses rising
and falling, warming and cooling, with tremulous question-
ings of their possible salvation alternating with triumphant
assurance. And not only artless, simple maids, but crime-
laden sinners and way-worn worldlings were stirred at his
words and rested on him for help and guidance, often bitterly
disappointing their leader by their falling away. That such an
influence as his and Whitefield's was sadly needed at this
period must be generally confessed. It broke up the spiritual
deadness and dulness that had fallen over the land; and
had the leaders gone back to the foundations of the Church
to which they belonged, and so made their religion less
personal and more humble, their work had been all reform
and no schism.

CHAPTER II.

WILLIAM DALE's children, Thomas, Anne, Mary, and Elizabeth, were left in the care of his wife's mother, Mrs. Smith.

The burden for an elderly lady of moderate means was a very heavy one; if she had hard thoughts of the children's father she may be excused. To the children she was all kindness, affection, and self-denial. She brought them up with strict notions of integrity and honour. She was a very religious woman, and to her training, and perhaps also by inheritance from her, Thomas Dale owed his steady principles and faith. She took into her family a child who went by the name of Anna Dale, and for whose maintenance she received a liberal allowance. This girl was no relation, but a connection of the family by marriage; she, however, clung to her adopted family, and hated to remember that the relationship was only by adoption. Mrs. Smith would not allow her to share the poverty of the other children, though even that exception was painful to Anna. She was especially fond of Thomas, whom all her life she addressed as "My dear brother." He returned her affection, but with a characteristic sternness and truthfulness would, after he learned she was not his own sister, never write to her except as "My dear Anna," and "Yours affectionately," one of those trifles that often show the character more truly than a greater action.

It can easily be believed that Mrs. Smith's family would not look on the burden so unjustly laid upon her with approval; no doubt she was blamed for accepting it, and

there was that feeling usual in such circumstances, that
the children ought to be very grateful, and to understand
that they were kept out of charity.   One of the relations
obtained a nomination for Christ's Hospital for the boy.
It is a school that has given many great men their education.   Coleridge and Lamb had passed through it, and
were at this period beginning to be known in the literary
world, though they were not famous enough to make their
example comforting to the little boy just entering.   There
was to him a great humiliation in accepting the nomination—a humiliation which the roughness of the school
accentuated.   There is a touch of pathos in the fact that
he bore all that had to be borne in silence, but to the end
of his life could never talk about the suffering of his
school days.   Coming from a refined and tender home
into the mixed society and harsh discipline of the blue-coat
school, he tasted to the full of that keen misery that belongs
to childhood, a misery so poignant that the scar never
faded, and the wound never ceased to be tender to the
touch.   Even the excellent education he received there
and all the honours he won could not soften his recollections or nerve him to recall them.   He worked hard,
he brought his prizes home to his grandmother, but his
boyhood was saddened by the struggle.

From school he went to Corpus Christi College, Cambridge.   While still an undergraduate, he earned a little
extra money by his pen.   He was above the average as a
classic, and his college was proud of him.   He took his
degree, and prepared to fill up the time between that and
taking Holy Orders by tutoring.   He had always intended
to become a clergyman, and his college friends and asso-
ciates were many of them, either then or in their after life,
leaders among the Evangelicals.   Of all these, Charles
Simeon was the most prominent.   For a time he seemed
to be unequalled in the strength of his opinions and in the

fascination of his personality, but the Cambridge movement was weaker than the Oxford one in that it possessed less dogma and depended more on its leader.

The romance of Thomas Dale's life came early before he was of an age to present himself for deacon's orders. He accepted the tutorship of the sons of a Mr. Richardson, a publisher. Mr. Richardson was a well-to-do man, with an important business that had an East Indian connection, and in the days of John Company India was far more full of gold and silver than it will ever be again. He had a large family of sons and daughters, and the young tutor found he was losing his heart to the only grown-up daughter, a girl of about seventeen. He explained the necessity he was under of resigning his tutorship. But Mr. Richardson was deeply impressed with the tutor's talents, and offered instead his consent to the engagement. Emily Richardson's consent was also gained, and the young couple were married in 1820, when he was twenty-one and she seventeen.

The step seems hasty and imprudent, but after that one period of boyish suffering fortune grew kind. With what little money he had of his own Mr. Dale earned a sufficient income with his pen and his pupils. He and his wife were suited to each other by contrast, and their twenty-eight years of married life were years of uninterrupted affection. She was clever, vivacious, and amusing, a great reader, with such a power of narration and gift of memory that she would keep her husband's pupils entranced by telling them the romances of Walter Scott. Thirty years after her death, a friend, writing to Mrs. Pelham Dale about the imprisonment of her husband, says of these narrations, "Thinking of food for the mind, fancy my first knowledge of the 'Waverley Novels' was the repeating of them, *without books*, by *his* mother to us boys at Beckenham. What an angel she would be to visit prisoners in gaol!"

Her husband, on the contrary, was quiet, even stern, in manner, with a great deal of impressive dignity that must have been of great service to him as a tutor. His features were firm and strongly marked, but his complexion was very fair, his eyes blue, his light hair thick and curling, and he was short, so that he required a great deal of dignity to prevent him appearing boyish. He had a strong sense of humour, and loved a repartee or a witty saying, but a practical joke or a personality of any kind aroused his anger.

Before he married his poems had attracted attention and praise. The *Monthly Review* spoke of one in the following terms :—"The Song of a Captive Jew in Babylon appears to us better than the attempts of Lord Byron or Mr. Moore in the same style."

The praise of the *Monthly Review* was, of course, exaggerated. We still read of poems that recall Tennyson at his best—of characters in novels that equal any Thackeray has ever drawn for us. But, apart from the exaggeration of the praise, the popularity of Thomas Dale's poems was only equalled by the rapidity with which they have been forgotten. They are still found in poetical collections or books of hymns. The longer ones are out of print and hardly known, and yet for the time they were famous, and ran through many editions. The poem alluded to above—a poem of three verses—is forgotten, while Lord Byron's and Mr. Moore's retain their hold on the public mind. The second verse will serve as an example :—

> " Alas ! we were warned, but we recked not the warning,
> Till our warriors grew weak in the day of despair ;
> And our glory was fled, as the light cloud of morning,
> That gleams for a moment, and melts into air ;
> As the proud heathen trampled o'er Zion's sad daughter,
> She wept tears of blood o'er her guilt and her woe ;
> For the voice of her God had commissioned the slaughter,
> The rod of His vengeance had pointed the blow ! "

It is smooth and sweet and flowing enough, but it lacks that sympathetic touch that ensures immortality. There is a fashion in poetry as in all other arts, and the tide of fashion has left some of the singers of the last generation stranded—not even remembered among the minor poets. The high estimation of their contemporaries was faulty ; their thoughts, their phrases, their very style have grown obsolete. The disciples of Wordsworth or Cowper have given place to the followers of Tennyson and Browning, and the wave has already gathered that will sweep away the mortals of this generation, and leave the immortals standing alone.

And yet perhaps if the dead bones should ever live again, or when the age is distant enough to be reconstructed as a curiosity, instead of being despised as being old-fashioned, some of these now silent songs may be sounded afresh, and wake echoes in hearts once more.

That Mr. Dale's poems were much in harmony with the thoughts and feelings of his time is proved by a letter found among his papers. It is written from America, by one who only knows him through his writings—not by fame or acquaintanceship, but who in 1843 has found a book published in 1835—" Found it and read it with so much pleasure," so runs the letter, "that I feel the same wish to express that pleasure to you which moves us to thank the giver of any good gift." Then follows the mention of certain passages that have particularly affected the reader, and the following "thrilling portraiture of suspense" is quoted :—

> " But oh ! what transient pang intense
> Can wound like sickening slow suspense ?
> It longs for tears —yet cannot weep—
> It sighs for rest —yet shrinks from sleep,
> Rends the rack'd heart with ceaseless strife,
> And looks for death, yet clings to life."

Such testimony as this is always pleasant to an author, but Mr. Dale took no pains to preserve a copy of his own poems, and probably rated them less highly than did his friends. A great many were printed in those silk-bound annuals that were so popular at that date. He himself edited several, "The Iris" among others, and corresponded on the subjects of the contributions with Crabbe, James Montgomery, called Satan Montgomery, after his great poem—which reviewers of that period classed with Milton's "Paradise Lost," and readers of this know by name only—with Alaric Watts, and many others.

The editing of such collections was, of course, merely "a pot-boiler," to borrow an artist's phrase. His more ambitious works were a poem, "The Widow of Nain," in which the touching Gospel story is reverently and gently dwelt on; "Irad and Adah," a story of the Flood, a period that gives a biblical atmosphere to a pretty love-story; and "The Outlaw of Taurus." He also translated the Tragedies of Sophocles into English verse—a work which was much praised by his fellow-scholars.

He always wrote poetry, though in after life he chiefly published sermons and books of devotion. That framing of verses and musical lines was an outlet to himself, but he discovered a gift that he possessed in a greater degree than that of poetry—a gift of which the desire for poetical expression was but an outcome—the magic of oratory.

Before leaving the subject of his poetry the reader shall have an example of the whole of a short piece, that has a very true ring about it. It is upon the seventeenth verse of the fifty-first psalm—"A broken heart Thou wilt not despise."

He intended at one time to make a new poetical version of the Psalms. Tate and Brady was then the version used in every church, and one that certainly lacks poetical feeling in most of the verses.

" My spirit sinks with darkness and distress ;
   I see Thee not, my Hope, my Light, my Lord !
   Oh ! let Thy gracious presence be restored,
   And rise once more my Sun of Righteousness !
   Still dost Thou cease my lowly heart to bless ;
   In tears of blood my guilt has been deplored,
   With keen remorse and bitterness abhorred.
   Oh ! leave me not thus dark and comfortless,
   But save me, ere I perish ! O'er my soul
   The tempter triumphs ; vengeance and despair
   On my devoted head in thunder roll,
   And yet Thou hid'st Thy face.   I cannot bear
   Thy wrath, my God !—Hell reigns without control,
   And fear appals my heart, and sin pollutes my prayer !
   And whither can I turn but to the throne
   Of Him I have offended ?—art not Thou
   My God ! A son's loved name I claim not now,
   But Thou art still my Father—Thou alone,
   Unchanging and eternal.   I have done
   A deed too dark to breathe, and on my brow
   The murderer's curse is stamped, and yet I bow
   And plead Thy mercies, oft in triumph known,
   In shame remembered still. Guilt's venomed sting
   Strikes deeper at the thought : Thy grace, adored
   In youth, I dare not now essay to sing ;
   My blood-stained hand would taint the sacred chord.
   One only plea—a broken heart—I bring ;
   Pardon Thy servant's sin, for it is great, O Lord ! "

These extracts are a sufficient proof of poetical power.
His was a poet's nature, shy and sensitive, a soft heart
under a stern expression, quick to respond to emotion.
This weakness, when once discovered by the needy and
unscrupulous, was apt to be taken advantage of, and his
purse was always open to relieve distress. A man of quick
imagination and ready sympathy is more fearful than
another, lest he should turn aside from want and misery.
It was doubtless the poetical side of his nature that made

his preaching so effective, that love of language glowing, eloquent, descriptive that is the poet's portion.

The principal source of income when he first married was his pupils. He had his brother-in-law and other pupils boarding with him in a house at Beckenham. It was a large, old-fashioned, picturesque house, now pulled down, divided from the road by a high ivy-covered wall. He did not move into this house until after he had taken priest's orders. His eldest son, Thomas Pelham, was born at Greenwich on April 3, 1821, but his childhood's recollections were all of Beckenham. The house was said to be haunted, and it was an amusement of the children's to lie hidden in the thick ivy on the wall and make unearthly noises to startle the passers-by. The ghost was one of those noisy spirits (probably rats) who are said to delight in dragging about furniture and playing tricks with the poker and tongs. There was a square stone hall with a gallery round, and in the hall a heavy oak table. One night, when Mr. Dale was sitting up writing, he heard a noise that he could not imagine to be anything but the table being dragged over the floor. He went into the gallery and looked down, but while he was there there was nothing to be seen or heard.

Here, in spite of her ever-increasing family, Mrs. Dale fascinated and influenced the pupils. The testimony of one has been already recorded. Another was Alexander Forbes, afterwards Bishop of Brechin. He always expressed his great debt to his tutor's wife, and after he left he wrote to her from Haileybury, to, as he himself puts it, make his confession to her.

It is as if the idle (by his own account) and sweet-tempered lad felt the impulse of that saintly devotion in which his life ended stirring in his heart. He said that he owed much of his strong feeling on religious subjects to those earnest talks with Mrs. Dale. His final development may

have been a disappointment to his mentor, for she had a
dislike that amounted to prejudice to what was then called
Tractarianism.

It is because his career was so honourable and his victory
over his youthful follies so complete that this letter can be
published without hesitation, for, though the hand that
wrote it is still, and all the writer's frets and troubles have
passed into eternal calm, the claims of confidence are
sacred. But this " confession" is but a step in the upward
development of a man's character, not the feeble struggle of
a weakling. It is the frank confession of one who cannot
blind his eyes or dull his conscience, the description of a
phase he lived to look back upon from greater heights.

> EAST INDIA COLLEGE, HAILEYBURY,
> HERTS, *August* 1835.

MY DEAR MADAM,—I have always forborne writing
to remind you of a long-promised letter, because I was
conscious that all your good advice would, like water
cast on the sand, be very unprofitably wasted, and
that amid the gaiety of my college life your kind
advice would be quite lost upon me, but I have lately
begun to think a little about my own folly, and my
eyes are now open to the evil of pursuing wicked
courses, while alas! the impression is too weak to
render me any permanent advantage, and I now
write this to you who have been so kind formerly
in giving me lots of advice, and to whom I can with
safety and comfort speak my mind, to put you the
question of the gaoler of Philippi, "What shall I do
to be saved?" I write this in perfect confidence of
your not making this public, and whether you do or
not, I am sure that it is but a false shame that makes

me dislike any third person prying into the inviolate
secrecy of a letter. Of course this does not apply to
my kind preceptor whose regard I shall always study
to retain, however unworthy my conscience tells me I
am of it. But to return to my subject, mine is, I fear,
a very bad case, for I dread that I am one of those
who knew his Master's will and did it not, and who
we know will be punished with *many* stripes; and yet
it is not from want of thought that I sin so deeply ; on
the contrary when a bitter consciousness of past crime
comes upon me, I pray earnestly (I trust) to God to
pardon me and for His grace to support me, and
as long as I have no temptation I get on pretty well,
but whenever the blasts of temptation blow the tender
shoots of conscience are blighted and leave nothing
standing but unprofitable wild oats. When the fit, as
I may term it, wears off, which I fear I never can
elevate to a true and lively repentance, seven devils
worse than before come back to their tenement, which
has not even the merit of being swept and garnished,
and the latter state of the man is worse than before.
Nay, such is the infatuation of my mind that, well
knowing the consequence (for it is not through carelessness and want of thought that I sin—that were
much more excusable), being well assured that the
wicked shall be turned into Hell and all they that
forget God, I still *bon gré*, *mal gré* continue in
sin and feel the miserable sensation that I cannot get
out of the slough of a corrupt mind even if I would.
Now I write this to you to give me a little advice, for
when left to myself my mind gradually leaves its own

peculiar case and wanders forth into mental specula-
tions upon abstruse subjects with which I have little to
do, and is tormented with evil imaginings derogating
from the dignity and might of the Most Highest, till I
quite lose myself.

Now I think I have scribbled more than you will be
willing to read and, accordingly, I will bring my letter
to a speedy conclusion, and having made my confession
I hope you will *shrive* me on the first convenient opportunity. By the bye, what a delightful religion Roman
Catholic is, if one could only persuade oneself to
believe it all, for, tho' I think them too harshly
treated by our strict Anglicans, there are some points
which I think it a moral impossibility for a sane person
to believe. But, on the other hand, there are certain
things in which we err, for instance the neglect of
extreme unction, James v. 14, sanctifying of water,
etc., 1 Tim. iv. 4, and a few other points. I returned
to Haileybury about 10 days ago from Scotland. I
would have paid my respects, but to avoid the temptations to expense, etc., in London, I went straight thro'.
At present, tho' doing little, I am enjoying to a considerable degree the *dolce far niente*, but as I intend
to do something I must really begin ; but the fact is, I
find my natural indolence growing so fast upon me
that, in spite of an attempt now and then to get rid of
it, I find I can work at nothing but what gives me no
trouble, as Classics and Pol. Economy.

I trust you will forgive this vile tissue of egoism
which I have penned to you, but what is writ, is writ,
so I must send it with all its iniquities on its head,

hoping you will pardon it. I hope your family are all
quite well from Tom down to the youngest, whose
name the deponent knoweth not. I must congratulate
Mr. Dale upon being made Professor in King's (which
I heard from Professor Jones, who is a jolly good
member of the Church triumphant). It will be nice
and convenient for him being near St. Bride's. Geo.
Miller I saw much of in Scotland. He is turning out
as fine a fellow of any of his standing as any I know.
I hope Miss Dale, whom Mr. Fletcher irreverently calls
Auntie, is well, with best regards to whom and Mr. Dale
and inquiries after your health. Believe me, *Votre*
serviteur obéissant,   A. P. FORBES.

One could not have a better example of confidence and
affection, ease and respect than this letter conveys, while
at the same time it gives such a clear picture of a light-
hearted popular collegian, who has within him those higher
stirrings and promptings that will not be smothered by
laughter and action, but from time to time stir both heart
and conscience to revolt. At such a time it is the picture
of the enthusiastic woman, religious above everything, but
still so bright, warm-hearted, and quick in speech as to
satisfy the vigour of youth, that comes before him as a
guide.

Nearly eight years afterwards he writes to his former
tutor a very different letter, but by this time he has chosen
his career—the doubts, difficulties, and hesitations have
been swept away. The boyish light-heartedness has gone,
but perhaps would never have been so freely revealed to
Mr. Dale as to his wife. At the same time it is evident
that his conclusions have led him to a different point of
view from hers. She was a thorough Evangelical, hating the

Tractarians and the Oxford party far more than did her husband. He, though a Low Churchman, held higher sacramental opinions than most of his party. Still in the former letter young Forbes does not hesitate to declare his opinion about Extreme Unction and the Sanctifying of Water. Did he look forward to the eager refutation of such doctrines from his correspondent with a touch of boyish mischief underlying the seriousness of his opinions?

He writes thus to his former tutor in April 1843 :—

MY DEAR SIR,—With reference to the conversation we had a few days ago, I can quite enter into your desire that I sh^d give some account of the views with which I am about to take Holy Orders, and yet I feel great difficulty in describing my sentiments by any other formulas than those of the creed, prayer-book, etc., so as not to give occasion to my being misunderstood, for all truth, and above all theological truth, is balanced on so fine an edge that it requires far greater caution than a note like the present can pretend, to avoid unintentional error. Moreover the Oxford system for many years back has always repudiated the idea of young men committing themselves to Theological opinions during their undergraduate career, requiring rather an assent of obedience than one of conviction, and rather maturing the mind for the formation of a sound judgement afterwards than guiding it directly: accordingly I have as yet made very little progress in Dogmatic Theology, and have not been over careful to read the many pamphlets that have come out, so that I can hardly be expected to pronounce on difficult points, and have formed rather conclusions of feeling than

those of reason, *prejudice* rather than judgements: at
the same time it would be uncandid in me to say that
I had not read somewhat, and have sometimes thought
deeply and anxiously on many of the subjects that are
at present agitating the Theological World.   But here
again the difficulty of *words* presents itself, for suppos-
ing that I were to tell you that I were a Tractarian,
I do not see that that makes matters clearer, for as
occurred in the conversation I had with you on the
11th, you said some people called you a Tractarian
and yet I heard you say many things opposed to what
I supposed was Tractarian.   The word varies much in
its signification, as every word of abuse must do, that
from convenience, custom or accident has passed into a
shibboleth and is *essentially* vague, so that I would willingly drop the expression, or else so define it as to make
it less liable to misconstruction in an individual case.

If the term Tractarian mean one who wishes to see
the influence of the Church cautiously and judiciously
restored so as to exhibit her as the great vessel of
Christian mercies, the organ of light and truth, the
great instructress of souls: if it mean one who vene-
rates the earlier and purer times of the Church, without
blindly following the opinions of any individual doctor,
or binding himself to observe as essentials ceremonial
practices or disciplines that have become obsolete: who
recognizes in the B. Sacraments something holier than
mere symbols or tokens of grace, who in short is an
aimer at unity, an opponent of latitudinarianism in all
its forms, who would have men more as they were in
ancient times, more charitable, more prayerful, more

obedient, more zealous, more ascetic.   If these explain
Tractarianism I cannot but admire it, and if these
things are judged wrong I can only say, *Errare male
cum Platone.*

But, while I admire the general principles of the
renaissance of older feeling, I cannot sufficiently
deprecate the inexpediencies that some zealous but
unwise persons have fallen into by intruding non-
essential ceremonies or doctrines on the consciences of
their weaker brethren, and so causing them to offend.
There are also many things in works published by
some of the divines of the School which I can by no
means assent to; and more things that have been
injudiciously said and written which I wish had never
been put in writing. I did not, I assure you, deserve your
sneer and the hard thing you said about estimating
persons not as their souls but as fine people. I am
willing to labour wherever I may be appointed to, but
it would be false in me to pretend that I should not
prefer being within reach of my friends, nor do I
think, that to one who has not the *domus et placens
uxor*, a little quiet society not only is not disad-
vantageous but an almost necessary relaxation after
the fatigues of a day spent in that most painful of all
things, the intercourse with human misery which one
cannot relieve. I return to Oxford to-day, and a note
addressed to Brazen-nose College will be sure to find
me. I hope that you will not esteem the trouble I
have put you to as irksome, for which I am truly
obliged to you.—Believe me, my dear Sir, yours very
truly,   A. P. FORBES.

These two letters indicate as well as such communications can the growth and inclination of the writer's opinions, and the sequel is the saintly life and strong ecclesiastical influence of the Bishop of Brechin. The influences of the house at Beckenham did much to foster the first opening of these religious convictions, as the Bishop always declared.

He writes thus in after years when the news of Mrs. Dale's death reaches him :—

DUNDEE.

MY DEAR SIR,—I owe you an apology for intrusion on the sacredness of your grief, yet something within me prompts me to express to you the deepness of my sympathy with your bereavement. And I feel sure that the expression of the sorrow of one who has, in the blow that has staggered you, lost one to whom at a dangerous age he owed much, and for whom he ever entertained much gratitude and affection, will not be painful to you. I know, my dear Sir, that I can say little that will comfort you in such a crushing blow as this. Resignation and conformity to God's Holy Will and the acceptance of the Cross laid heavily on us is the only solid ground of assuagement of a sorrow which, even at heaviest, is lightened by sure and certain hope of everlasting life, and by the subdued comfort of the thought of the end of trial and the withdrawal of the cares of Earth. And yet how much could I say by way of affectionate reminiscence, of kindly words, of good advice, and wise warnings, neglected at the time but not forgotten—of the happy days spent under your roof, where she even to our young hearts was the charm. It is enough that you knew how *one* on whom her influence bore feels to estimate what others do likewise. Poor George Miller will be very sorry, for he has a kind heart. With every kind wish for your consolation, believe me, your affectionate Pupil,

ALEX. BISHOP OF BRECHIN.

Before he left Beckenham Mr. Dale began to be much sought after as a preacher. He used to drive from Beckenham to the church where he was to preach. His manservant was an amusing character, and was often hailed by Mr. Dale's friends with the question—

"Where do you preach next Sunday, George?"

"We preach at such and such a church, sir," George answered, with a pompous emphasis on the plural pronoun.

His mistress corrected him—though vainly—for a habit he had of receiving every order with "Werry good, mam."

"You need not say very good to me, George; I prefer 'Yes, mam.'"

"Werry good, mam," returned George, more emphatically than ever.

But George's most amusing speech was his explanation of his infidelity to his betrothed. He jilted the housemaid for the sake of the landlady of the inn.

"I can hardly believe, George," said his mistress severely, "that you can have the heart to treat poor Jane so ill."

"Well, you see, mum," said George confidentially, "it's like this. If you was to have two plates put before you, and one was full o' wittles and one was empty, which 'ud you take?"

From Beckenham the Dales moved to Grove Lane, Camberwell, a smaller house, but they took fewer pupils, as Mr. Dale's engagements for clerical work became more numerous and his family larger.

In 1828 Mr. Dale had been elected Professor of English

Language and Literature at the University of London, and later in the year became Divinity Lecturer at the same University.

There was one day-pupil at Grove Lane, an account of whose schooling is to be found in Mr. Ruskin's " Præterita." Every day his father walked with him from Herne Hill, and left John Ruskin at Mr. Dale's house. As he went home to half-past one dinner and to prepare his lessons, he mixed very little with the other boys, but the acquaintance thus formed between the families lasted for many years. Later on John Ruskin attended Mr. Dale's lectures on Early English Literature at King's College. The affectionate letters he wrote to his tutor from abroad have already been published, and need not be quoted from here.

In the January of 1835 Sir Robert Peel " being desirous of placing in the Parish of St. Bride's a resident Clergyman of high Character and eminent as a Preacher," to quote from Sir Robert's letter, offered Mr. Dale the living, which was accepted, and the family moved into a house in Lincoln's Inn Fields.

At this time Mr. Dale and Mr. Melville were the popular Evangelical preachers in town. The conductors of the omnibuses used to shout out the two names as rival destinations for wandering church-goers.

About this date, 1835, Mr. Dale was preaching at St. Mary's, Cambridge. Dr. Carus of Trinity College writes thus to congratulate him on his appointment to St. Bride's :— " None will more sincerely rejoice with you and indeed with the whole Church of Christ in this early act of our new ministry. . . . May I be allowed also to add, that, whilst we are all here rejoicing in your appointment we are more earnestly than ever looking for your residence once more amongst us, and whilst we pray for your prosperity at St. Bride's, we desire also a large portion of grace on your coming ministration at St. Mary's."

The sermons were preached and printed, and Mr. Simeon wrote the following acknowledgment of them:—

MY DEAR FRIEND,—I feel extremely indebted to you for your kind present of the Sermons you have recently delivered before the University. In truth I have had a rich treat in the reading of them. Never in my whole life did I see so striking a Contrast to my homely style of writing. But God gives to every man his proper gift: and we should all be thankful for what we have, and not be envious on account of what we have not. But this I feel in reference to your forcible and brilliant statements: that they ought to be delivered with a corresponding energy to give them their proper force; else they will pass off from the minds of the hearers too rapidly: but if delivered suitably to their vast import, they must produce (humanly speaking) a very strong impression. Yours are not words but matter; and very much cleared of the redundancy of tropes and figures, which rather characterized your earlier productions. My only fear is that you will not allow yourself time to give them their full effect. They will require indeed *occasional* rapidity, but long and frequent pauses, as well as very diversified intonations. It is not isochrony that will improve them, but pauses at *certain places*, to give effect to what you have spoken. Of the places you yourself (I was going to say) will be the best judge: but I must recall that, because the ideas having emanated from your own mind, you will scarcely be able to judge when the mind of your hearers needs relief. But, by reading one or two of your sermons to a person who has not heard them before,

you will acquire that discernment, or I should say,
that *feeling*, which will instantly commend itself to
your judgement. Mr. Foote read his plays to an old
servant, and he was sure what she enjoyed his whole
audience would enjoy. So if you mark the eyes and
features of one to whom you read your sermons, you
will see what your diversified pauses and intonations
will effect upon your hearers at large. But it should
be to a person unused to your delivery: and then you
will see the truth of the observation that *Actio, Actio*
is almost all: it will give force to statements simple as
mine, and will give tenfold weight to statements grand
and beautiful as yours.

I trust you will excuse these hints from, Dear Sir,
Your very affec^te and much indebted friend,

C. SIMEON.

K. C., CAMB., *June* 8th 1836.

Those who remember say that the sermons when printed
lost much that they gained from the power of the
preacher's delivery. There is a story told of him that at
one time when he was preaching his attention was attracted
and he was much disturbed by a young couple who had
chosen the crowded church as a place for meeting and
flirtation. Gradually, without any personal attack, more,
as it were, in sorrow than in anger, by the magic of his
glance and intonation, he drew attention to them, and they
sat miserable and self-conscious under the solemn rebuke
that, addressed indefinitely to such triflers, yet seemed con-
spicuously for them.

In February 1841 he was appointed to the Golden
Lectureship—a course of sermons preached on Tuesdays
at St. Margaret's, Lothbury, the appointment to which was
vested in the Haberdasher's Company. In 1843 Sir Robert

Peel was again Prime Minister, and wrote to offer Mr.
Dale a canonry at St. Paul's. The pompous condescension
of Sir Robert's letter forms an amusing contrast to the
style of a present great statesman; but in those days prime
ministers wrote from Olympus to the mortals below. The
letter runs thus—

SIR,—When in power in 1835 I appointed you the
minister of an important and populous district of the
Metropolis in the confident expectation that your appointment would promote the spiritual welfare of that
district.

My expectation in this respect has been fully justified,
and I have had the satisfaction of receiving ample
testimony to the zeal and ability with which you have
discharged the duties of a Parish minister.

For the purpose of rewarding your successful exer-
tions and of encouraging others in the faithful discharge
of their several functions, I have recommended to Her
Majesty that you should be selected for the vacant
Canonry of S⁺ Paul's, and Her Majesty has been
graciously pleased to approve of my Recommendation.
I am, Sir, your faithful Servant,   ROBERT PEEL.

Thus rewarded—*pour encourager les autres*—Canon Dale
took possession of the fine old house in Amen Court. In
those days it had a grand oak staircase which was destroyed
in a fire a few years later. Canon Liddon had the same
house in after years when he became one of the chapter.

The Canons were an illustrious body at the time of Mr.
Dale's election. Amongst them were Sydney Smith,
Thomas Barham, the author of "Ingoldsby Legends," and
Montague Villiers, afterwards Bishop of Carlisle. Unfor-
tunately the repartees and witticisms that brightened their

meetings have been forgotten. Sydney Smith once showed them how appropriate to each man's case were the headings of the Psalms put over their stalls. The great Canon was, however, in a state of ill-health at this date. In his letters about chapter business he alludes often to his probable inability to preach at his next turn, and finally writes to Canon Dale the following characteristically cheerful little note :—

MY DEAR SIR,—What a man does well he in general has no dislike to do. You give so much satisfaction and attract such large congregations at the Cathedral that it would be a public benefit if you would take my turn on Sunday Evenings. I do not mean to offend you by offering any Honorarium, for that I think ought not to take place between one Canon and another. I shall pay the M. Canon in waiting precisely as if he had officiated for me—therefore you have only to consider if what I am asking is as agreeable to you as I am sure it will be to those who hear you. I am far too unwell to do any duty, but am always, Yours truly,
SYDNEY SMITH.

Canon Dale went from St. Bride's to St. Pancras'. He had resigned the Lectureship at Lothbury before this, and was annoyed at the outcry against Mr. Melville succeeding him. Mr. Ruskin writes to him on this subject :—

DENMARK HILL, 22nd *March.*

DEAR MR. DALE,—I was much struck by your appeal and interested by your report, respecting your enormous and oppressive charge and burden in that unhappy parish. I will send you the other half of the enclosed note to-morrow—or perhaps, I had better wait until you favour us with a single line saying you have

this. I am afraid I may not be able to get into town
on Tuesday or I would not give you this trouble. I
trust Mrs Dale is better and gains strength. With
sincere regards to her and to all my friends, ever faithfully and gratefully yours,   J. RUSKIN.

I am very sorry both for the cause and the fact of
your leaving us in the city—and the more so because I
am vexed at the way in which people take up the question of choice of a successor;—instead of simply considering who would be most useful, and who would
leave you least cause to regret the necessity of your
own abandonment of us. I hear everybody talking
about clergymen's incomes as if the founder of that
lecture had meant it only to provide a poor clergyman
with a living. What business have they with that
matter? The man that preaches most truth and with
most power is the man that should have it—if he had
a million a year besides, though of two good men one
would of course give it to the poorest; but it is a bitter
shame, in my mind, and a foul want of charity to accuse Mr. Melville of avarice because he comes forward
for this thing. Cannot they understand that such a
man may feel it painful to hold his tongue, and may
feel that he has no power of doing the good he was
meant to do and this is the thing he needs?

From this period Canon Dale's life was occupied fully
with parochial work, preaching, and the building of churches
to serve the various districts he formed from his great parish ;
but as his son was now working with him, it would be better
to give the details of St. Pancras and its organisations in a
future chapter.

CHAPTER III.

THOMAS PELHAM was the eldest child of Thomas and
Emily Dale. His mother was but eighteen at the time of
his birth, and between her and her son there was ever the
greatest affection and confidence.

In some respects he was born to a life of far greater
happiness than the majority of mankind enjoy. He had a
wide intelligence and an eager love of acquiring knowledge,
that made the world full of interest and romance to him.
To the day of his death he kept this gift fresh and full of
zest. He was always ready to learn, and what he learnt he
could produce again at pleasure from the storehouse of his
memory. Except when idleness was enforced by illness,
the days never dragged with him. He often said that he
came into the world at an interesting period, when his two
favourite sciences, chemistry and engineering, were advanc-
ing with strides.

His earliest recollection of himself was in petticoats and
red shoes. The red shoes were a trial to him ; he did not
consider them manly, and he and the brother next him
escaped into the yard to dabble them in the mud and dim
their brilliancy. When his portrait was painted, he made it
a special request that his shoes should be represented as
black, and was very indignant when he found the painter
had broken his promise, and the detested red shoes were
conspicuous.

Another recollection was of passionate outbreaks, for which he was punished by being shut into a cupboard. Then, when he had calmed down in his solitude, he would sit on the floor and read by the light that streamed through a large crack in the door. He learned to read early, and was seldom without a book in his pocket.

A trouble of his childhood was the terror inspired by a certain dark archway. He could not define the fear, but so strong a hold had it on his imagination that when he was too old to be willing to confess to such a weakness, it was with an effort that he passed the place without quickening his steps. Then there was the haunted hill, down which at sunset he often raced, urged by the hobbling step he fancied he heard, and dared not look round to face. This was supposed to be an old woman, who had left directions in her will that she was to be buried upright, to be ready for the day of judgment. Popular superstition declared that she walked out at sunset, and to race down the hill at that time was a fearful pleasure.

Chemistry was his first love among the sciences, and he had a clear remembrance of a painful burn, the result of his early experiment with phosphorus, a hurt he concealed for some time. His mother had more sympathy with these pursuits than his father. She herself was fond of discussing the insoluble problem of perpetual motion, and her son was soon eager for the discovery. Electricity, of course, fascinated him, and, boy-like, he delighted in giving his brothers and sisters shocks.

Only one of his childish letters, probably his first, has been preserved. It runs as follows —

MY DEAR PAPA,—Have you received a letter from me. You must excuse blots for I have spoilt a sheet of paper. I should like to come and stay with you for then I should learn to swim. I hope you are able to

get the Guls. Is your house facing the sea. Farn-
borough aunt is here. I have heard that you are
gowing to stay where you are we have bought 19^d
of pots of which I subscribed 1^s. 2^d. I went to aunt
lorford's (Lawford's) and she gave me a Chesboard
and we tea in the garden and with it a cake. Henry
Andrews was there and Uncle Lorford gave him a
bow and arrows he has got a pretty house and a large
garden. I liked little Willy Fenn verry well only he
was rather to playfull but that he meant for kindness.
I hope you are quite well. Give my love to Mamma
and I hope George and cook are both well. Send me
an answer wether they have got a good harbour. Jem
has drawn Mamma a likeness of Huttan's house we
are all well. Mr. Torriano came here yesterday and on
Jem's birthday we had the orange wine and I did not
like it at all.—I remain your affectionate son

THOMAS P. DALE.

P.S. Excuse bad writing for my pen is bad and it
is getting dark.

Spelling and punctuation leave much to be desired, but
there are some characteristic touches in the letter. The
question about the harbour is one he would all his life have
been ready to ask, and would have received the answer
with interest. Had he been with his parents the harbour
would have been a constant source of amusement. From
such misplaced kindness as Willy Fenn's we have most of
us suffered at one time or another, and also from similar
disappointments to the treat of the orange wine on Jem's
birthday.

One of the pleasures of childhood was the village fair,
where there were sure to be pictures of the "Dook" and

Buonaparte, and the favourite description of the showman was, " There's the Dook a-leadin' of 'is men to victory, and there's Boney 'iding be'ind the trees for fear of the bul-lets " —a description eminently satisfactory to the village mind.

The children's life at Beckenham was uneventful, varied now and then by visits to uncles and aunts. Tom, as he was called then, had a vivid recollection of long visits at St. Mary Cray, where his father's sister lived. She had married a Kentish squire, who farmed his own land, and who was the picture of what a yeoman farmer should be—stout, red-faced, cheerful, with a voluminous neckcloth, white breeches, and blue coat for a Sunday costume. His nephew recalled him, in his character of churchwarden, being asked for assistance by the clerk on Sacrament Sunday. It was a slovenly service at the little parish church. Aunt Mary was constantly at war with the parson on the subject. On this occasion the bottle of Communion wine had not been opened, and the clerk was seeking for a corkscrew. The churchwarden stood up, plunged his hand into his pocket, and produced, to the great interest of his little nephew, a sample of wheat, a pocket-book, a knife, some string, and finally a corkscrew, with which the clerk then and there drew the cork, and returned the instrument over the pew with thanks.

It was at this church that the persistency of Aunt Mary forced from the unwilling parson service on saints' days. Her nephew never forgot the meaning look at her with which the parson, who had a muffled nasal voice, repeated a verse of the Psalms for the day—" *Are* your minds set upon righteousness, O ye congregation : and *do* ye judge the things that are right, O ye sons of men ? "

It was probably at this church that the parson's pronunciation led the young listener to a firm belief that Abraham's servant was called Putt, because " Abraham said unto his servant Putt—thine hand."

As a child Pelham Dale's education was desultory. His father's time was occupied with his pupils, and his mother was fully employed in the cares of the house and family. For a great reader, however, liberty has its advantages; if the knowledge thus acquired is not so systematically arranged as examiners expect, it is thoroughly comprehended, and is gained without weariness. The scientific discoveries of the day were his favourite romances, and he could remember all his life the different stages of the developments of railways, electricity, gas, photography—all that he had watched from his boyhood.

As a lad he came off victorious in an argument with an engineer, who, to excuse some defect in a pipe, talked imposing but erroneous technicalities about hydraulic pressure; but under the boy's searching questions, and determination to understand the matter, the man was reduced to confessing to a mistake.

When they moved from Beckenham he learnt with his father's pupils, until, on the appointment to St. Bride's, they were given up.

As soon as he was old enough he went to King's College, and then, by his own wish, was apprenticed to learn engineering. To be an engineer was his ambition at this time.

The gentlemen apprentices were in the same workshop, and heard all the coarseness and blasphemy that the workmen indulged in; but though this was a trying experience, especially to a home-bred boy, he did not let it turn him from his purpose. It gave him, however, a knowledge of the British workman and his ways that was of considerable use to him in after life.

He was, however, growing fast, and his health failed under the long hours and manual toil. He was persuaded to relinquish the profession, and was sent to college.

Of his religious feelings at this time there is no record,

nor was he ever of a nature to love open discussion and analysis of his personal emotions. If he talked to any one in such a fashion, it would have been to his mother; but his deepest feelings were the most carefully concealed. He did not pass through those bitter storms of doubt and uncertainty that assail so many minds when they first learn to think for themselves. Probably, from his constant habit of eager inquiry on all subjects that interested him, he never experienced that shock that makes so many falter, when they first realise that what they have thought fixed and unalterable has been and is a subject of dispute. He took a wider view of matters, religious and scientific, than most men, and could never see that science and religion could be opposed to each other. When a limited interpretation came into collision with a limited scientific knowledge, it was the fault, he held, of the statement, not of the truth. He never forgot that as yet we are far from complete knowledge, and there are as many unknown wonders waiting for us as those that master-minds have revealed.

At the time of his college days Pelham Dale's opinions were at one with his father's. He was somewhat more of a sacramentalist perhaps, and yet Canon Dale's views on that subject were firm and ecclesiastical, considerably more so, judging from the books of devotion he compiled, than those of many a Low Churchman of the present day. Briefly, it might be said that, while he did nothing to dethrone the all-important sermon from the position it had attained, those sermons taught that the Blessed Sacrament was necessary to salvation. In order to lessen the crowds of communicants that sometimes prolonged the monthly service until far into the afternoon, he determined to administer the sacrament every fortnight. But his teaching bore fruit, for many of the congregation received at each opportunity, saying, as a reason for doing so, " Can I turn my back on the table of the Lord?" The spirit was already there, if the more definite Church teaching were not yet general.

Pelham Dale was entered at Sidney Sussex College, Cambridge, and had for his tutor Mr. Colenso, afterwards a bishop well known for his beliefs, or unbeliefs, but at this time chiefly famous as a mathematician. On writing to congratulate Mr. Dale on his appointment to St. Paul's, Mr. Colenso added that he was glad to say his son seemed very ready and desirous to work. He was not only ready to work, but fascinated by the study of mathematics, and delighted to invent different methods of working out problems, so much so that his tutor, who appreciated his talents, said to him, " Dale, you ought to write a treatise on the Romance of the Differential Calculus."

Of the great Dr. Whewell (familiarly termed Billy Whistle by the undergraduates) he saw little, and did not like that little. He resented an unnecessarily severe reprimand for leaning over a bridge to look at the water below, and was indignant that the master never returned an undergraduate's salute, though he sternly exacted it. His set at college was composed of reading men, who by no means despised a good story and a hearty laugh. A favourite recreation was the reading of Pickwick. All his life Pelham Dale was a great admirer of Dickens, and was fond of quoting from his books, more especially the wisdom of Sam Weller and the sayings of Mrs. Gamp.

There are no letters of his of this date, so the records of college life are very scanty. He was happy and worked hard, but, he always said, without system. He had his time of engineering, which had stopped regular study, to make up for, besides the irregularity of all his work from boyhood. His tutor thought he should be second wrangler, he himself doubted if he should attain the height of a senior optime. He was disheartened after the examination by remembering that in the anxiety of the

moment he had written a familiar formula wrong. Therefore the lists were no disappointment to him: he was
twenty-fifth wrangler, and was elected to a fellowship. This
fellowship he held but a short time, for during the vacation,
spent with his family at Reigate, he had become engaged
to Miss Mary Francis, with the understanding that the
marriage was to be deferred until he had a living.

Except in their religious views—and even they must
have had such dissimilarity as comes from differently
constituted minds—there was not much resemblance
between father and son. Pelham Dale was tall, close
upon six feet, thin always, but fairly broad-shouldered;
he had a slight stoop, the stoop of a constant reader,
blue eyes, fair complexion, and light brown hair. His
forehead was broad, well developed at the temples, his
eyes deep set beneath level brows. The forehead and
eyes were those of a mathematician; one sees the same
formation in portraits of men with similar tastes. As a
young man he wore whiskers, but later in life let his beard
grow, partly to defend his throat, which was delicate, partly
to avoid the trouble of shaving.

He was an eager talker on any subject that interested
him, and had a trick of laughing and rubbing his hands
when he was amused or pleased. He was nervous and
sensitive on some points, and in his youth had the reputation of being irritable and quick-tempered, a failing he set
himself to conquer, so that it became but a tradition to
those who knew him in later life. A certain sensitiveness
of constitution always troubled him. It was rather sensitiveness than delicacy, for he seldom intermitted his work,
and did not suffer from physical strain nearly so much as
from mental worry. His weakness took the form of dyspepsia and a delicate throat. The former was a trouble to
him all his life, and made him dislike any but the plainest
food, and of that he ate sparingly.

Many of the Dales were musical, most of them could play by ear; some studied thoroughly; but though he appreciated good music it was not the delight to him that form and colour were. Drawing and painting were favourite recreations with him, and his colouring was often praised for pureness and tenderness. From the first he was an admirer of Turner, and most unfortunately resisted the strong temptation to extravagance in the form of a longing to buy David Cox's sketches, which, not sufficiently appreciated at that time, are properly valued, now—a little late for the artist. From the age of sixteen to seventy he never missed an Academy. As a rule landscapes had a greater attraction for him than figures, though now and again some figure-subject would make such an impression on him that he could describe it long after. One of Holman Hunt's early pictures struck his fancy in this manner. Some years later he took lessons from Mr. Buss, and gained a facility of expression with the brush that increased with practice. The occupation was of course an amusement and relaxation, but at one time he sold many of his oil pictures to a dealer, which may be taken as a proof that for an amateur they were above the average. Afterwards he gave up oils in favour of the more portable water-colours, and his sketches have the merits of atmosphere and sweetness.

As a boy one of his favourite books was Spenser's "Faery Queen;" he used to say he was one of those few persons who have read the poem through. Milton's "Paradise Lost" was also a favourite, but with these exceptions poetry and fiction took a very secondary place compared to his favourite science. Southey's "Doctor" was a much-read volume. Walter Scott he had read as a boy, Dickens he always enjoyed, but with the exception of Anthony Trollope and Mrs. Oliphant, he seldom read the works of any later novelist. He had a dislike, in fact, to those numerous plots that turn on crime or faithlessness; his family used to

say laughingly he could not appreciate a good villain. Out
of deference to his father's wishes he never at college played
cards, and only once went to the theatre when he grew
up. He did not share the prejudice, however, and when he
became master of a household made no rule against such
pleasures.

He took his degree in '45, and in the same year was
ordained deacon and went as curate to the Rev. Daniel
Moore, then at Camberwell. Mr. Moore wrote to Canon
Dale in praise of his son, adding that the "common people
heard him gladly." He did not, indeed, inherit his father's
powers of oratory, but his sermons, plainly delivered, were
full of thought and scholarship. He wrote them at first,
and in after life learned to preach extempore from a somewhat curious reason. A little mad woman, very like Dickens's description of Miss Flite in "Bleak House," fell in
love with all the men of the Dale family. Unfortunately
her affection took the form of attending church, and whenever she caught their eyes, nodding and smiling and blowing kisses. The sight of the strange little figure nodding
at him while he preached made Mr. Pelham Dale so nervous
that he preached from memory and shut his eyes. He
broke himself of the last habit when the cause was removed,
but he had learnt to trust his memory.

Soon after taking priest's orders he was presented to the
living of St. Vedast, alias Foster, with St. Michael-le-Querne,
by the Dean and Chapter of St. Paul's. The church stands
in Foster Lane, behind the General Post-Office, and was
built by Wren, after the original church had been burnt in
the Great Fire. Its tower is very narrow and curiously
white, so that one can distinguish it readily from the other
towers round the cathedral. The interior is flat ceilinged,
of Italian design, the cornice and ornaments being beauti-
fully moulded. The square form of the church, with an
aisle on the south side, sends the altar and east window

very much to one side of the building. The woodwork and wainscoting is of dark oak—the pulpit and reredos finely carved, the work of Grinling Gibbons.

In those days the pulpit stood at the north side of the building, and the organ was in the west gallery. In front of the gallery the lion and the unicorn fought for the crown. The oak, carving and all, was painted and varnished, very probably in the first instance to conceal repairs with an inferior material. There were high wooden pews, with red curtains hung on brass rods, to make their privacy complete; and yet these pews were not fit for slumber, the seats were so high and narrow that without a large hassock no one with legs of an ordinary length could have kept his position on them if he relaxed his muscles. On Sundays the charity children, in their picturesque dress, sat on appropriately humble forms in the centre aisle. The dark wood wainscoting was enlivened by gold-lettered lists of churchwardens and charities, and by two shelves of baker's loaves, which were given at the end of the service to certain poor widows. On the white-washed walls above the wainscoting were pagan memorials of ancient citizens— little fat cherubs weeping and drawing back veils to reveal Death's heads, all sculptured in black and white marble, lettered slabs with urns on the top, and less pretentious slabs, lozenge-shaped, white on a dark ground—" In memory of——." Colour was supplied by the red curtains and cushions of pew and gallery and by the east windows, the centre of which was The Ascension, the principal figure surrounded with cherub's heads in grey clouds.

There was an unfortunate circumstance connected with this church at which want of experience prevented its young rector being alarmed. St. Michael-le-Querne had been likewise burned down at the Great Fire, but never rebuilt. The parish was joined to that of St. Vedast, and brought with it its complement of churchwardens, so that

the small church and parish had four churchwardens, and
none of the four in the rector's appointment.

Having accepted the living, he was married at Reigate
Church, and the young couple began housekeeping in the
residentiary house at Amen Court. Canon Dale was living
in Gordon Square, the Rectory House of St. Pancras,
and so lent Amen Court to his son, whose living had no
house. Here he began his married life, which, though
otherwise full of troubles and difficulties, was one of uninterrupted affection.

The servants in charge of Amen Court were a man and
wife. The former (somewhat of a character) obtained afterwards, through Canon Dale, the appointment of verger at
St. Paul's. He was at first refused as being too short, and
wrote an amusingly anxious letter, assuring the Canon he
could attain the necessary height by thick but light shoes
to raise him half-an-inch, and "to have hair on my head
by means of a Scalp which would give me at least one and
a half, if not more, which would bring me to the height
which you said would do." Such pleading could not be
resisted; he obtained the appointment, and, as verger,
escorted some of the Royal Family up to the Cross of St.
Paul's. One of the princesses leaned on his arm in the
descent, and he went about for some time after, proclaim-
ing, like a happy ogre, "I have touched Royal flesh!"

At the time of Pelham Dale's appointment to St. Vedast
there were a fair number of city incumbents of his own age.
The parishes were not yet deserted; junior partners and
head clerks still lived over the offices with their families,
and formed congregations for their parish churches. Several
of these younger incumbents joined together and had week-
day services, with sermons at their various churches in turn,
meeting together afterwards to talk over and discuss the
points raised in the sermon. It was a good training for
both preachers and critics. A sermon by the rector of St.

Vedast on the text, "In that day shall there be upon the bells of the horses HOLINESS UNTO THE LORD" (Zech. xiv. 20), attracted attention and was long remembered. These services were well attended until the resident laity began to disperse. Gradually the rise in the value of land caused every available foot to be used for office work, until on Sundays and holidays the busy city became a deserted place, where a few housekeepers and watchmen kept guard over empty premises.

But for many years after this exodus the air still vibrated on Sunday morning to the chiming of the fine old bells swinging in the clustering towers. It was a beautiful sound, musical, full, harmonious; here a chime dropping one note after another, drowned for a moment by a clash from a neighbouring steeple, and undertoned by the booming base of a great bell ringing down. It has ceased now; it became an annoyance and expense, and has given place to the railway whistle and the shout of the newspaper boy.

Training in parochial work, after the wants of his own parish had been seen to, was to be had in St. Pancras parish, and until Canon Dale resigned the charge in 1860, his son worked under him. The parish was very large, populous, and poor. With his great influence and powerful supporters, Canon Dale was enabled to build churches and cut off many districts, so that it became possible for church ministrations and parochial aid to penetrate into the densely populated courts and alleys. A large part of his private fortune was spent in the building of these churches.

The schools of the parish were also extremely well organised and very efficient. In these Pelham Dale took much interest, gladly giving instruction to those who showed talent in any subject they wished to follow further than the school course took them. To this day there are many who

remember gratefully the St. Pancras schools, and some who
have attained high positions from the start in life thus received. But though now the good results are remembered,
at the time the overwhelming poverty and neglect seemed
hopeless, the most strenuous efforts left a large portion
untouched, and the committees of rich and willing helpers
found a heavy task before them.

The usual fate of reforms attended the work, and a powerful opposition was roused, which was the final cause of
Canon Dale's resignation after fifteen years' labour.

At the time, however, of his son's marriage the work was
still in its infancy, and the opposition not yet strong enough
for annoyance.

The August after their marriage Mr. and Mrs. Pelham
Dale were burnt out of Amen Court. The fire was caused
by the carelessness of the nurse, who put the candle against
the curtains of the bed where Mrs. Pelham Dale was. The
panelled walls caught fire, but no lives were lost, though
it was rumoured in the crowd that the three weeks' old baby
was burnt. The only person in danger was the page-boy,
whose deafness made him difficult to arouse; but he was
seen escaping over the roofs, having saved his new livery
hat, which he was wearing, an ornamental finish to his
fluttering night-shirt. The old oak staircase and the contents of many of the rooms were destroyed, and the Pelham
Dales removed into a furnished house in Guildford Street,
while 3 Amen Court was rebuilt.

Early in the next year '49, Canon Dale lost his wife,
a grief that was as deep as it was inexpressible. Their
youngest child was not three years old at the time of her
death, though she had lived to see her first grandchild.
She was one of those who, from their vivacity and activity
of mind, leave a great blank in the lives of those they
love.

In '51 Pelham Dale became librarian of Sion College,

and moved from Amen Court to the librarian's house, which
with the library and almshouses was enclosed in a yard by
London Wall.   The place has all been swept away within
the last ten years or so.   The library has been removed to
the Embankment, and offices cover the old site.

Sion College was founded by one Thomas White, D.D.,
for the benefit of city incumbents.   There was a reading-
room, and members were allowed to take out the books to
read.   The state of the library gave plenty of scope for
work.   Pelham Dale catalogued the books—no light task,
working single-handed—and invented a simple but effective
method of keeping a check upon the volumes that were
borrowed.   Each book had its place and number, and when
it was taken out a slip of wood took its place, holding a
paper with spaces for the name and address of the borrower,
and dates of taking out and returning the book.   The title
of the book was on the wood, and the paper was removed
when filled up.

For a scholar life in a library has its charms, but for a
young man it has great drawbacks.   To sit working from
ten to four, and to fill up the rest of the time with services
and lectures, leaves but a little while for air and exercise.
The natural consequence of such an existence is dyspepsia
—a trouble to which he was naturally subjected.

In '56 he resigned the librarianship, and removed to
14 Torrington Square, where, to eke out his income, he
took pupils.   This was the only work he ever found posi-
tively distasteful.   To force an unwilling boy to learn, to
explain to some one who does not care to understand was
an arduous and unpleasant task to one to whom learning
was a pleasure and no trouble.   The teaching, however,
restricted to certain hours, might have been bearable, but
hobbledehoys in a London house require constant super-
vision ; they are neither boys nor men, and their grown-up
moods are broken by lapses into boyish mischief.   There

were, of course, bright exceptions, and some of his pupils were always among his personal friends. In '59, however, he gave up tuition; and in order that Mrs. Pelham Dale might take care of her mother, they joined housekeeping with her at 5 Woburn Square.

During this period Pelham Dale continued his scientific studies; he belonged to the Royal Society, of which he was made a Fellow. He also from time to time experimented with considerable success in the laboratory of a friend.

In a history such as this there are many details of family life that cannot be entered into, and yet have so much influence that there seems a sense of injustice in passing them over. Let it suffice to say that no one could have met the troubles of daily life with greater self-denial or self-effacement. The love and confidence between him and his wife were perfect—they bore their troubles together, and they needed the mutual help and sympathy to enable them to bear them. In the same way the money troubles that are inseparable from a family and a small income must be passed over, merely giving as an example of the self-denial he practised the fact that, at a time of difficulty, he resigned his Fellowship of the Royal Society rather than spend any money on his own pleasures.

In 1859 Canon Dale meditated the resignation of St. Pancras. Montague Villiers, then Bishop of Carlisle, wrote thus on the subject :—

I see your Christmas address is printed in *The Times*. I fear you are out of sorts. I wish I were nearer you to cheer you. I am truly sorry you feel bound to resign. You know it is not a post I *coveted*, but still you have done such great things. The Lord has made you so useful in the midst of a Godless Vestry—in the face of

opposition where support ought to have been looked
for, that I for one would have you refuse to lay down
your armour till you are summoned to that rest which
remaineth for the people of God, and where you will
rejoin one who supported and cheered you in many a
dark and weary hour. I trust we may very soon meet ;
the trouble has decided me to preach at St. Pancras in
February. I could not help sending you a line to tell
you my thoughts as I was reading the *Times* this evening.—Always affectionately yours,

H. MONTAGUE CARLISLE.

What are the arrangements? I hope you won't
have as a successor a pragmatical, perpendicular prig,
as Sydney Smith defined a Puseyite.

The Bishop's letters are always bright and amusing. He
says in another :—

" I think the Bishop's charge is as I once heard a Scotch
sermon described, ' Very like a Scotch night, clear and
fearfully long.' Was the Dome cold? I thought of the
first line of a school-song—' Domum, Domum, Dulce
Domum !'

" I wish Carlisle Cathedral worked as harmoniously as
St. Paul's."

In '60 Canon Dale accepted the living of Therfield, near
Royston, and retired from St. Pancras and its worries, and
his son's work there naturally ceased also.

Therfield Rectory was a handsome old-fashioned house,
the kitchen built into part of an old monastery wall. It
was a damp, finely-timbered country, so damp that the
freshly dug graves were generally half-full of water, and
one of the clergy said he could never get over his horror of
the splash that attended the lowering of the coffin. The

population was poor and agricultural. At one time the villagers suffered greatly from fever, caused by bad water. They drank and cooked with water from a green and stagnant pond. Canon Dale sank a well at his own expense and put a pump to it, but for a long time the pond was preferred to the pump, for the reason that it was easier to dip a pail than to work a stiff handle.

Dissent was very active, and the Rector, while promising an equal distribution of flannel petticoats, tried to persuade the villagers to keep to either Church or Chapel. But the country mind is slow to alter; they had always been accustomed to pay court to the Church and attend the Chapel, or else to snub the one by going to the other. A quarrel over a vacant pew, for example, caused a lapse into Dissent. Two farmers claimed the pew; the one had spoken to the churchwarden, the other had had the use of it suggested to him in the course of conversation by one of the ladies at the Rectory. They both came to take possession and met in the pew—a high one. They had a whispered dispute; from words they came to blows;—they were not noisy about it, but rolled together, punching each other's head as quietly as the action permitted in the shelter of the pew. The final decision was in favour of the churchwarden's nominee, and the defeated farmer retired to the chapel in great wrath —only to return to his parish church when a suitable pew fell vacant.

However, in the ten years that he spent there, Canon Dale improved both place and people. Evangelicalism carried with it a great deal of solid charity—roast-beef and Welsh flannel. He was generous by nature, and, as has been said, far more soft-hearted than he looked. His curates complained that he was found handing cake over the hedge to the naughty children who were forbidden the school-feast.

The religious feeling that was the motive power of all

this organisation and charity found its own expression in
well-kept Sundays, long and somewhat dull services, termi-
nating in a powerful sermon; self-denial and a dread of
pleasure, with a curious preference for personal feasts and
fasts in the place of those ordered by the Prayer-Book.
Many excellent persons, who would not for worlds have
profaned the Sabbath, as they called the day of Resurrection, thought fasting on Good Friday a Papistical practice.
As the fervour that animated them died out in their suc-
cessors, it left in many cases only the dull service and the
neglect of holy-days—those who carried on the same fervent spirit began to go forward, to fear the error of Biblio-
latry, and to seek for their doctrine in the teaching of the
ages nearer Christ.

CHAPTER IV.

THE DEACONESSES, GREAT NORTHERN HOSPITAL—CANON
DALE BECOMES DEAN OF ROCHESTER—HIS DEATH AT
AMEN COURT.

IN the account of Pelham Dale's studies one important
subject has not yet been mentioned. This was the study
of Hebrew. He began it as necessary to a thorough knowledge of the Bible—he ended by becoming a Hebrew
scholar of some note. He added Arabic and Syriac to
Hebrew with the same object, and these two languages
were learned chiefly in his journeys on the Metropolitan
Railway. He kept a grammar in his pocket to take advantage of such unoccupied moments.

When his father's resignation of St. Pancras closed that
field of work to him, he turned his attention to an organisation which had long been in his thoughts.

One great need had been suggested to him by the scenes
of misery he had witnessed in the parish of St. Pancras.
Over and over again he had visited some bare room, where,
without the comfort of warmth or cleanliness, and with
all the squalor of poverty and terror of starvation casting
its shadow over their last moments, lay those dying of the
scourge of consumption. "What I want," said a doctor in
conversation with Mr. Pelham Dale, "is a place where such
as these can be nursed, and their weakness solaced by comfort and care."

It seemed to Mr. Dale that here was an opportunity of
utilising the energies of a band of willing, if hitherto un-
trained, workers.

In those days, and in these too, for the matter of that,
all great parishes were worked through the agency of the
women of the parish—those with money and leisure being
generally ready and anxious for occupation in what may
be collectively called " good works."

Of course there are great difficulties to be overcome in
the task of utilising and arranging the variety of material
forming this band of workers.   There has always been
much sarcasm and contempt bestowed upon the "district
ladies," especially at this period, when tracts and grey water-
proofs were supposed, in addition to angularity of figure
and plainness of feature, to be characteristic of the class.
However, the fact remains, that, in spite of the type of girl
so amusingly drawn in one of Mrs. Oliphant's novels, who
takes to parish work for the sake of the curates and possible
" chances," there is a great deal of devotion and energy
among these workers.   There comes a time when the home-
duties in the life of a single woman may cease—when her
parents are dead, and the married brothers and sisters do
not need her services.   Even one who is thoroughly imbued
with the notion that a woman has no distinct existence, but
comes into the world only for service—first her parents,
then her brothers (as for sisters, the more in number the
greater the division of labour) may realise that the much-
talked of home-duties have ceased to exist ; that only their
isolated useless selves are left, with so much income—or so
little—to keep themselves from " being a burden."   It was
a favourite phrase of the time, " being a burden."   Life has
grown freer for women within these thirty years.   In those
days many were condemned to a narrow life, with limited
literature, limited interest, close boundaries of "right"—so
many pleasant things were " wrong " in those days—limited
education, with smatterings of accomplishments, and home-
life, with all its trivial hours and duties magnified into deities,
its solid, substantial food, and its solid, ugly furniture—all

made a close, cramping cage for the humble-minded, timid, middle-class women, who might have blossomed into something happier, and even better, under a sunnier rule.

So left, with no more rigid duties than to be punctual, especially for breakfast, and to see that their maid or maids performed their household work properly, many of these ladies were anxious to pass from their district-visiting and Sunday-school teaching into a more complete life of devotion to their fellow-creatures; but from life-vows and convent walls they shrank with all the horror of a reader of Protestant literature. It was perhaps the spiciest reading in a narrow range of fiction, but it was not reassuring to an aspirant for a life of devotion.

Mr. Dale's first plan was to utilise this army of workers for the scheme that he had at heart. Why should not these ladies cast in their lot together? They had no vocation for the religious life of a sisterhood, but a great wish for a life of good works. Let them take a house together, and there nurse the sick, train servants, and devote themselves to parish work. There was to be no vow; it was to be nothing more than a society of ladies who wished to occupy their time in charitable services to Christ's poor. When they wearied of it, or were called by other duties, they could go back into the world; they were to be in no wise bound; it was merely an outlet for their energetic benevolence.

In these schemes he probably overrated the powers of those he meant to work with; he idealised their virtues and ignored their narrowness. Partly from humility, he all his life failed to make allowances for the poverty of mind that so many suffer from. He could not believe but that every one was actuated in religious matters by a carefully-weighed decision and a good motive; that every one had the power of thinking, and at important crises used it. He did not recognise the jealousies and prejudices that would risk the harmony of such a household as he proposed.

In planning out the scheme, however, it became evident that, to work freely, these ladies must have some recognised position, and he began to consider the possibility of reviving the deaconess of the primitive Church. He went to Germany to study the working of the Kaiserwerth Institution, and was very courteously received by the pastors and sisters. Being very undemonstrative, he suffered a little from the return visits of these pastors, especially on one occasion, when, in gratitude for his hospitality, a little pastor stood on tiptoe and kissed him, in spite of his unbent head, on both cheeks, saying, "Farewell, my brother." The scheme for the Deaconess Institution grew and began to take form and shape. Miss Ferard, a connection by marriage, took up the work, and became eventually Head-Sister, not without hesitating greatly over the title, and discussing its superiority to Sister Superior, Senior Sister, and the like.

The Bishop of London's (Dr. Tait) sanction was obtained. A prospectus was issued, which, beginning, "It is proposed by a clergyman, assisted by some ladies, to establish an Institution which, as far as circumstances admit, shall be on the model of the Protestant Deaconess Institution at Kaiserwerth," went on to describe the character of the work to be undertaken, and announced the Bishop's promise that, "after due probation, the ladies undertaking it shall be recognised by him as deaconesses."

Another paper, printed for private circulation, defines a deaconess as "a woman having the *Bishop's authority* and officially recognised by him as a servant of the Church, her duties being to minister to those gathered in prisons, hospitals, asylums, and the like; or, if her work be parochial, to visit the sick poor, to teach in schools, &c., under the direction of the Incumbent. It is understood that she is to give herself wholly to the duty so long

as she exercises her office; at the same time that, being untrammelled by religious vows, she is the better able to show to the world an example of womanly earnestness and piety."

The revival of the order of deaconesses was well received by those to whom it was submitted. A good committee was selected, and a long list of patrons and patronesses drawn up. Funds were collected, and the society began its existence on November 30, 1861. Three ladies were admitted as candidates, to be deaconesses after due probation. They took 50 Burton Crescent, and began there to nurse sick people and to train girls for service. Two more ladies joined shortly after, but one of the most efficient fell seriously ill, so the working number was only four. At the end of their first report, the committee congratulated themselves that their experiment—for it was not yet beyond that stage—had proved the immense advantage of *organized* women's work.

In accordance with the original scheme, the principal work of the society was a nursing-home. It opened with a ward of three beds, and was advertised as "specially for the benefit of females of respectability in need of careful nursing, such as domestic servants, assistants in shops, and others who cannot be nursed at home, chronic incurables, and persons in the concluding stages of consumption." Drawing up the rules was a difficult matter, as the rules for a republic always must be. The Head-Sister, too, was a manager of decision and power, and not inclined to brook interference, especially in household matters. Rule 7, which named her as supreme in the house, added, "She will therefore rule, but in that Christian spirit by which the chief must count herself servant of all."

Rule 10, dealing with the religious life of the sisters, decreed that "daily prayer, morning and evening, was

to be used. The prayers, taken from the Liturgy, together
with one or more special prayers to be approved by the
Bishop, being said, in the absence of the chaplain, by
the Head-Sister or the Sister in charge." The sisters
were to meet also together each day for reading the
Scripture, meditation, and private prayer.

Rule 13 stated that "the sisters should dress alike
in a plain and inexpensive manner, avoiding all singu-
larity and display." The result of this rule was the now
well-known deaconess dress of blue serge, with a white
close cap indoors, and outdoors a grey cloak and brown
cottage bonnet with a brown veil. "Tell Mary," wrote
the Head-Sister, "that the bonnet is as ugly as she could
wish." Every sister was allowed a holiday of a month
or six weeks. The time of probation was a year at least,
and a deaconess was understood to devote herself to the
work for a period of five years, and at the end of that time
to devote herself for another equal period. However, each
Sister had uncontrolled liberty to leave the Institution at
any time, though a three months' notice was suggested.

All the rules were capable of alteration by future councils
of sisters.

From the first, Mr. Pelham Dale, as chaplain, made
strenuous efforts to keep to his original designs. His
examination of sisterhoods had brought Wantage, Clewer,
and Ditchingham under his notice. He was favourably
impressed with the system of Anglican sisterhoods, but had
no wish to found an Evangelical rival to the existing societies ;
his object was to provide a home and organization for women
who, having no vocation for the life of a "Religious," yet
wished to devote their energies to charitable works. But
at the commencement of the work many of those who
joined hardly did so in the acceptation of this view; they
were, many of them, really anxious for the life of a sisterhood, but had been hitherto restrained by prejudice.

The Head-Sister, in a letter on the subject, puts the matter thus :—" I much fear that the very simplicity of your scheme would be a difficulty. I think to most of those who are disposed to become sisters, a certain degree of form and peculiarity is essential, something to separate it from common life ; where this is not the case, they immediately leave and join other stricter sisterhoods. Obedience to the superior is, of course, necessary, but it is, of course, a hard trial to many to give it who have always been inclined to follow the bent of their own inclination," &c. The letter goes on to argue the necessity of authority and discipline.

The chaplain, on his part, saw no objection to those who had a vocation passing from this Institution into a sisterhood. He worked with interest at the promotion of the society on the lines drawn out ; but as time went on, the Head-Sister's prejudices in favour of autocratic rule became stronger, and her conviction that strict authority was necessary, and, if the work was to prosper, must be in the hands of the Sister Superior, became firmer.

The argument that they were simply adding one more to the list of religious houses and not benefiting the class for which the Institution was founded, was urged in vain by the chaplain, who saw his cherished scheme fading away. Finally, finding that the Head-Sister and he were not likely to agree on this point, he resigned the chaplaincy, and was succeeded by Mr. Berdmore Compton, of All Saints, Margaret Street.

This failure—for, as far as his plans were concerned, it was a failure—was a great disappointment to Mr. Dale. He had thrown himself heart and soul into the work, as he invariably did in all he undertook ; he had had the whole scheme clear in his mind, but had failed to convince his fellow-workers, who had only sought for new names to soothe groundless prejudices.

One of his objects had been to send out from the Head Institutions workers for parish and hospitals, but under the new regime the workers were recalled for a time to live under the rule of the house.

One of the works given up was a small and struggling hospital in a crowded part of the town, and to this Mr. Dale now devoted himself. The nursing was done by three sisters, ladies by birth; Dr. Cholmeley gave his service as visiting physician, and Mr. Pelham Dale was chaplain. He found much subject of interest not only in the various types to be found in the patients, but also in treatment and the science of medicine and surgery. His love of science prompted him to learn the causes of both suffering and alleviation. He was present at some of the operations, and he obtained a knowledge of anatomy and physiology; but though he steadied his nerves in his determination to master the mysteries revealed in the operating-room, so far from hardening him, it gave him a horror of inflicting unnecessary pain on any living creature. He would never accompany sportsmen, or willingly see the fluttering agonies of a wounded bird. He did not, indeed, condemn sportsmen or denounce sport; he took it for granted that no man would wish to inflict unnecessary pain; but his knowledge of suffering restrained him from any risk of inflicting it himself.

In illustration of hospital work, a scene may be quoted from a novel he wrote for his own amusement at this period. The story was of sisterhood life, the principal scenes being enacted in the environs of an hospital where the heroine was learning nursing; the hero, a gentleman engineer, reduced by family troubles to earning his living as an engine-driver; the villain was a manager at a foundry. One of the principal incidents was the heroine's ride on an engine, in company with the hero, to carry help to some injured persons. All the descriptions of the foundry, hospital, and inhabitants of Creek Town are true to life and experience. He never offered the novel for publication, as he fancied some of the descriptions and scenes might be considered personal. Nor was it, except among friends, a picture he cared to present to the world of religious life. He wrote with an appreciation of the faults and humours of community life—faults and humours that are common to every human society when little tempers creep in ; but we can only afford to confess failings in what we reverence to those who share our feelings—we do not make them public for the benefit of antagonists. The following is an account of an accident that is of frequent occurrence, whose victims are generally to be found in hospital wards. It is clearer and more truthful than any description that could be drawn without actual experience.

LIZA.

Easter had fallen early this year, and now, though the spring was well advanced and Whitsuntide drawing near, it was still raw and chilly. It was, however, the custom—probably with an eye to the cheap railway trips which mark the season of the year—that the young ladies of Creek Town should, whatever the weather, appear in summer costume ; and muslins, as being at once cheap and dressy, were greatly in demand. Rodgers the moulder's position among his fellows entailed the social necessity that his children should be, as Mrs. Rodgers expressed it, dressed respectably. Of this Rodgers entirely approved, and would no doubt, even when heavy castings were on at Smith's, and the evaporation from his person unusually profuse, have dispensed with one or two pots of his favourite eightpenny rather than his children should not have their Sunday things. For it must be observed by the way that this respectable dressing was entirely of a Sunday or holiday character. On the first day of the week, Alice and Eliza Rodgers looked like young ladies in their feathers and muslins, nor could the most critical examination of the exterior of the costume have detected any fault, except perhaps that the colours were a little too vivid, and the make of the dresses a little over fashionable. Possibly had a school-feast been suddenly announced in the week, it might have been discovered that the children's Sunday things formed part of the mortgaged property already alluded to, but even your uncle, though apt to be close, is human, and would no doubt have consented to some little arrangement by which Mrs. Rodgers' feelings would have been spared.

At Whitsunday Alice and Eliza appeared in pink muslin frocks and tulle bonnets, and very pretty they looked in them. It was quite an open question, and one which Mrs. Rodgers decided in favour of her own children, whether they were not quite as elegant and fashionable as little Miss Jones, about their own age, who sat in the chancel pew at St. Dunstan's. On their return from Sunday-school they sat by the fire discussing Sister Clare's lesson and her allusion to a fatal accident that had occurred to a lad employed in one of the factories. The minds of the class had been so full of this accident and its details, that the teacher had preferred to dwell on the sufferer with pitying respect rather than ignore the subject of all the whispered gossip.

Baby Rodgers was just sufficiently recovered from a recent attack of croup to be left sleeping in his cradle, and father promised to mind him while mother went out, if she would look sharp and let him have his tea, for which he declared the cold weather had given him a *h*appetite. As ill-fortune would have it, Mrs. Rodgers was only just out of the house when a friend put his head in at the door and asked Rodgers to step a little way down the street ; he had a disputed bet to settle, and Mr. Rodgers' large experience in such matters was desired in order to satisfy all parties. Alice was to mind the baby. But just as father was out of the way Eliza found she was on fire. No one could ever give a clear account of the matter—no one ever can. St. Dunstan's Hospital officials had often inquired into what to them was an interesting matter of scientific statistics. The account was always the same. Mother was away for a minute—just a minute—and then it happened. And so now. Alice screamed and ran into the street calling for help. Sister Clare was on her way to St. Alphege, and an agonised word put her in possession of the truth. She rushed into the cottage in time to find the child's head and shoulders in a blaze. The woollen habit was flung round the little girl in a moment and the fire extinguished. She caught up the child, already insensible from the smoke, in her arms, and ran off at once to St. Dunstan's Hospital.

Tom, the porter, verified what metaphysicians might call his perceptive faculty, in virtue of which he knew her at the bottom of the street, and, scenting a casuality, ran at once at full speed to meet the dark figure labouring under her unwonted burden. He took the child gently out of her arms (Tom could have carried both together if it had been necessary), and hastening with her to the hospital, laid her down gently on the table where so many accidents had been placed. He gave a scrutinising glance at the little insensible figure, and turning to Clare said with a tenderness that surprised her, "Sister, she's burnt to death. Whose child is it?"

"Rodgers'," said Sister Clare; "will not some one send for him?"

"I'll take care of him, Sister," said Tom.

"Oh, he was so fond of his twins!" exclaimed Sister Clare. "His children are all alone, but I cannot leave this little one."

Sister Agnes came in at that moment, and Tom, with her assent, proceeded on his mission. He knew pretty well where Rodgers was likely to be found. When he entered the bar-room of the public-house, there he was, listening to a statement of the sporting difficulty.

Tom was too often the messenger of evil tidings in Creek Town for his arrival not to cause an immediate interruption in the conversation, interesting though it were.

"An accident down at your place," said Tom to Rodgers.

"Which?" said Rodgers.

"A burn," said Tom.

"Which on 'em?" said Rodgers deadly pale.

"The little girl."

"Is it bad?" said Rodgers.

"They hadn't done examinin' her when I left."

"Come along then, mates," said he, "if it ain't much"—and his voice trembled slightly—"we'll settle this 'ere little matter this evenin'."

As he turned to go, Tom gave them a look. It was evidently no more use thinking about the bet. Tom's face showed them that Rodgers would not come back that evening. The two men walked rapidly and in silence towards the infirmary. Ill news, it is said, flies apace. A crowd, many of them school-children, had already gathered round the door of the infirmary. Mrs. Rodgers had come and gone home to look after her other darlings.

The child, moaning with returning sensibility, lay upon the table. Not a trace remained by which to recognise the pretty Eliza. The face was a ghastly mixture of black and pallor, its features seared and blistered to a shapeless mass, hardly human in expression. The hair was no longer waving in golden tresses, but shrivelled and mixed with singed and half-burnt muslin. The artificial flowers, late so resplendent, were reduced to tangled masses of crooked wire and ashes—except one rose which the fire had capriciously spared amid the general wreck, and which still seemed to bloom in faint remembrance of its former lustre.

The house-surgeon, assisted by Sister Agnes, was busy with the application of the proper remedies, for though they were quite aware the case was hopeless, the surgical art zealously clutches at even the slightest chance in its favour.

The father looked at the poor misshapen features and groaned audibly.

"Which is it?" he said. "Is it Halice or Liza?"

"It's Liza, father," said a faint voice, "but I can't see you."

The fire had destroyed her eyes.

Rodgers stooped down to kiss the disfigured forehead. Sister Agnes checked him gently—"You would hurt her," she said.

The tears rolled down his cheeks and he was silent. At last with a violent effort he gulped down his sorrow, and turning to Sister Agnes he said—"Is she very bad?"

The sweet voice replied, "I fear so." And she handled the poor child with a tender dexterity—her firm deft fingers showing no tremor or apparently influenced by the emotion visible in her gentle face.

But Rodgers needed to ask no further questions—he knew his doom. When Tom looked grave, Sister Agnes sorrowful, and Mr. Robinson, the house-surgeon, was silent, it had come to be understood in Creek Town that they expressed no hope because they had none. He understood now that Tom's evasion in the public-house was only that the ill-tidings should not break on him too suddenly. He waited patiently therefore, prepared for what he knew they would soon have to tell him.

The little girl was soon removed to the ward. It was one in which there was a single bed, for the Great Enemy was expected that night, and it was better he should meet Eliza with her friends alone.

Sister Agnes took Rodgers a little aside and spoke

in a low voice—"Your child is in a very dangerous state. I fear there are small hopes of her recovery."

"You think she will not get well?"

"I must tell you," said Sister Agnes, "that we do not think she will survive the night."

"Sister," said the faint voice in the child's cot.

Sister Agnes was at her side in a moment.

"What do you want, my dear?"

"Is it Sister Clare?"

"Sister Clare shall come to you.'

And Sister Clare, who was standing just outside, entered the ward. Her right arm was red and swollen.

"I am here," she said, and she took the child's hand in her own.

"Is father here?"

"Yes, Liza dear," he replied, and Sister Clare put the little cold hand in his.

The father bent over the child. A mask of lint, very hideous to those who see it for the first time, concealed her face, and Rodgers sobbed and rocked himself to and fro in the chair as he gazed on it. He gave way to grief with the consciousness that none but sympathising eyes were looking on.

"Father!" said the child, "don't. Sister Clare, tell him what you told us—about the glories of the other world."

The text "Them that sleep in Jesus shall God bring with Him, wherefore comfort one another with these words," painted by a patient who departed to his rest before he saw the Easter the text was designed for, hung upon the wall. Sister Clare pointed to it.

"Yes," he said, "there is a little comfort. May I stay with her?"

"Yes," replied Sister Agnes, "you and her mother may come as you please. She will not suffer much. And see," she said, as the child dwelt upon Clare's words, "see how bright the child's hopes are. She is not afraid; she knows she will soon be with the Lord."

And then, aware how good it would be for Rodgers to have some occupation to distract his thoughts, she put a glass into his hand and said, "Give her that a spoonful at a time. If she should sleep longer than ten minutes, call me," and then she left the father alone with the child.

She dozed off, and a strange husky breathing was the only sound heard in the ward. Her mother came in, but after a while had to return to the other children. He would not let her give the medicine to the child, but administered it himself as directed. Sister Agnes looked in from time to time and felt the cold hands, but they grew colder and colder, and the sound of the breathing came more and more faintly. The father sat as the shadows of that Sunday darkened round him, and the infirmary became as quiet as infirmaries and hospitals ever do, even on Sundays. About midnight Sister Agnes looked in again. She put the little figure straight in the bed and covered the face with the sheet.

"Your little one," she said, "is with the Lord. Go home now, and God bless you and comfort you."

Rodgers went home, looked as he passed on the sleeping Alice, and then with the exhaustion of sorrow threw himself half-dressed upon the bed and fell asleep.

PART II.

MAKING A "WASTER."

O sacred sorrow, by whom souls are tried,
Sent not to punish mortals, but to guide.
—*Crabbe.*

Rodgers awoke at his usual hour on Monday morning
with a heavy sense of his calamity upon him and a
remembrance which even sleep only dimmed and
dulled but did not obliterate. He did not dream,
he did not even awake and go to sleep again, but
he knew all the while that when he did awake a
bitter remembrance would at once overtake him, which
in his deepest slumbers he could not altogether throw
off. So when five o'clock came, Rodgers was broad
awake and thinking what he had better do. Should
he lie there, at any rate till breakfast-time? But he
could not rest; he would, he knew, only toss about
from side to side, and the extra hours, which on any
other morning would have been so pleasant, were
to-day dreadful to contemplate. He would dream
now, and see with horror *her* face turn into the
hideous mask, or worse still, dream that the sweet
Sister Agnes had taken off the lint and shown him
the beautiful face of Liza all restored again, and then
wake up with a start to the bitter realisation of his
loss. No, he could not lie there, he would get up,

at any rate he could go to the works. He had a casting to get ready; it was one of peculiar difficulty, and would take a great deal of scheming to make the pattern leave the mould. This he considered would be the best occupation; it would prevent him from thinking. No one at the works would speak to him about *her*; his mates would respect his grief.

Accordingly at six o'clock he appeared at the factory, the first to enter the gates. The gate-keeper as he marked him saw the change a single night had made in his appearance. There was also something noticeable in his coming so early, for it was to be remarked that the hands "knocked off" with vastly greater punctuality than they began. Rodgers and his sporting friends especially would commonly be only just in time to save the "quarter," and often entered the gates in a body, still engaged in keen conversation, keeping up to the very last moment and until the machinery began to revolve the discussions incident to their favourite pursuit. This morning he passed at once into the foundry, and before his mates had taken off their coats was already creeping on hands and knees over the black sand which formed the floor of the foundry. His mates respected his sorrow; they let him work apart, speaking to one another on ordinary matters; but no sooner had the blowing-fans commenced their monotonous roar than they began to narrate in an undertone (they could hear a whisper where others not used to the place would have been deafened with noise, such is the force of habit) the sad occurrence of yesterday to those—and they were not many

—who were as yet unacquainted with its details. They all agreed that Rodgers was hard hit, and they all sympathised with him; most of them were fathers, and had boys and girls of their own, and though they often threatened these boys and girls, and sometimes gave them "a good hiding," they loved their children notwithstanding, and possibly, though their treatment of them might be sometimes rough, loved them not a whit less than fathers in a higher social position are wont to do. The work on which Rodgers was engaged was a casting for a railway station at Wilchester, which, as it was situated close under the cathedral, was, of course, to be Gothic. A group of two angels' heads—possibly a little out of place in a railway station—formed the centre of the work. Rodgers, who had a good deal of the artist's feeling about him—it was this which made him especially valuable as a workman at Smith & Co.'s—was making the mould of these angel faces in the sand. He touched it lovingly with an artist's interest, working round with extra care and attention. He was glad also that he had such a piece of work assigned to him; it seemed soothing and pleasant to mould the sweet angelic faces; he fancied he saw a likeness in one of them especially, and he could not feel satisfied until he had given to the mould the most perfect form that his material admitted. True it is that cast-iron compared with bronze is but a sorry material to work in, but art is art, whatever be the medium. Rodgers could so far forget himself in his work as to find a solace in it, yet it was not the art that offered him the best solace. He thought of the words his dying child had repeated after Sister Clare with such confident expectation, and the angel-face cheered him not so much by the beauty of line and form as by the conviction he felt that his "Liza was now an angel." For though art is a great civiliser, it is powerless indeed compared to Christianity, and it was the words, not the form, which solaced Rodgers in his trouble.

In this occupation the two hours before breakfast wore away, and Rodgers knew that the time of emancipation was drawing near by the restless looks which the men cast towards the door of the foundry, near which a lad had stationed himself and was intent on watching the bell. He returned with feigned interest to his work as he saw Mr. Smith enter the foundry, rather an unusual thing with him to appear so early. He passed on, and stood with his back to the lad near where Rodgers was at work, and began to admire the angels' faces and the dexterous way in which the whole casting was managed.

"I don't know," he said to Rodgers, "when I have seen a better mould than that. If the Wilchester Company ain't satisfied with that, they don't know good work when they see it."

Rodgers could not help being pleased with his old master's admiration of his work, which he knew was genuine enough, and he looked grateful, though he did not make any very audible reply.

"Bell oh!" called out the boy at the gate, and in an instant the men threw down their tools, and by the time the bell was heard not a man except Rodgers was at work. It was to gain this extra moment of idleness that the boy watched the bell so attentively. Soon after the machinery stopped, and there was a silence in the factory. The men crowded out of the gate and were already at horse-play with one another. Rodgers still lingered, for he could not bear to join them, and he and "Old Billy" were left alone together.

"Rodgers," said his master as the last man disappeared, "it was kind of you to come to work this morning after all that has happened to you. But mind, though I want the Wilchester Company to have their station open, I'd sooner do without them angels than you should work when you've no mind to it."

"All right, gov'nor," said Rodgers with a kind of respectful independence. "But I'd rather work just now."

"Yes," said Mr. Smith, "it takes away your thoughts, and they're sad enough, I know. However, if you want a quarter or two this week or a day away" —he put an emphasis on this, for he knew he would want one sad day at least—"you are to do as you like, mind that."

Rodgers made no answer; he took up his coat and put it on in silence, but his look, as his eye moistened, showed that he saw what was in his master's mind. Mr. Smith walked up to the foreman's little office and gave some directions. Rodgers knew that the purport of these was to secure him the liberty promised.

"If," muttered Rodgers to himself, as he walked home, "all our masters was like Old Billy, there'd be more work done in our factory, I'm thinking."

At first sound of the factory-bell Rodgers returned to his work. He still kept apart from his fellow-

workmen, but plied his task with so much diligence
that even the watchful spectacled eyes of Fordyce
(nicknamed Four-heyes), the manager, saw there was
nothing to be got by looking after him. Fordyce was
not that day in the best of humours. The castings
were wanted in a hurry, and the fact becoming known
to the moulders, they indeed intended that they should
be ready, but at the same time saw a favourable opportunity for making overtime. He and Old Billy had
had some words about our friend Rodgers. Old Billy
informed Fordyce of the directions he had given to
the foreman, and requested him to see they were
carried out. This he was pleased to consider an
invasion of his own peculiar province, and had characterised it as d—d nonsensical sentiment.

"Do him," said he, "a great deal more good to be
kept to his work than loaf about at home or drown
his trouble at a public-house. If he wants a quarter,
take the (expletive) castings out of his hands altogether and put another man on the job."

Old Billy demurred to this, it would vex Rodgers,
and he'd rather do without the angels than that should
happen. Fordyce still persisted, and the consequence
was that Old Billy lost his temper, told him he was
a conceited fool who didn't know how to manage his
hands—added that he might do what he liked with
the new ones, but he'd be somethinged if the old
hands should be put upon. Fordyce would have
liked to swear in return, but it would have been a
dangerous experiment ; he wanted to be a partner
in the house in place of a salaried officer, and he

must not provoke his senior too far; so he only said, "Let the angels go to somewhere; I don't care if you don't!"

This little difference, however, had deprived Fordyce of one of his mainstays when in a difficulty like the present. He used on these occasions to get old Mr. Smith to come into the shop, and get from him, in the hearing of the men, an expression of his desire for expedition. This, as Old Billy was never hard about overtime, always had the desired effect, and the men would fall to with a will—at least the old hands would, and the others were obliged to follow. To-day, however, any appeal to him was out of the question, and Fordyce became more and more irritated as he contended with a kind of passive idleness, which, as it was general throughout the shop, was more aggravating than if one or two could have been laid hold of and made examples to the other offenders. He mentally determined several times in the course of the day to dismiss some of the workmen, but the hands knew they were masters of the situation, and so "the sack" had no terrors for them; they were wanted just then, and could not be dispensed with.

He took no notice of Rodgers except once or twice to growl at him for spending so much time over the angels, which, notwithstanding their beautiful appearance, judged by the epithets he applied to them, he seemed undoubtedly to consider to belong to the category of fallen angels.

The men this time succeeded in their plans. They made at least two hours overtime. Six o'clock struck,

and still the blowing fans hummed their monotonous
tune, and still the furnaces glowed and roared.   At
length, however, after a good deal of blasphemy on
the part of Fordyce, the moulds were ready for the
metal.   Several of the castings were unusually large
and heavy, and there was a little extra excitement
in the foundry.   Rodgers' angels being delicate work
were to be run first, and then the large castings were
to have their turn.

The furnaces still roared on, and as the shadows
of evening deepened, a peculiar lurid light poured
round the foundry.   A vast cauldron full of molten
metal, the surface of which quivered and glistened
with the heat, was drawn from the furnaces and then
hoisted up from the furnace mouth and passed with
easy dexterity to a distant part of the foundry, the
huge cranes holding out their arms as wanted, and
handing, as it were, their vast fiery burden from one
to the other, until the glowing mass was just over
the opening into which the molten metal was to be
run.   Into this, under the direction of Rodgers, who
seemed in the excitement of the scene to forget his
sorrow, a fiery stream was poured with as much ease
and precision as a young lady might use when watering
her favourite plants in a drawing-room window.   As
the metal ran away into the black sand and disappeared, smoke and gas issued from many openings
which a dexterous spurt of molten metal from a ladle
in the hands of Rodgers ignited.   In a few moments
the operation was complete, the flames died down at
the openings, and all was by comparison quiet again.

It would necessarily be many hours before so large
a casting would be sufficiently cool to be withdrawn
from the sand; it might even now be a failure, and
all the work have to be done over again; but this
did not seem probable, no untoward signs such as indicate a "waster" (the technical name given to abortive
efforts of the engineering art) manifested themselves
to the experienced eye.

The smaller castings were disinterred from their
beds of sand. Rodgers looked with some anxiety
to see how his own particular work would turn out.
The sand was removed, and there were the two angel
faces, but one was "blown;" some defect in the sand or
some sudden jar had disturbed the mould and made a
"waster." One of the faces came out clear and sharp
in all its beautiful lines, the other was little more than
a misshapen mass of iron. Rodgers trembled as he
looked; the mask of lint came back to his mind, and
the great strong man, the sweat still streaming down
his face, turned pale and shivered.

A malicious triumph gleamed in the eyes of Fordyce.

"You blanked stupid blunderer," said he, "I thought
you would do better than that. Blanked if I don't
give you the sack and give the job to a better man."

Rodgers made him no answer, took out his handker-
chief, slowly wiped his face, then deliberately put on
his coat and walked to the gate.

"The Gov'ner," said he to the gatekeeper, "said I
wasn't to stop if I hadn't a mind to."

"All right," said the man, and opened the gate.

Though Rodgers left the factory thus suddenly, it must

not be supposed that he was very much hurt at the speech of Fordyce. Unfortunately hard words were so common at the factory, that they had lost their hardness by reason of their commonness, and so a few more or less did not make much difference. He did not like Fordyce any the better for them, and probably, had he felt up to the mark, would have risked the sack and given them back with interest; but the unexpected appearance of the face in the sand—it was the face, too, he had considered like his Liza—had given him a sudden check.

This description of Rodgers the moulder carries truth in every word of it. It is not very often that one gets so clear a perception of the working-man with his virtues and faults, his follies and his manliness. Here he is looked in the face, not from the heights above or from the sentimental view of the writer of tracts. Rodgers is a fellow-creature, to be got at in a straightforward, practical way, as far as the author was concerned, to be talked to about his work and family in a thoroughly sympathetic manner, to have his faults condoned on account of his temptations, and his virtues strengthened by the hand of friendship. Here is one paragraph more, where, in the further development of the story, our friend Rodgers meets Bill the engine-driver.

Bill held the opinion very strongly that fat sorrows are better than lean ones, and that whether in sorrow or in sickness, if a man could but eat and drink, he was sure to come round the quicker. He soon proposed, therefore, as a benevolent carrying out of his own theory, that they should adjourn to a public-house frequented by brethren of his craft.

"Just a 'arf-pint of eightpenny," said he, putting the matter modestly, "will do you good."

Rodgers assenting, they entered the parlour of the public-house. The engine-driver ordered a pot, for of course he no more intended to confine his friend to a single half-pint than if you ask a friend, dear reader, to take a glass of wine, you intend to limit him to a single one, even if it be a bumper.

This same 'arf pint, though the writer does not exaggerate into depravity the hospitality which leads to its consumption, was a source of great trouble at the hospital.

"How did your accident happen?" the chaplain would ask. "Were you quite sober at the time?"

"Sober, sir! I should think I was; why, I'd only 'ad 'arf-a-pint."

"It always is a 'arf-pint," the chaplain was forced to retort, and very rarely would the patient confess to more. Perhaps it was only the last 'arf they remembered.

Often the drunkenness came from over-kindness on the part of his fellows. The man had been treated. Once in answer to an expostulation on over-treating a man who was young and weakly, easily overcome, the chaplain received the following explanation.

"Well, sir, you see it's like this. A chap comes and tells me he's down on his luck. I'm sorry for him, and I says, 'Wot'll you take, mate?' and I stands him something to drink, that's all I can do for him."

Money and food were not equally included in the etiquette of sympathy, unfortunately. Let us trust that the temperance man's hospitality will take the form of bread and butter as well as coffee. A "lemon" is somewhat wanting in support.

The account of the gradual growth of the Great Northern Hospital belongs to its history. It grew out of infancy into a big place, with its staff and committees and Ladies' Association, and when it had as it were grown up, its tutors and nurses left it.

Another movement in which Pelham Dale was greatly interested was that of higher education for girls of the middle-class. Miss Frances Buss began the work which is now so widely spread, with the North London Collegiate School for girls, and in its early and less prosperous days it could always command Mr. Dale's assistance as lecturer, teacher, or examiner.

All these were additions to his clerical work. He never adopted the convenient plan of some City Incumbents, who shut up their churches for "cleaning" in the summer. He either provided a substitute or returned for Sunday duty when his family were taking their seaside holiday in August and September.

In 1869 Canon Dale received the offer of the Deanery of Ely. The letter from the Prime Minister forms an amusing contrast to the pompous style of Sir Robert Peel in the letter quoted in a previous chapter.

VERY REV. AND DEAR SIR,—I take the liberty of proposing to you that you should be appointed to the Deanery of Ely, vacant by this, or rather about to be vacant by the nomination of Dr. Goodwin to the Bishopric of Carlisle.

I am led to think that, after a long career of memorable and distinguished labour in the Church, it may be pleasant to you to associate yourself with that venerable and beautiful cathedral in the tranquil spot so broadly contrasted with the turbulent site of St. Paul's. *Sit mea sedes utinam senectæ.*

In any case I am sure you will not interpret this offer otherwise than as a mark of cordial respect.

Should you as I hope accept it the matter may be taken to be concluded, as I have obtained Her Majesty's approval.

Forgive the irregularities of a note written in the railway carriage, and believe me, Very Rev. and dear Sir, Your sincere and faithful,

W. E. GLADSTONE.

I know not by what ludicrous and unconscious anticipation I have written Very before Rev. But as it is there I will not erase it.

The death of his wife had left a host of sad and dear memories round the old house by St. Paul's and his life as Canon. He was unwilling to transplant himself, and said to his family that he would die there. He was persuaded to reconsider the matter, and made inquiries concerning the work and duties of the Deanery. He finally wrote to decline—"with deep and unfeigned regret, that on the ground of impaired health and increasing infirmities he must forego the acceptance of the arduous and responsible dignity."

In February 1870 Mr. Gladstone wrote again to propose his appointment to the Deanery of Rochester. This time the offer was accepted, since the other members of the Chapter were older than he, and it would not have been a suitable post for a younger man.

He preached one sermon as Dean of Rochester in the Cathedral on the Life to Come—a remarkably beautiful sermon, long remembered by those who heard it. He returned to Amen Court, meaning to move to make way for Canon Melville, who was his immediate successor, but this was prevented by illness. He was attacked with inflammation, and died after a short but painful illness.

His eldest son and others of his family were in attendance upon him. From Dean Dale's grave in Highgate Cemetery may be seen many of the churches he caused to be built. His wife had been buried in the vaults of St. Pancras, but being convinced of the danger of interment in crowded centres, he had put aside his strong wish to be placed beside her in death, and given the weight of his influence to the sealing up of the vaults. His own funeral he wished quiet and unostentatious, and desired that no Life or Memorials should be published. The reserve and shyness of his life he carried with him to the grave, and yet few men have been more sought after and admired as a spiritual guide and preacher than he was. His correspondence with those seeking for advice and direction in sin and sorrow was very large ; for, by whatever name it is called, to hear confession and give direction are the inalienable offices of every leader of religious thought. We have seen how Wesley discharged these offices. Thomas Dale had much of this work to do. He received—and bore it unmoved— that constant adulation and praise that follows successful preaching. His parochial works and organisations were highly estimated. The fine bust of him by Sir Edgar Boehm was presented to him among many other testimonials ; but he kept no notes of these and similar tributes of respect among his private papers, and unfortunately the bare record of facts is now all that can be given, instead of that proposed by his son, which would have been clothed with personal knowledge and affectionate recollection.

CHAPTER V.

IN 1869 the Woburn Square house was found too small for the combined households. They moved, therefore, farther west, taking 6 Ladbroke Gardens, Notting Hill, where they lived for eleven years, until the death of Mrs. Pelham Dale's mother.

The distance from St. Vedast was greater, but a season-ticket to Aldergate Street made it as near in point of time as it had been before.

Mr. Pelham Dale was still chaplain to the Great Northern Hospital, a post he did not give up until seventy-two or seventy-three. It was some little time after his work there had ceased that a friend told him of a dying man to whom he had been called. This man, anxious for the last consolations of religion, had explained that he had been led to think seriously on such subjects through the impression made on his mind by hearing the Bible read in the wards of the hospital, where he had been taken after an accident. It had, he said, been read so clearly that the words came to him with a fresh force, and he understood their meaning as he had not done before. The chaplain was Mr. Pelham Dale, who, in addition to a pleasant voice, had a scholarly comprehension of what he read, and, while avoiding the error of being over-dramatic—a vulgarism in reading that he much disliked—never missed conveying the meaning he desired a sentence to bear by a carefully-modulated emphasis.

99

He was at this period at work upon his Commentary on Ecclesiastes. This was the only book of the kind he published, though he left a mass of material; notes of studies in the Hebrew and Greek Scripture, courses of teaching derived from these, with papers on the relation of science and Scripture, and much else. An account, however, of his studies in this direction will be given by the abler pen of one of those friends and pupils to whom he wrote, and with whom he worked in that pure delight of giving and gaining knowledge that was one of the—perhaps the greatest—pleasures of his life.

This Commentary on Ecclesiastes was published finally with the generous assistance of Dr. Gladstone, a friend of many years' standing, with whom he worked out scientific problems, and with whom he corresponded, after he had left London, on his favourite subject of the refraction and dispersion of light.

Of the enjoyment of family life Mr. Dale's constant activity gave him but little. He was often out, especially after he went to Ladbroke Gardens, from five in the morning until ten or eleven at night; those less active days, when more time was spent in the house, he was generally at work in his study. In spite of this, there was a strong bond of sympathy and friendship between him and his children. His wife was always the sharer of his plans, and, so far as her home-duties allowed, of his work. His children were eager for his companionship when the opportunities came, and were neither timid nor constrained with him. When they were little, they walked proudly to church holding by his finger. One of them has a clear remembrance of being carried home in his arms, sobbing with the pain of an earache, from a children's party. He was not demonstrative, but in times of pain and trouble he was very tender. He would tell fairy tales—the favourites were " Catskin " and " Falada,"—

repeat portions of "Rejected Addresses," or the ballad of
"Old King Cole." The partisan feeling for Nancy Lake, left
behind for "distressing her aunt" while taking revenge
on her brother, seems ludicrous in connection with the
burlesque ; but to this day the description of the horses—

> " The tails of both hung down behind,
>   Their shoes were on their feet,"

brings a picture of "poor Nancy, not going!" to the
writer's mind.

During the holidays at the seaside there were long walks
to be taken with their father and his sketch-book. Nor
was there any pursuit or hobby to which he refused a
sympathetic attention, not a feigned one—young people
are quick to detect the superiority that patronises. He
was really interested, and joined with a real enjoyment,
and he invariably knew so much, and suggested so many
improvements, that partnership with him was as profitable
as it was agreeable.

Practical joking he disliked, as his father disliked it
before him, and the teasing each other, so favourite
an amusement in most families, vexed him often much
more than it did the victims he protected. All joking
on religious subjects was forbidden, but there were very
few rules or prohibitions else. His religion was neither
gloomy nor alarming, and as his children grew up they
passed into friends and companions with no gulf to be
bridged over between them. He was always young—young
in interest and enthusiasm, young in his belief in others
and in the world in general ; so much so, that when in time
there were grandchildren among his household, they too
carried their pursuits and interests and requests for information to the study in the same spirit of comradeship that
their elders had shown before them.

The Church of St. Vedast, open on the silent, deserted

Sundays and closed on the noisy, crowded week-days, was a constant subject of anxiety to the Rector. From time to time he made efforts to use it in connection with those other works in which he was occupied, for services for his fellow-workers. Then, with the help of these, he determined to start a Bible-class for the benefit of the women employed in the City. There was at this time no particular agency or centre for these women, who worked, many of them, in the ribbon and flower factories in or near his parish, and had their lodgings in the cheaper suburbs.

The first idea was to form a society to be called The Young Women's Christian Association, and to make it a centre for the City. A circular was put out suggesting the formation of such an Association, and proposing to begin by a Bible-class, to meet every Monday at 8 P.M. in the vestry-room of St. Vedast.

The objects of the proposed Association were stated to be :—"The study of Holy Scripture, and the gathering together of women like-minded, and thus to provide a society for mutual support and companionship. To supply a centre of union for Christian women in the City, and especially to furnish to such as are strangers a ready means of becoming acquainted with those of more experience than themselves. To obtain the co-operation of those who, having had experience of the difficulties and temptations incident to their particular calling, are willing to help those who are as yet young and inexperienced."

With these objects the class was started. Probably because the title of Young Women's Christian Association was already adopted by others, it was called the Women's Bible Union. The meeting was transferred to Sir John Johnstone's school-room, and the first half hour was spent in singing hymns.

The following appeal was put out, which explains simply and clearly the spirit of the work :—

ST. VEDAST VESTRY,
FOSTER LANE, CHEAPSIDE.

This paper is put into your hands to invite you to
join with us in a great and much-needed Christian work.
We wish to gather together those who will be cheered
by mutual Christian communion and sympathy, and
who are desirous also of holding out a helping hand
to the ignorant, the unhappy, and the wavering—in a
word, to form a UNION of earnest Christian womanly
hearts, desirous first themselves to grow in grace and
the knowledge of God, and then, after the example of
holy women of old, to render loving service to the
cause of their Lord and Master.

We wish to find this union in a triple cord—first, in
the study of the Word of God, knowing that there we
shall discover those rules and precepts which will guide
us aright amid the temptations, dangers, and sorrows
which beset our path through life. The second bond
we shall form by seeking to bring those who are
ignorant and suffering to the knowledge of the Saviour,
the Guide and Comforter of all. And the third bond
shall be mutual prayer and supplication one for another.

Come with us, then, and we will do you good. If
you are in sorrow, we will try and comfort you. If you
are in distress, we will try and help you. If you need
guidance and direction, such as we can give shall be
yours. In all things will we labour to sympathise with
you, bear your burdens, and so seek to fulfil the law of
Christus.   T. PELHAM DALE, *Rector*.

This paper was published after the first year of the establishment of the Bible-class. The attendance, though not

very large, was regular, and the members devout; the
difficulty still being that so few of the workers lived near
their places of daily occupation, economy took them to
Islington and Holloway and the like suburbs, for their
lodgings.

The churchwardens viewed the use of the school-room
with dislike; they wished it to be let, and not wasted unprofitably on small beginnings. In 1873 they succeeded, being
four to one, in regaining possession of it. The vestry-room
of St. Vedast was not a portion of the church, but a room
opening into it, long and narrow, surrounded by red-
cushioned lockers, with a large arm-chair on a stand to
give dignity to the chairman's seat, and a green-baize-
covered table. It was lighted by a skylight, and at one
time had a door, that was afterwards built up, opening into
Priest's Court. When this door was closed, the only
entrance was through the church. The stiff arrangement
of the fixed seats made it an awkward place for a devotional meeting, the members being obliged to sit on the high
narrow lockers with their backs against the wainscoted wall.

Sir John Johnstone's school-room was in Priest's Court,
and was a portion of the property which belonged to
the united parishes. For this property the Rector and
four churchwardens were trustees. The value of the rents
amounted to some fifteen hundred a year, and the unsatisfactory expenditure was a subject of anxiety to the Rector.
He was, however, always outvoted on such questions, but
the inquiries he made about the use of this school-room led
him to suspect that his rights over the trust-moneys were
stronger and more clearly defined than he had hitherto
believed. He was, he discovered, chairman by right—not
courtesy—and principal trustee. His efforts to see the
trust-deeds were unavailing; it is one thing to have a
right to demand, and quite another to be able to enforce
the right. To submit with patience, to close his eyes to

proceedings he could not approve, was the only way to
keep peace and harmony in this little parish. It was a way
recommended by most authorities, ecclesiastical and lay,
of that date. Expediency was the watchword, but to-day's
expediency is to-morrow's stumbling-block, of which truth
the Public Worship Regulation Act is a good example.
It soothed public opinion on its noisiest, therefore in the
estimation of statesmen its strongest, point. It caused its
promoters a great deal of trouble and annoyance in its
attempted execution, and the Church was disgraced by acts
committed in the name of justice as defined by the Act.

However, the Public Worship Regulation Act was not
yet passed, and even if he could have seen its shadow in
the future, it is certain that the Rector of St. Vedast's conscience would not have permitted him to take the course
of letting ill alone. He did not expect to succeed in his
suggested reforms without incurring some disagreeables,
but a vestry meeting is not often a pleasurable affair; he
was, however, convinced that if he put his case fairly he
would get a fair hearing. Custom had blinded his co-
trustees to the impropriety of expending charity-money on
anything but charity, and they had not realised any more
than he himself had done how strong was his right to be
heard. He had before voted on equal terms with the
others, and was of course always in a minority ; he now
pointed out that his responsibility being greater than he
had imagined, he must do more—he must protest. His
knowledge of his responsibilities was far from perfect, nor
did he obtain a sight of the trust-deeds until a Royal Commission was called, some years after, to inquire into the
trust-moneys and their expenditure. Then, when the
responsibility was ceasing, that most fickle of deities—Law
—gave him power to enforce his rights.

One of the first expenditures to which he objected was
the obviously improper one of an audit-dinner given out of

the funds, and costing some thirty pounds. The Rector felt
a little delicacy in putting the matter before his co-trustees,
inasmuch as he was well aware that what was a penance to
him was a pleasure to them. A man with a delicate diges-
tion and small appetite, the City banquets, to which he was
often bidden in his position as a City Rector, had no delights
for him ; but to his co-trustees the matter appeared differently—to dine well has always been the great object of a City
merchant. Who does not remember Leech's picture of
the citizen who for many days "has not tasted turtle-soup"?
From the first they refused to listen to his arguments, and
were ready to compromise the matter by going without
their grace and clinging to their dinner. The Rector, for
his part, could not feel that he had made much advance
inreform by withdrawing his own presence under protest.
He hoped, however, that on consideration they would feel
the force of those protests, and that in the future the custom
of dining out of the proceeds of charitable bequests would
be more honoured in the breach than the observance. It
was not so, however ; year after year the protest was made and
angrily refuted, until at last the quarrel became public and
the *Times* made merry over the St. Vedast "love-feast."

The dispute about the dinner was an ancient one ; there
is no means of tracing its actual commencement, but it
was about this date, 1870, that the Rector was informed
that he could speak with more authority on this and other
subjects of expenditure than he had imagined. In spite of
his efforts to retain the school-room for the use of his Bible-
classes, he was forced to give it up, but succeeded, for a
time at any rate, in securing it so far to its original uses
that it was only let at a moderate rental to a City clergyman
for an infant-school. Mr. Pelham Dale also covenanted
that the keys should be returned to him if the room was no
longer needed as a school. This agreement was not kept,
and the keys were held by the other trustees, who were

anxious to build more offices to increase the large funds
at their disposal. While explaining these matters, it will
make future statements clearer to add that a letter concerning this dispute about the schools contradicts the
Rector's objection to the vaults under the church, declar-
ing them to be empty and in good repair.

Meanwhile, the members of the class formed a congregation for the church. The services were as bright and
musical as limited powers permitted. There was no choir,
but the singing was led by a lady who was being trained
for the profession of music. The organist, paid by the
parish, was an elderly lady, stout, grey-haired, and cheerful.
In spite of her age (she was over eighty when her connection with St. Vedast ceased), her playing was vigorous and
correct. The writer has a vivid recollection of the thundering and joyous voluntaries with which the services ended
when Mrs. Mounsey Bartholomew was at the organ. At
this time, and until the Vestry forbade it, she gave her assistance to the practices and week-day services.

Though the best that could be done under the circumstances, these services fell far short of what the Rector wished.
Those at All Saints, Margaret Street, were considered by
most Churchmen to be the best rendered and most devout
of any. It was a representative church, and St. Vedast
would have followed its example but for lack of material.

In 1873 the opportunity Pelham Dale had long wished
for came. On one of his numerous journeys by the Underground Railway, a friend told him in conversation that Mr.
Cowie, of St. Laurence Jewry, having been promoted to
the Deanery of Manchester, the choir were seeking work
elsewhere. Dean Cowie's successor intended to alter the
services, and at his suggestion the choir took time to consider whether they would continue to work under such
different conditions.

" If they are leaving, I wish they would come to me,"

said the Rector of St. Vedast. This speech was repeated
to them, with the result that they offered their services
and were accepted. They were of the class Mr. Dale had
always felt ought to be served by churches in the position
of St. Vedast. They spent their working hours in the
offices and warehouses of the City, and they were members
of those crowds which, except on Sundays and Bank holidays, stream through its quaintly-named streets, lanes, and
alleys. The so-called parishioners spent less time in the
City, for they were not obliged to attend the offices they
rented with the regularity of their clerks.

Mr. Turner, the choir-master and precentor, wrote a
letter to the *City Press* explaining their reason for leaving,
and doing justice to the courtesy and kindly consideration
of Mr. Walrond, Mr. Cowie's successor. This letter was
afterwards printed as a leaflet with the heading of St.
Vedast, Foster, and St. Michael-le-Querne, and a note to
the effect that the Rector of the above-named parishes had
accepted their services. Their reason for leaving St. Laurence Jewry, was "the proposed alterations in the manner
of conducting Divine service, chiefly in the position of the
celebrant at the time of Holy Communion, and the disapproval of non-communicating attendance, by assenting to
which they would practically deny the doctrine of their
Blessed Lord's holy presence in the Eucharist."

The editor's comment on the letter from which this extract is quoted was :—"We consider that a body of men
maintaining such a doctrine as that set forth in the above
resolution are not fit to hold any official position in the
Church of England, and that the sooner they transfer their
services elsewhere the better."

This comment is printed in a parenthesis on the leaflet.
The services at St. Vedast are announced to begin on
Advent Sunday, November 30. The leaflet was for private
circulation among the members of the choir and their friends.

The Rector of St. Vedast issued a pastoral to his congregation that explains clearly his position and views at this time :—

To the Parishioners and Congregation.

DEAR FRIENDS,—It is well known to many of you that I have for some years past laboured to do what I could towards supplying that which is evidently one of the most pressing spiritual wants of our great city, viz., the adaptation of the services in our sanctuaries to the needs of the fluctuating working population, which, no longer resident, is gathered each day from the surrounding suburbs. To this end was established the Women's Bible Union, as inquiry showed me that there was no special provision for the female workers, analogous to those agencies which had already been so happily established for young men. Thus I hoped to enter a harvest-field in the Church as yet but little reaped, and one where I was not likely to interfere with other men's labours. I thank God that our work, though small and unobtrusive, has not lacked tokens of His acceptance in the earnestness and heartiness of spirit with which we were enabled to drink in the sweetness of His Holy Word.

But I was alone and single-handed ; nor was I able, though I made many efforts to do so, to make our services—and these are the special glory of a sanctuary—so bright and cheerful as I wished. If earnest, the worshippers were few, and there was nothing to attract those I specially wished to benefit. Quite unexpectedly, however, I received the offer from a large number of Churchmen to give me the

help I desired, and thus carry on the work on a more
extended scale, and include both young men and
women in the scope of our efforts to edify. This help
I most thankfully accepted, and already, although our
arrangements are incomplete, have we a large choir
of communicant members of the Church, and an increasing congregation, who have given to our worship
that which it needed to make it what Christian worship
ought to be, beautiful and harmonious, and, above all,
spiritual and heart-stirring. The hours of service are
such as experience has shown are best adapted to
those engaged in the city. The week-day services
will be short and cheering, commencing and concluding also punctually at the hours named, that those
who are not "slothful in business" may also be
"fervent in spirit, serving the Lord."

The order and ornaments which we shall use in
these services will, I trust, commend themselves to all
earnest Churchmen. In these accessories of worship
it is best to follow ancient precedent, especially in
these days of changes, that we may thus visibly set
forth to those without that the Catholic Faith can never
wax old or vanish away. The unthinking may not
have considered this; the unbelieving deny it; the
prejudiced misunderstand it. But the reverent Christian, well instructed in the faith, will delight to
remember that in our venerable Liturgy he is wor-
shipping God with the same words and forms which
those saints of old who, centuries ago, fell asleep
in Jesus, were wont to use. To him it is a visible
reminder of that Communion of Saints in which,

notwithstanding heresies, schisms, and disunions, he firmly believes.

I must, however, here remind you that the Church of God has from the first foundation rested on the Holy Word of God. Without that Gospel, most firmly believed amongst us, there can be neither Church, nor Sacraments, nor Saviour. Thus, then, the study of the Word of God must ever be a principal object with all true Christians. "They must consider how studious they ought to be in reading and learning the Scriptures, and in framing the manners of themselves, and them that specially pertain to them, according to the rule of the same Scriptures." Never was this more necessary than now, when we are told that Science has irrefutably shown that the Gospel is but a beautiful myth, by which is meant that very same thing which the Apostle speaks of more plainly as a cunningly devised fable. The best method to refute such sophistries is to study the Scripture itself. Its wonderful adaptation to human needs; its inner harmonies; above all, the testimony it gives to Christ, and the testimony it receives from the Spirit, point to those who will prayerfully study that it *is* the pure engrafted Word which is able to save our souls. The better to promote this study, Bible-classes have been instituted, which all who are able are invited to attend. These, with the sermons of those who will address you from the pulpit, will, I trust, teach you the true and right way.

But with the Word of God are joined sacraments by an inseparable bond, and not even the devout hearer of

the Word of God can be looked on as other than a cate-
chumen and babe in Christ if he be not baptized and a
participator in the holy mysteries of the Sacrament of
the Body and Blood of our Lord. None, therefore, who
are of age can be admitted to the choir except they be
devout, regular, and consistent communicants, but those
who are such, and have the time and ability to lead the
praises of their brethren, we entreat to join us. We
propose that all such members of the choir as can
possibly attend should meet at the early celebration at
eight o'clock on the morning of Advent Sunday, in order
that we may formally begin our work with mutual supplication one for the other. If any are unable to be
present, they are requested to communicate elsewhere,
that, though absent in the body, they may be present
in spirit at that Holy Eucharist which is also the holy
communion of all the faithful. I do also most earnestly
entreat every member of the congregation either at
once to make full use of these their Christian privileges, or at least use all diligence according to the
Church's rule to prepare themselves thereto. Remember that those who, being able, refuse to communicate,
have excommunicated themselves : that soul is cut off
from the visible body of the faithful.

And now I commend you to God and the Word of
His grace, which is able to build you up and give you
an inheritance among them that be sanctified. Brethren,
pray for us, that the Word may have free course and
be glorified, as I trust it is with you.—Your faithful
servant and minister in Christ,

T. PELHAM DALE.

The following is the general order of services which will be held in the Church on and after Advent Sunday next :—

Every Sunday, Celebration of the Holy Communion at 8 o'clock A.M.   Matins, second Celebration of Holy Communion with Sermon, at 10.45 A.M. Litany and Sermon at 3 P.M.   Evensong and Sermon at 7 P.M.

Every Wednesday, Litany or Te Deum and Short Sermon at 1.15 P.M.   Evensong at 8 P.M.

Every Friday, Litany or Te Deum and Short Sermon at 1.15 P.M.   Short Evening Service at 7.30.

On all Holy Days, a Short Mid-day Service at 1.15 P.M.   Evensong at 8 P.M.

All the services will be choral, excepting the first Celebration on Sundays.   Bible-classes will be held in the Vestry for men on Wednesday evenings at 9 o'clock ; for women on Friday evenings at 8 o'clock.

The mid-day services were among the most useful and best attended of all.   It meant that on Wednesdays and Fridays many men gave up a portion of their luncheon-hour to attend the service, and in after days a grateful mention was made of these half-hours of worship in several letters to Mr. Dale in prison ; the best consolation the writers could have offered him.   This mid-day service, especially in Advent and Lent, was afterwards adopted at St. Paul's Cathedral, where congregations of City men still meet.   In 1873 St. Vedast was always well attended, for it was about the only church in the City whose doors were open at that hour.

It had been found that the offertory at St. Laurence Jewry was sufficient to pay an assistant-priest, and Mr.

Nicholson, who had been Curate there, now came to St.
Vedast. Thus Mr. Pelham Dale found one of his earnest
wishes fulfilled; his church was used once more, and his
ministry gladly accepted by those he had been anxious to
serve. But the ratepayers were indignant at this invasion of
their church. As their homes were not in the City they
never attended it themselves, but they were ratepaying
parishioners for all that, and felt it right to protest against
week-day services. One of the parishioners—also non-
resident—welcomed the change heartily, and presented the
Rector with a brass cross for the altar. This cross and two
candles were the ornaments, usual enough now-a-days, but
the right to use them has not been won without a struggle.
The altar itself was an oak table, with four angels supporting the four corners. It was supposed to have been
originally a credence table, and was small and low. The
Rector, however, appreciating its beautiful workmanship,
preferred to keep it in its honourable position; it suited
the rich carving of the reredos, if only its size had not
rendered it insignificant. The altar with its cross, two
candles, and flowers on festivals, raised the anger of certain
people. Now-a-days the hatred of the cross as a symbol is
less than it was then; it has been accepted, but there is still
a prejudice against stone figures even in the restoration of
old works, when the empty niches show where of old time
the statue stood. The curious ornaments with which some
persons can conscientiously decorate their churches are
defended on the ground that no one would worship them.
Protected by such arguments, the signs of the zodiac have
been found suitable, and pagan monuments have been raised
with never a religious memory or hope betrayed in their
sculpture. This shrinking from all religious symbols is
surely a sign of terrible decadence in religion and art. It
is a prejudice hard to account for and hard to remove; it
may be perhaps an involuntary protest against the intrusion

of religion into week-day life. There was certainly at one time a very strong dislike to letting the religion of Sunday, generally called the Sabbath, rule over any but the one day. Religion was respectable and necessary; but for the comfort of those who submitted to it for the sake of respectability and example, it must be limited.

There is a story which, true or not, describes accurately the popular feeling about the cross as a Christian symbol. There was once a rich man who built for himself and his co-religionists an exceedingly magnificent chapel. Since money was no object—a grand phrase that!—the architect employed was allowed to indulge in the most florid Gothic he could invent. The building was rich with crocket and pinnacle, with buttresses that strengthened nothing, and gargoyles that grinned for grinning's sake. Over the gargoyles in their grotesqueness he spent his best imagination, and finally finished off the spire, merely for ornament, with a cross. With much pride and more trepidation he watched the effect of his ornate building on his patron when it was first shown free of scaffolding. He had no cue to his client's artistic tastes; he knew only that he expected money's worth for ready money. Among the plans submitted, those with the most substantial outline had always been received with the greatest favour. Now he saw the great man's face darken.

"This'll never do, man!" he exclaimed in the impatient abrupt manner of one to whom time is money.

The architect imagined the wave of the hand directed to his beloved gargoyles. "I assure you, sir," he began, "those grotesque figures——"

"Pooh! pooh!" interrupted the other impatiently, "let the devils alone, man! It's the cross that must come down!"

This was the feeling with regard to the cross at St. Vedast. From a case decided at that time it appeared there was no

illegality in a movable ornament, so one day the cross was
carried off. How it was done was not known. From a
letter from the donor it appears that some one had stated
it was by order of the Bishop. He writes to ask if such a
fact were possible. "I gave it to you personally," he says;
"if the parties have removed and kept it, it is to my mind
clearly a theft, and should be so treated." It was not,
however, within the experience of High Churchmen that
legal decisions were ever in their favour—the treatment of
the rioters at St. George's-in-the-East enforced this lesson—
so after consideration the matter was allowed to drop, and
for some time a floral cross supplied the place of the stolen
one. In this threatening of storms the year 1873 drew
to a close. The Public Worship Regulation Act was in
the air, the days of the Ritualists were said to be numbered.
The Archbishop himself was forging the weapon that was to
destroy them; and, strangely enough, all the time these very
strong measures were being taken, the clamour was against
the intolerance of Puseyites and their re-lighting of the fires
at Smithfield.

St. Alban's, Holborn, was the church most directly attacked. It had been consecrated in 1864; since then
schools and parochial works had grown up round it, the
courts and alleys about it were comparatively civilised, its
services were crowded; but in spite of this, not an authority
put forth a hand to prevent the attacks made upon it or
showed a willingness to frustrate the attempt to stop such a
great work. With this example before them, humble com-
mencements like that of St. Vedast had reason to tremble
for their very existence; but this persecution was also a
purification. Every member of the congregation knew that
the work was done for the work's sake; that the incumbent
who undertook it forfeited all chances of Church preferment;
that closed doors with few dull services meant safety, respectability and a smiling recognition from authorities who

loved peace. It gave a brotherhood, a devotion, an earnestness to these worshippers; but, as all evil things do, it
worked great harm among the weaker souls. They shrank
from ridicule; they doubted, naturally, of powers that did
not believe in themselves, who claimed for the Church no
more than her value as a society for inculcating good
manners and a decent observation of the Sunday—say
church at eleven in your own cushioned pew—and, confus-
ing the Church with its representatives, they found it difficult to believe in a body that did not seem to believe in
itself.

CHAPTER VI.

HAVING carried the history of Mr. Dale's work to the most troublous period of his existence, it might serve as a better explanation of his opinions than any that his biographer can give, to insert here a paper of his on the development of ritual. Had the original scheme of this book been carried out, the mental development of the movement would have been traced side by side with its history. This paper contains the gist of the arguments intended to be used, though their form—that of a paper read at a clerical meeting—necessarily restricts and limits them.

THE DEVELOPMENT OF RITUAL A NECESSARY OUTCOME OF EVANGELICAL REVIVAL.

That there has been a development of ritual not only within the Church of England, but also beyond its borders, even among Dissenters of the strictest puritan traditions, is a fact which is patent to every one. We see the signs of it in Gothic Dissenting chapels with spires and towers, their choirs arranged chancel-wise, and in their services: for example, the announced Christmas carols of a neighbouring chapel—the very thing which in my own case has been adduced as an instance of

ultra-ritualism. This development has been uniformly
progressive during the last fifty years, and indeed long
before. To begin with one's own recollection, the Dissenting chapel built in the earlier years of the present
century was invariably plain. In a few cases perhaps
a portico with Doric columns might be attempted. But
a steeple-house!—it was to every puritan a nauseous
abomination. In the same way every one recollects
that peculiar style of church architecture—technically
called churchwardenism—which culminated in such
striking art effects as a high deal pew for the squire
lined with green baize affixed with brass nails—or a
Grecian reredos, presented by my lord, with painted
columns, either starved or gouty as the taste of the
noble giver suggested, and of far commoner materials
and very much worse design than his own portico,
which was usually in the very poorest classic taste.

The material fabric corresponded but too accurately
for the most part with the state of the spiritual life
within it. Communions three times a year—triennial
confirmations—no daily or even week-day services—
were quite the rule. There were some noble exceptions to all this, but they were few and far between.

I will give a sketch of the state of things in the
villages where I spent much of my early life not twenty
miles distant from St. Paul's.

C. cum F. was an All-Souls' living of some value,
with a good rectory or vicarage-house. The incumbent was *bene natus, bene vestitus*, and might have been,
as far as I know, *mediocriter doctus;* but he was far
too great a man to associate with any but county

people, and I have no recollection of ever seeing him.
However, the nearest church to us was F., and here we
had a succession of curates, carelessly selected and of
doubtful reputation.   There was, as might be expected,
little earnestness in the worship at F.   We generally
attended there in the morning, but walked over, if the
afternoon were fine, to D., a distance of three miles.
We were attracted, not indeed by ritual, but by simple
earnestness.

O. cum C. was another united parish.   O. was a
large village, and C. still larger, with a mill in it em-
ploying a considerable number of hands.   The vicar
kept no curate, so we had service one Sunday at O.,
the next at C., morning and afternoon alternately.   We
went to church of course when visiting a relation who
lived in C., but the old vicar mumbled so that his sermons were quite unintelligible ; it was hard to follow
him even in the prayers.   Of course there was no
spiritual life.   The mill-owner prospered greatly, and
being a Dissenter, built in a style of architecture of
his own a chapel which he called the Temple, one
of the ugliest buildings I ever saw.   The erection
of this building caused a large amount of bitter
feeling.   The poor old vicar, always eccentric, at last
died hopelessly imbecile, and a better state of things
began.

P. C. was held by an Evangelical, a good man, but
almost as crazy as his neighbour at O. cum C. ; nevertheless there was spiritual life and earnestness there.
It is true that the old gentleman, instead of reading
the Lessons, would expound special verses to the

congregation, and make such startling alterations in the
service that even the farmers were aghast. But, as he
said, he was an old man and the Bishop would excuse
him. I believe his Evangelical peculiarities were not
commented on by the Bishop. They were certainly
not made the subject of an ecclesiastical prosecution.

The church at which I attended oftenest was that of
B., now almost a suburb, then a country village. This
was the church of our home. We sat high up in a
gallery in deep pews, which effectually concealed inde-
corous behaviour. I was carefully instructed that the
church was God's house, and reverence was incul-
cated, and when necessary enforced. But as a practical
homily on this, whenever the weather permitted we
walked three miles to S., because there the Gospel was
preached. Of course, child though I was, I naturally
drew the inference that at B. the Gospel was *not*
preached. However, I used to listen to the sermons
at S., some of which I remember to this day. The
curate at B. (for the rector was a pluralist and non-resident) was especially brief, one of his sermons lasting
for what was then the marvellously short period of
seven and a half minutes. Short as they were, they
seemed to me to be tedious. My impressions of B.
were of dirty surplices, and the pre-communion service
read from the desk, and not from the altar, which was
never used except at the infrequent celebrations, and
when I was, of course, not present.

My first impressions of ritual were experienced at
St. Mary-in-the-Castle at Hastings. Here the Communion Service was read from the altar, which was

covered with a bright crimson altar-cloth of velvet, and
there were two clergymen in clean surplices with hoods
and black scarves. Now I submit that the difference
between St. Mary's and B. was quite as great as that
which at present obtains between any two Kensington
churches of different schools you choose to name—nay,
it was far greater; it was not the difference between
high ritual and low ritual, but between reverence and
irreverence.   I do not believe, however, that St. Mary's
with its earnest Evangelical sermons, monthly communions, week-day lectures, &c., was in great favour.
The name by which all this was called in those days
was Methodism.   I may add, however, that I entered
B. again after I know not how many years' interval.
The harvest festival evensong had just finished, the
church was lighted with gas, and was most tastily de-
corated with fruit and flowers. My old gallery was
still in existence, but the square pews had disappeared
from the chancel, and there was, I think, in their place
an ornamental chancel screen with its gate still open.
Yet I maintain that the revival at B. is but the outcome of what I witnessed at St. Mary's nearly half a
century before.

For I believe it was quite impossible that awakening
spiritual life should be content with its old surroundings.   I do not believe it would have been possible
even if there had been *no* art revival outside the
Church.   But we know that a very strong art current,
both musical and pictorial, had set in; and this time
not confined to the cultivated and wealthy, but involving
the less educated classes. Witness our shilling concerts

and Bethnal Green Museum. Our age has been said
to lack the art feeling, but surely a country that can
give birth to a Turner and welcome so enthusiastically
a Mendelssohn, cannot be devoid of feeling for art. It
was not, then, likely to allow its religious worship to
remain in the state of utter coldness and colourlessness
existing at the beginning of the century. The Church
had already been growing stronger, for, at the time I
speak of, the Evangelical revival had caught hold of the
people, and the place had become too strait for her.
She must advance in ritual; the only question was
how and in what direction?

The genius of the English Church and people determined the lines on which this development was to
take place. Our Church, though reformed, has never
broken, as the Continental Reformed Churches have
done, with the traditions of the past. The answer to
usurpations, whether of popes or kings, puritans or
republicans, has always been one *Nolumus leges angliæ
mutari*.

Thus then it was, I believe, inevitable that the necessary development of the externals of religious life should
take the form of a revival of ancient ritual. We must,
to satisfy our devotional needs, either invent or restore;
that the latter was the course that would be taken is, I
think, sufficiently proved by the universal contempt that
is expressed for what is called "fancy ritual." We may
preach in our gowns or in our surplices, but no congregation would submit to the ordinary coat, because the
coat has no past to support it. Our choirs may appear
either in their ordinary dress or in the surplice, but no

enterprising ritualist has ever advised black gowns for them. And so in the same way vestments mean albs and chasubles—that is, the ancient vestments in their ancient forms. The injunction to use the cope in cathedrals is only valued by the High Church party as admitting the principle of a Eucharistic vestment ; what they desire is *the* ancient Eucharistic vestment, which both parties know, if Eucharistic vestments should become general, will assuredly be the ancient chasuble, &c.

But now, it may be asked, why should such a sudden desire have displayed itself—shared in by so many of the clergy—for a distinctive Eucharistic vestment ? What has made this and the so-called eastward position the badge of a party ? Is there not a cause, and that deeper than the æsthetic and antiquarian proclivities of Englishmen ? In truth there is. Let me point out what I believe it to be.

Every fresh movement in the Church is, I believe, the outcome and complement of some corresponding movement outside.

The Church and the world develop side by side, but then within the Church this development cannot result in producing new doctrines. Erroneous and strange doctrine, that is, heresies and novelties, are all in the same category, and are equally to be driven away. Development of the faith then can only exist in the more clear and perfect exposition of doctrines already existing. This fact has been abundantly insisted on by writers upon Church history, and numberless instances have been pointed out by them. If, then, this

be so, we must look outside the Church for the complement of the Evangelical movement.

I maintain that the Evangelical revival was the
Church's effort to shake off the effects of the deism
of the preceding century. Butler and Paley—the last
dear to the memory of old Cantabs—represent the
scientific side ; Venn, Simeon, and their followers the
popular emotional and religious side of this effort. The
people were sunk into a cold and heartless indifferentism.
They were awakened by a fearless and heart-stirring
appeal to the great doctrine of Justification by Faith,
and the weakness of their chilly and semi-heathenish
morality was exposed by the announcement of the great
doctrine of human corruption and the absolute necessity of a personal Saviour. To use the French phrase,
the Evangelical revival conquered for us those half-
forgotten doctrines of the Gospel. What we used in
days gone by to call Evangelical sermons are now heard
everywhere, and with equal distinctness in High and
Low Church pulpits.

But though one phase of infidelity was attacked and
defeated, the monster is and ever will be hydra-headed ;
and another development was taking place. David
Hume's works gather dust on the shelves of our
libraries, as do those of deists who went before him.
But now Tyndal, Darwin, and Huxley are in the
ascendant, and there are more dangerous enemies
still; Strauss and Renan have their followers in
England, and a so-called scientific criticism has done
its utmost to weaken and undermine the very foundation of the faith itself.

The Evangelical of old prided himself on the fact that he followed the ancient method by proving from the *Scriptures* that Jesus was Christ. But the world now laughs at this method; it doubts the historic Scriptures and disbelieves in the historic Christ. It scoffs at the evidences of miracle and prophecy—both miracle and prophecy are with it simply impossibilities. Find a clear prediction in Scripture of some future event! The very evidence (so this school of writers affirm) proves that the date of the writing is erroneous. It is, of course, a *vaticinium post eventum*. Hence we have a school of thought of which Matthew Arnold is a popular exponent, widely disseminated and having followers within the Church itself. Now, it would lead me too far away from my main subject to show how this school of thought acts and reacts upon modern religious opinion; but the result is patent; it is a lowering of our conception of the divinity of our Blessed Lord, and a denial, more or less complete, of the supernatural in religion. In a word, then, Rationalism has superseded Deism. Philosophical unbelief has given place to scientific scepticism.

Now, in the face of this change of attack, the Church is forced to change her mode of defence. Whereas before faith was opposed to unbelief, now the supernatural is set over against the natural. It is no new doctrine which affirms this supernatural character, both in the past and present; it is the oldest of them all, revived and reinforced to meet the rising tide of heathenism and Sadduceanism which is around us.

The Church always has claimed supernatural powers

and a divinely-appointed order, and these claims are
now asserted. She is not only the guardian and
keeper of Holy Scripture, the point which came forward so prominently in Evangelical teaching, but she
is besides the dispenser and minister of supernatural
grace conveyed by sacraments. In these she sees the
real presence of her ever-present Lord manifested to
her faithful members. Thus the sacramental system,
as it has been called, has necessarily risen into highest
prominence. The Evangelicals—to use a simile borrowed from our church arrangements—placed the pulpit
before the altar. It was perhaps well that it should
be so then, for they had not only to teach men how to
approach the altar, but they had also, as it were, to
fence it from those who had hitherto neglected so mar-
vellous a means of grace. Now if, at this present, the
pulpit stands a little aside, it has lost none of its dignity on that account, only the Holy Table rises to its
proper eminence. The Church has had her Matins in
the earlier days of her revival, let the higher liturgy of
the Celebration now begin. Let the faithful know that
the Lord is with them of a truth. If they have known
hitherto that where two or three are gathered together
in His name, there is He in the midst of them, let
them now see that of the Holy Table especially can
we say is the promise fulfilled, "There will I meet with
thee and speak unto thee."

It is, then, this felt want of the divine in the surrounding denial of the supernatural—this now marked
contrast between the heathenism and the Christianity
of these times, and which Evangelical preaching has

brought into such prominence, which has caused the revival again of what I may call Eucharistic religion.

As of old it was the celebration of the Eucharist which made the final separation of heathen and Christian, those who were not Christians then leaving the sacred building and its door closing on the faithful alone, so is it—allowing for the altered circumstances —even now.

Eucharistic celebration is regarded more and more as the turning-point of Christian life, as the external mark and sign distinguishing the believer from the unbeliever. For it is just here that the antagonism of those who do and those who do not believe in historic Christianity comes into the strongest relief. Whatever views we take of the Divine Presence in the Holy Eucharist, it is evident that that Holy Mystery has a special significance, as a showing forth the Lord's death, καταγγέλειν, till He come, which is utterly opposed to naturalism. Most of all, the ancient Church view of the Holy Supper, which taught her worshippers that there was something more than mere bread and mere wine before them, is opposed to it. So then in an age when the contest between belief and unbelief was at its height, it was natural that the controversy should, as it were, be associated with the pulpit, alleging that " this same Jesus which we preach unto you is Christ;" so now that the front of the battle has shifted, and it is a contest between naturalism and supernaturalism, it is equally natural that the altar should come into prominence, for it is at the altar that the supernatural in our religion receives its most emphatic testimony. In the Sacrament of the Altar is the testimony to, first, the supernatural in the PAST as witnessing to a Divine Saviour—the God-man suffering for our redemption—a Christ who did so suffer, so die, *so rise again*, even as it is declared in the Gospel. Secondly, to the supernatural in the PRESENT, to a Christ continually and in the Sacrament really present to His people. Thirdly, to the supernatural in the FUTURE, to a Christ about to come (even as prophets have declared) with power and great glory to judge the world in righteousness. Hence I think we find a reason why our age—the age of Darwinism and Tyndalism—that is, the age in which the world will know of pure naturalism and nothing else—should be the same age in which the Church displays afresh the power of Eucharistic Mysteries. Thus the sacramental revival has extended itself alike to all sections and schools of thought within the Church.

In sacraments, and especially in the Eucharist, we have, according to the belief of all Christians who venerate sacraments at all, the nearest realisation possible of the supernatural. If we take as our guide Catholic doctrine, I mean the doctrine of the first six centuries of Christianity, we shall have to affirm a real presence of Christ, a supernatural grace derived from that living presence, to the faithful something more than a mere commemoration of an event in the past, though that event was essentially miraculous in the highest degree—something which brings the supernatural to the level of present experience, and thus gives most emphatically the lie to that modern form ot infidelity, which surely takes this for its fundamental principle, that "all things continue as they were from the beginning of the creation." I can indeed conceive a man who disbelieves the historic miraculous Christianity of the Gospels being possibly a devout worshipper. I cannot conceive it possible that he should be a devout communicant. I think also I see a reason why the faithful laity should now cling so much more to sacraments than before—not that the best Evangelicals, as I know, ever were guilty of undervaluing the Eucharist—it is the instinct of the unlearned, often truer and better than the reasoning of the learned, clinging fast to the rock of the faith where it affords surest foothold and shelter in the present storm. They hide themselves in the cleft of the rock, in the wounded side of Jesus, till this tyranny—this cold-hearted scepticism—be overpast.

Thus then I think I have shown that the revival of the so-called Sacramental System is due to the spread of naturalism. It is a fact that the age of Darwinism and Tyndalism has witnessed a wonderful revival (and that, remember, not confined to a particular ecclesiastical school of thought) of sacramental observance. I have endeavoured to show that in this case *post hoc* is *propter hoc*—that we have a consequence, not a coincidence. I have shown also why this revival must be accompanied with a ritual development, which, while embracing our whole liturgy, should culminate at Eucharistic Celebration.

I have, in conclusion, to remark very briefly on the causes whence arises the resistance that this

development is encountering not only within, but
especially amongst Christians without, the Anglican
Communion. But this, again, is, I think, easily accounted
for. The Roman Communion, as was to be expected,
has preserved far more of the ancient ritual than we have.
They have never done otherwise than use the eastward
position and the vestments—they have retained the
lights and the incense which we have disused, though,
I trust, *not* abolished. Hence these things are considered to be distinctively Roman, and are classed by the
general and ill-informed public in precisely the same
category as are Papal supremacy, transubstantiation,
the immaculate conception and Papal infallibility. Both
Romans and Nonconformists have a direct interest in
the continuance of this illusion, for the former will
assuredly gain if they can confound the primitive and
the Roman together, and so advance, as indeed they
are diligently doing, their own uncatholic tenets under
the guise of Catholicism. They use the mixed chalice
—we do not; they hold Papal infallibility—we do not.
It is easy to transfer, by a kind of rhetorical leger-
demain quite as effective with the reasoner as with those
whom he wishes to convince, some of the hoary honour
of the one to cover the intrinsic modernness of the
other. Monsigneur Capel makes it quite a point, I
believe, that High Churchmen imitate him and his
communion. The answer is seldom heard that we
have as much right to primitive ritual as he has, and
that these observances have in them nothing essentially Popish. An answer which, in the midst of a
senseless " No Popery " cry which some who ought to

know better join in, it is difficult to obtain a hearing for at all.

Again, the Nonconformists are equally interested in preventing this ritualistic manifestation. They decline to appeal to antiquity at all; they reject the apostolic succession of the priesthood; they are for the most part Zwinglians in doctrine. There is this weakness inherent in their system, that if they are not Protestants they are nothing. Witness that very curious current phrase, the Protestant religion, as though religion could consist in a protest against the errors of others. It is indeed true that this is but a *façon de parler*, but it has far too much truth in it, all the same. No wonder, then, that they should instinctively recoil from a ritual which incidentally sets forth the apostolic character of its priesthood, and which is opposed at every point to that of Zwinglianism, which regards the Eucharist as commemorative and nothing else— a ritual which, at every turn and gesture, goes back to the ages of primitive Christianity, which takes in all that was best and purest of that mediæval Christianity which they have been taught to regard as at once the very darkest ignorance and the very mystery of iniquity combined. Nevertheless, I do not believe that we shall find in Nonconformity where it is earnest and sound in evangelical belief—where it is *truly Christian*, a very implacable adversary. Fortunately, we have ceased to attempt to control our Nonconformist brethren with the machinery of bit and Conventicle Acts. They are free to build their chapels with spires and chancels if they will, but then, if they do, how

very little will it cost to turn them into churches?
Verbum sap., for I can pursue this topic no further.

I must say, then, that I anticipate, and at no very
distant period, success to the so-called ritualistic
movement, so soon as the public are sufficiently well-
informed to understand the real state of the case.
I think something of this kind will happen. According to the last judgment, the mixed chalice is illegal.
If this should be affirmed, we shall perhaps have a
clergyman or two suspended for using it—that is, for
doing what nearly all the Western Church, and all the
Eastern too, has done before him for eighteen centuries.
I have some idea that such a *reductio ad absurdum*
will be too much for English common-sense. And the
same is true, *mutatis mutandis*, of the eastward position, the lights and vestments, and, perhaps in a somewhat less degree, of incense also. There are heresies
which have died a natural death. This prohibition of
ancient ritual does not even rise to the dignity of a
heresy; it is the result of a senseless panic, a misap-
prehension. The opposition it now causes will fade
away in a while, vanishing into the limbo where opposition to the surplice in the pulpit, intoned prayers, and
stone altars has already vanished.

The most important question yet remains. Will
the success of ritualism—that is, of a more æsthetic
and magnificent development of ritual observance—be
accompanied with a real advance of Gospel truth?
This will depend upon the depth of spiritual life within
the Church herself. Ritual, being the external shell,
the symbolical act which implies the devotional feeling,

can do no more than express that feeling. It is to
spiritual religion exactly what words are to thought;
and as poverty of thought is often masked by exu-
berance of language, so may spiritual deadness be
covered with excess of ritual. Moreover, the analogy
may be pushed further. Just as language in such circumstances becomes verbose, so does ritual become
tawdry and degenerate into slovenliness. If, however,
there be within the Church a real increase in spiritual
life, then the ritual, like well-ordered and noble words,
will rightly set forth the value of noble thoughts.
It is the persuasion that the ritual is for the most part
a genuine expression of devotion on the part of those
who use it, and the personal experience that the adoption of it in due measure helps, and does not hinder
devotion, which has made me a ritualist. I do verily
believe that I and my people are certainly benefited by
these things, and that the spiritual life is really deepen-
ing amongst us. I believe that the ritual does set forth
the doctrine, and the ancient ritual the ancient (that
is, the true Catholic) doctrine. I believe that, as we
use the ceremonies which have been used in the
Church for so many centuries, even though disuse had
made them to some—yes, to myself, till better instructed — appear strange and questionable, we do
very vividly and consolingly bring back to our remembrance that Communion of Saints which unites us in
spirit with that noble army of martyrs—aye, with that
wider, nobler company still, the Holy Church throughout all the world who have lived before us in the faith
and fear of Christ. I verily believe that these ancient

ritual observances have no inconsiderable influence towards inducing us to hold fast to that faith once delivered to the saints which alone can stand against the scoffs and persecutions of an ungodly and sceptical world.

If it be true, however, as some think, that these ritual observances we prize so much are but superstition, if there is no life in them, if they are but rubbish to be swept away, then have I greatly erred. If they be not as the furniture of that Tabernacle in which God dwells, if this progress in ritual be not for His glory or the advantage of the souls of His Church, then I can only say very sorrowfully, " If Thy Spirit go not with us, carry us not up from hence."

CHAPTER VII.

EIGHTEEN hundred and seventy-four was the year of the
London Mission, the first of those general calls for reflection and repentance which the Church has since repeated
to the great benefit of her people.

The Mission services at St. Vedast began a day earlier
than elsewhere, for the 6th of February is St. Vedast's day.
St. Vedast, although of French origin—he was Bishop of
Arles—seems to have been a popular patron saint in England. This church bore as an *alias* the anglicised form of the
saint's name, Foster, which is frequent all over the country
as a surname. To the Fosters, perhaps, as builders of
churches, are due those dedications to their patron saint.
The German Faust has the same derivation. There is no
other church of this dedication in London, but there are some
two or three in the Lincoln diocese, *i.e.*, St. Vedast; the
alias Foster is unique. "Aliases are never respectable, Dale,"
a friend whispered when the name was called at a visitation. St. Michael's surname, Le Querne, as all Londoners
know, means that the church was in the cornmarket.

It seemed especially advantageous to a new work like
that at St. Vedast, that the mission should come so early
in its existence to establish and strengthen it, and choir and
clergy entered with energy into the preparations for the
services for their dedication festival and the Mission.

The distance of his house from the church was at no

time allowed by Mr. Dale to excuse himself from attendance at the services, or to prevent his adding any extra clerical work that appeared useful to the congregation.

The Mission at St. Vedast was conducted by the Rev. R. J. Ives of Clewer. The following is the invitation to the Mission given in full, for these addresses and pastorals show the object and spirit of the work :—

DEARLY BELOVED IN CHRIST,—In bringing before you the order of services which, if God will, we propose to hold during the ensuing Mission-time, let me remind you of the objects we have in view, and the benefits which we hope will result from them to ourselves and others.

The Mission is a combined effort on the part of faithful members of the Church to deepen the spiritual life in themselves and to seek to arouse the careless and indifferent. The method by which it is sought to do this is (1) first of all, earnest prayer and intercession for grace, as well publicly in the sanctuary as in the privacy of the home and the seclusion of the chamber, and then (2) secondly, by a combined effort on the part of those who are conscious that they have received the gift, to minister the same, in their several orders and degrees, to others who are doubting, careless, or unbelieving.

By a happy coincidence, our Commemoration Festival falls on the day before that appointed by the Bishop for the commencement of the Mission. Our parish church is dedicated to the glory of God in special memory of one who was a Missionary Bishop to a neighbour country, at a time when history shows us that the Mission work of the Church was making the most striking progress. We may remark, however, that St. Vedast was not a martyr, nor even what is usually meant by a confessor : the greater part of his life was spent as a simple missionary priest. We may surely be encouraged by the thought that the same Word of God, and the same faith in Christ which proved so efficacious in the sixth century, will not fail of success now. The Lord's promise, "I am with you always, even to the end of the world," belongs as much to us as it did to our forefathers. The same heartfelt faith, then, relying on the same promise, will assuredly manifest both to ourselves and the world that real Christianity has lost nothing of its power and efficacy; for if HE be for us, who shall be against us? Thus, then, ought we to be stirred up to renewed and more earnest effort, as well by the recollection of the past as by confidence in the future. The Gospel goes forth conquering and to conquer.

Let all of us, then, who are convinced of this, endeavour to realise the power by which we shall prevail. It is not ourselves, it is not our own strength; it is the Lord working with us and in us. Thus must we, first of all, strive to deepen our own spiritual life; we must earnestly seek an increased penitence for, and hatred of sin; a more lively desire after holiness; a greater nearness to God in devotion; an increased love to Christ; a more complete dependence upon His grace, and a more hearty submission to His will. Now the chief means of obtaining grace is a diligent use of the means of grace, and to this end let us carefully and to the utmost of our ability use those opportunities afforded us in the more frequent services, Eucharistic and otherwise, which the Mission-time will afford. Then, having thus ourselves tasted anew that the Lord is gracious, let us with all earnestness of heart, with one accord, intercede on behalf of the doubting, the careless,

and unbelieving: thus may we, in full confidence of a
happy result, go forth and show the sincerity of our
prayers, by seeking to influence those with whom the
providence of God has placed us, and by word and deed
stir up in them also the gift of God, or, if they be ignorant, lead them to the knowledge of truth.

How much some of you may do, and how extended is
your sphere, I need hardly remind you. In our great
commercial centres how wide and promising is the Mis-
sion-field open to an earnest soul ! Sometimes you can
speak and hold not your peace ; at other times silent
sympathy may be more eloquent than words. Do you,
especially who are older and more experienced in the
ways of city life, and to whom is commended, as it
were by a special Providence, those who, young and
inexperienced, often friendless and strangers, enter on
its awful dangers and temptations, consider afresh if
you have done your utmost to advance your Master's
kingdom. Did it ever strike you that you must watch
for their souls as one who must give an account ?

We, your ministers, for our part, will be ready. We
will, if you will allow us, advise those of you who are
in doubt, comfort those who are in sorrow. Sympathy
and counsel you shall have, as far as our poor power
extends. To the anxious and conscience-troubled we
say in the words of our Church, " Let him come and
open his grief, that by the ministry of God's Holy
Word he may receive the benefit of absolution." This
high gift and prerogative of ours we exercise with the
more confidence, because we do it not as those who
have dominion over your faith, but as partakers of

your joy. As "ambassadors for Christ, as though God
did beseech you by us: we pray you in Christ's stead,
be ye reconciled unto God."

Come, then, you who are by God's grace confirmed
and steadfast in the faith; the love of Christ will con-
strain you. Come, you that are doubting and despond-
ing; the love of Christ shall comfort you. Come, those
who are careless and indifferent; the love of Christ
shall quicken you. Come, you who gainsay and dis-
believe; the love of Christ will convince you. Come,
you who have even to this time hated that Holy Name;
the love of Christ will win you. There is none other
name given among men whereby we must be saved but
only the name of the Lord Jesus Christ. Let him that
is athirst come and drink of the water of life freely.

Your faithful servant in Jesus Christ,

T. PELHAM DALE.

The year 1874, beginning with additional spiritual life,
was one of increasing trouble and annoyance in other matters.
The differences between the Rector and churchwardens
grew more bitter, instead of, as the former hoped, gradually dying out. The facts of the matter were briefly
these. The charity funds of St. Vedast were carelessly
kept, being paid into the senior churchwarden's own banking account, and audited by the churchwardens themselves.
This churchwarden was the man in whose name all the
legal proceedings against Mr. Dale were undertaken. He
was the only one of the four resident in the parish, and was
a shoemaker in Gutter Lane—not so low a neighbour-
hood as the name implies—but he was the poorest of the
four, the other three being men of good means, successful in
their various trades, and living in the suburbs. Mr. Sergeant

did not attend the church (until the close observation of
the Rector became a part of his duty) except sufficiently to
qualify for the post of churchwarden, and was by choice a
Dissenter. For a man in any position to have trust sums
paid into his own account was, as the Rector pointed out,
unbusinesslike. The accounts of St. Michael were kept in
a better manner, but the expenditure was not satisfactory.
The dinner before mentioned averaged from £30 to £40
a year; the officials had large salaries and small duties; the
vestry meetings voted large sums towards the poor-rates,
though not a ratepayer in the parish required pecuniary assistance either from or towards the rates; the church property
was let on long and easy leases; and, in short, the managers
of this money had drifted into a belief that they had the
right as well as the power to do what they liked. The church
was not in good repair, though from time to time sums appeared in the accounts as spent upon cleaning. From this
year to 1881 nothing was done to the building in spite of
frequent representations from the Rector. The stone-paved
aisles were full of dangerous pitfalls and curious holes, while
the rats that found their way into the church showed that
there were certainly openings in the vaults below. The lead-
ings of the windows were no longer weather-tight, and walls
and glass were in want of cleaning. The gross income of St.
Michael's parish was £568, 1cs., of St. Vedast £800, and
the salaries of organist, sexton, and parish-clerk were paid
from these funds, but not a single other expense. The
organist was forbidden to play except on Sundays, Good
Friday, and Christmas Day. While on this subject I will
add Mr. Pelham Dale's account of the dispute about the
Sir John Johnstone's School.

This school was let to the Rev. M. Gibbs at £20 per
annum, and he covenanted to teach any who should
present themselves under the terms of the foundation.

In effect the school was an infant-school, and was valued by those who were afraid to allow their children to go across the crowded thoroughfares. I was often requested to grant a lease, but declined on the ground that the person holding the school ought not to pay rent at all. I did propose a scheme to the vestry, and offered myself to teach in the school, but the matter was adjourned *sine die*. When Mr. Gibbs gave up the infant-school I took it, but almost immediately the school had to be temporarily closed during the rebuilding of the adjoining premises. The keys of the school were given over to the builder, and the school and churchyard used as a depository of material and as a carpenter's shop without any rent, and contrary to my wishes. On my obtaining the keys from the builder, who of course had no authority to hold them, the lock was secretly altered. I was lately applied to by some lads to give them classes, and wrote desiring admission for this purpose, but was refused. I repeatedly asked to see the deed by which the site is leased to the Rector and churchwardens and was refused.

The unenviable position of the Rector with regard to his four churchwardens is easily understood in such a plain statement of facts as this of the schools; and as with this so with other subjects. The vestry meetings had no bright side to them. The Rector, sensitive, quiet, refined, hated disputes and hated rudeness, and the language of the vestry was no more choice and complimentary than is the majority of the meetings as reported in local prints. The only reporter allowed to be present was from a paper favoured by the churchwardens, but even there their speeches do not appear remarkable for restraint or refinement. Pelham Dale was

not a good fighter in such warfare, the triumph of having
said anything cutting or severe gave him no pleasure, and
he returned from these contests exhausted and weary. No
amount of work, no legal prosecution, not even prison itself
could compare in weariness and mental exhaustion with that
inflicted by a vestry meeting.

The mid-day services were a great success, and continued
to be so until they were adopted at the Cathedral, when the
smaller churches lost their congregations, but could hardly
regret the growth of a movement so quietly begun. The
increase of the congregation only made the discomforts of
the church more conspicuous, and in the first flush of their
new prosperity the Rector and his workers had visions of an
improved St. Vedast. That the large funds were not available was very evident, but it seemed possible that money
might be raised by the worshippers. With a view to this,
plans were prepared, and a faculty was to be obtained for
certain alterations and additions inside the church. The
plans were brought out in March, submitted to the Bishop,
who made some objections which were attended to, and thus
altered they were to be submitted to the vestry. Attempts
were made and frustrated to call this meeting before the
Easter elections. At the election a ratepayer writes to the
Rector to regret that " Mr. Horwood has been elected junior
churchwarden for St. Michael's ; he will be an opponent."

From a letter from this same friendly ratepayer it is
evident that the first meeting was a very stormy, not to say
abusive one. There is also another letter belonging to this
date so characteristic and amusing that it must not be altogether passed over ; it is from a dissentient parishioner, who
writes :—" I was perfectly astounded from receiving on Saturday from our house in the City specifications of certain alterations your aiming to make in the Church of St. Vedast."
After an allusion to old days, when the writer considered
the congregation quite large enough for a City church, he

goes on—" But oh ! what a mighty change has come over you ! I fear you have been studying in the school of Colenso, who has done all he can to prove that the Bible is a myth. Now, sir, I solemnly and seriously ask you if you believe the Bible to be true? If so, I am bound to tell you in all faithfulness that your present actions are entirely at variance with all the principles and doctrines of Scripture as I understand them." The beauties he finds were not intended irreverently, and shall not be quoted (he commits the common error of stating that our Lord never spoke rebukingly or in anger). These beauties he compares to the sounding brass and tinkling cymbals of the present day. He goes on to describe a poor widow who has just lost her husband, and a venerable old sinner who is nearing eternity, wandering into St. Vedast on the Sabbath-day, and is of opinion that they will return to their desolate homes "having been fed with nothing but husks which the swine eat." From this he commits himself to the frank opinion that " keeping peace with your vestry is the road to salvation," and ends with—

" But if you are determined to pursue that obstinate and pernicious course which you have done lately, I sincerely hope that every member of the vestry will obstruct your course by every legal means which may be at his disposal.— Believe me, Rev. Sir, with all Christian affection, yours very sincerely,   ——."

This letter of Christian affection is a specimen of the spirit in which the proposed changes were met. The faculty was not only opposed, it was delayed in every possible way. It took from March to August to get through the first step. Meanwhile, for the convenience of the choir, some of the side pews in the chancel were altered, the reading-desk was lowered by a board being taken out, and the floor was raised by a board being put in.

An arrangement so temporary and unimportant was made without any question of danger.   For many years no faculties had been obtained for any slight, or even important, alteration in the church.   But the Rector had his lesson to learn, and soon found that while one man may steal a horse, another may not look over a hedge.   So the first case of Sarjeant *v.* Dale was begun, and in his ignorance of legal possibilities the Rector felt very little alarm at the Chancellor's probable opinion of his plan for lifting the choir above the walls of the uncomfortable pews.

On the 25th January 1875, the case was to be opened ; therefore an appointment was made for the Chancellor to see the church.   If Dr. Tristram could have been made to sit even for a quarter of an hour in a pew without a footstool, it might have influenced him.   A gentleman with a strong Cockney accent and a curious habit of his own of disproportionately emphasising certain words in his sentence said of these seats, " My friend, sir, 'as a *wooden* leg, and gettin' *down* from these *seats* is *'orrible* to *'im."*

The case, however, was decided against the Rector.   He was allowed only one altered pew, which was considered sufficient to hold the boy-choristers ; the comfort of the platform was to be for a limited number of boys—the rest must stand upon footstools.   There was notice given of an appeal, but it was not prosecuted, and on September 9th the Court ordered that the platforms (excepting from pew 18) were to be removed by the Rector, or the churchwardens could take them away to prevent their being used on Sunday.

Before this decision was given, Mr. Pelham Dale had incurred the anger of the attacking Low Church party, and in consequence the court was held specially during the vacation, and opportunity was taken of commenting on the "use of these altered pews for practices which the churchwardens objected to, and which had led to the

differences between the churchwardens and the Rector."
Just at this time the strongest difference between Rector
and churchwardens was the dispute as to the using of
the schoolroom in Priest's Court for the object for which
it had been given, or the letting it to swell the total of
the funds.

Mr. Mackonochie, of St. Alban's, Holborn, was suspended in June 1875, and a determined attempt was made
to put an end to the great work being done in this poor
and crowded parish. The incumbent of St. Alban's was
being prosecuted under the old Act—a new one was ready
to complete his defeat when the force of the old was exhausted.   Mr. Mackonochie confined himself to one course
of action, to do what he thought right, and leave the rest in
God's hands.   He had a straightforward and determined
mind ; he was unhampered by money difficulties, the income from his church was merely nominal ; his own mode
of life was ascetic and simple ; he was the very man in his
strength and uprightness to be the leader in such a case.
But there is no doubt that the hard clerical work, which
by itself would have been a refreshment and a pleasure,
was unduly increased by the constant strain and anxiety to
which he was subjected ; so that at last the fine steadfast
mind began to bend under the pressure, but never the pure
religious spirit ; and his sad but beautiful death in the High-
lands, with the snow for his winding-sheet and the faithful
dogs for his watchers, may be traced to these heavy burdens
born uncomplainingly.   At this time, the Rector of St.
Vedast, admiring the calmness and determination with
which the incumbent of St. Alban's met the attack upon his
work, came forward to show an active sympathy.   The
services at St. Alban's—at least the Great Service—had to
be discontinued, for the clergy would not compromise the
rights of their branch of the Church Catholic by submitting
to uncanonical powers or admitting the illegality of their

worship. The sorrow and dismay of the crowded congregation at this deprivation was very great. The alienated laity,
whose protection was so much talked about at this time,
meant at St. Alban's a large band of very earnest Church-
people, who, because a very few grumbled at the manner of
conducting services, which there was no need for them to
attend, were to be driven out from their church with scornful recommendations to go to Rome, or infidelity, or indifference, so long as they went away. To these despised
worshippers Mr. Pelham Dale offered his church. After
matins at St. Alban's, clergy, choir, and congregation
walked to Foster Lane. The church was full to overflowing, some of the worshippers kneeling on the church
steps. Two of the St. Alban's clergy officiated, and
no doubt the result of the persecution was to fan the
flame of ardour and devotion that animated the kneeling
crowd.

Before next Sunday Mr. Stanton was forbidden by the
Bishop to officiate at St. Vedast's, but the congregation
continued to attend there until Mr. Mackonochie could
resume his duties at St. Alban's. When he did return, he
published a characteristically straightforward remonstrance in
the form of a letter to the Bishop of London. The following
extract refers to the services at St. Vedast :—

Your Lordship's demands, although in some points
greatly exceeding the decrees of the Court, were without question minutely obeyed by the St. Alban's clergy.
But to minister the Holy Sacrament of the Eucharist
was impossible, even if your Lordship had asked it of
them, when they could only do so standing at the
north end, with no priestly vestment—with a surplice
only, not even a stole. Some will say, "Well, but
surely the consecration of the sacrament is valid even

so." Yes, my Lord. Just as a subject needs only personal soundness to serve truly and loyally his sovereign, but would be thought hardly respectful if he therefore went in dressing-gown and slippers instead of court attire to the levée.

In this dilemma, the kind offer of Mr. Dale—a kindness which I hope will never be forgotten, either by St. Alban's people or by Catholics at large in the Church of England, and for which it has been my privilege to return him, in their name, hearty thanks —enabled them to direct the people to a church in which the Sacrament was to be found ministered in a manner which did not shock their religious sensibilities or in any way compromise your Lordship. Accordingly, the congregation went to St. Vedast's, and, by the request of Mr. Dale (partly in order to facilitate the addition of a celebration for the better accommodation of our people), two of our clergy officiated, strictly according to the usages of that church. Your Lordship was aware of the fact that they had thus taken part in the St. Vedast services on Monday morning, and, on the same day, of the fact that they would again take part in them on St. Peter's Day. You did not, however, express any disapproval of their doing so, or any wish that they should not do so; you did not see Mr. Stanton about it, or write to him asking him to desist, till on Saturday after mid-day, when all the arrangements for Sunday had necessarily been made, a *quasi*-formal letter came from your Lordship directing them not to officiate there, and that in terms which practically, as I have said, extended the direction to a prohibition, during my absence, from officiating in any church in the diocese.

The following letter was the acceptance of the offer of the use of St. Vedast :—

June 25th, 1875.

REVEREND AND DEAR SIR,—As Secretary to a Committee of the Clergy, Churchwardens, and Congregation of St. Alban's, Holborn, I am desirous of offering you the thanks of the Clergy and people for the generous and noble way in which you have come forward to help us in the present crisis, which is neither more nor less than a prohibition of the Celebration of the Holy Communion at our Church, for neither Clergy nor people will ever consent to have that Sacrament desecrated by a conformity to the " Purchas " Judgment. Our distress can only be understood by a consideration of our position as being deprived of all that Christian men and women hold most dear, and your offer to alleviate that distress has called forth our deepest and most heartfelt thanks, which I am unable adequately to convey to you.   I am expressing the sentiment of every heart when I say that we pray Almighty God to bless you in your own fight for the Catholic Faith, and to bless you for the noble Christian spirit which has prompted you to lend us a helping hand in our very deep trouble.

The 26th was the Sunday described. On the Monday Mr. Dale received an abusive but anonymous letter from "Yours, very disgusted!"   But the episode did not end here.   From this time the Church Association lent an ear to the complaints of the four churchwardens, and by next year a prosecution for ritualistic practices began.

In 1874 a Mr. Norris made the generous offer of Eucharistic vestments as a personal gift to Mr. Pelham Dale, and in the March of 1875 they were sent to Ladbroke Gardens; they were first used in the church at the Christmas festivals.

The Pastoral issued for Advent 1875 was as follows :—

MY DEAR FRIENDS,—Again we have arrived at the beginning of another Christian year, and in looking back upon the events which have occurred during its course, we have great cause for thankfulness. Surely we have reason to say, " Hitherto hath the Lord helped us." It is true that during the past year we have had to endure many hindrances, for the most part, however, of that petty kind which consists rather in slight annoyances and petty inconveniences than in overt acts of direct persecution. But these, though painful to all of us, and giving opening to the Tempter to solicitations towards a fretful, irritable, and uncharitable spirit, are, if we endure patiently, no sign of anything else than God's favour towards us. If we are accused falsely for our Master's sake (and we have the testimony of our conscience that it is so), we are indeed blessed. Only let us be sure that patience has her perfect work amongst us.

There is no doubt that we *are* accused. This is the charge specially directed against myself, viz. :—That I am consciously unfaithful to the Church of my baptism and ordination, in that I desire surreptitiously to bring in Popish practices; and that, with this object, I violate systematically laws which I am bound to obey. Now, such a charge as this is very grave indeed. Stripped of all disguise, it is a charge of conscious hypocrisy, and this because we adopt practices, novel indeed to an age just aroused from religious indifference and neglect, yet really dating from apostolic and sub-apostolic times. Yet to lie under such a charge as this is most painful, because it shows that my whole principles and motives are utterly misapprehended by those who urge it. I know, however, that the real matter at issue is not a detail more or less of ritual observance, but hinges upon great fundamental truths which touch on the very nature of sacramental grace itself.

Judging from my own experience, the special opposition to our ritual emanates from two classes: from those who dogmatically deny the existence of sacramental grace, regarding the Holy Supper as a mere commemorative act of faith, and also from those who take so low a view of the Eucharist that they imagine it may be safely neglected altogether without forfeiting their position as members of the Church of England. Now I would remind the first of these, that a careful examination of the Prayer-Book shows that the view they hold is not that of the authorised formularies of the Church of England, and that consequently they have no right to bring a charge of faithlessness against Churchmen who hold opinions which the language of their own formularies supports. That this is so is evident from the testimony of those Nonconformists who denounce our Prayer-Book (and from their point

of view they are quite right) as hopelessly and irre-
mediably ritualistic.   To that other class, the uncom-
municating Churchmen, I can only speak, as I am
bound to do, in the language of remonstrance.   Habitual
non-communicants have no title whatever to any voice
in questions of ritual at all.   Their own Church calls
on them to repent and amend, and bids them, *as they
love their own salvation,* to be partakers of this Holy
Communion.   I must reiterate here what I have said
more than once, that it is a monstrous act of tyranny,
worthy of the worst ages of persecution, that those
who by their own act are practically excommunicated
should pretend as matter of conscience to regulate the
worship of the faithful in God's Church.

It would be impossible in the compass of a pastoral
to enter into the proof that what are supposed to be
Popish practices in our method of conducting the service are really CATHOLIC and PRIMITIVE.   I have
treated on those points very fully of late in my sermons
and classes.   I am at special disadvantage because so
very few of those who are in the eyes of the law
parishioners ever attend the church.   The more reason,
surely, that they should abstain from judging on hearsay evidence, certainly insufficient, perhaps interested.

I gladly turn, however, from this painful subject to
facts more immediately bearing on our work.

The mid-day services have been well attended during
the past year, and are, I know, much valued by many
who make habitual use of them.   It appears to me
that a City Rector, whose parish has in the course of
years almost wholly lost its resident inhabitants, but

has become, if reckoned by those who pass through it, one of the most populous in the world, should adapt his ministrations and services to this flowing population. I could wish indeed that the seats of our church had been better arranged to meet the wants of those who may well be supposed often to need rest of body as well as refreshment of soul, but somehow or other the cause of Evangelical truth is imagined to be identified with the hideous architectural eyesores which encumber the floor of our otherwise beautiful, and, for this purpose, most commodious sanctuary. The voice of public opinion has, however, very properly pronounced against high-pew exclusiveness in the house of God, and will, no doubt, in due course make itself heard at St. Vedast as elsewhere. I wish to draw special attention to the service for the young on Sunday afternoon at 3.30 P.M. This service gives promise of some usefulness to those for whom it is adapted.

The Working Association commenced its labours on St. Michael's Day, and has already a stock of work in hand. Subscribers and workers will be thankfully welcomed. Any ladies desirous of enrolling their names and receiving materials to make into garments should apply at the Vestry before or after Evensong on Monday evenings.

The Communicants' Meeting takes place on the first Monday in the month after Evensong; all communicants of both sexes are invited. It is at these meetings that the special works connected with the church are arranged and fresh ones inaugurated. On the other

Mondays of the month the Women's Class is held, and the members are invited to introduce those who in their judgment would be benefited by the teaching given.

I cannot refrain from taking this opportunity of thanking my choir, both men and boys, for their services during the past year. Though an item appears in the accounts as "Choir Expenses," it must be remembered that not only are all the Choir, without exception, volunteers, but that they contribute largely both to the Special Fund which bears the expense of music, &c., and to the General Offertory. I have also the most certain conviction that the spirit which actuates them all is a real earnest desire to set forth the glory of God and the good of souls, by promoting a worship in which beauty and taste shall be the appropriate outward clothing of deep spirituality and devotion of heart.

The Offertory accounts are appended, and must, I think, on the whole, be considered satisfactory; as much, perhaps, as, considering all things, we could expect. I had feared at one time a considerable deficiency, but He who never forgets the weak has not forgotten us.

In conclusion, I must exhort you, as indeed the Church's season exhorts you, in her Lord's own words, "Behold, I come quickly, hold fast that thou hast, that no man take thy crown." Resolve, then, that by God's grace, your prayers shall be more earnest, your fasts more sincere, your feasts more full of thanksgiving ; and especially do you pray for me also, that grace may

be given me, so that with all boldness I may minister
to you the Gospel of the Grace of God ; and may the
peace of God, the Father, Son, and Holy Ghost, keep
your hearts and minds through Jesus Christ our Lord.
—Your faithful Priest and Servant,

T. PELHAM DALE.

The offertories at St. Vedast never equalled those of St.
Laurence, but still, considering that the class of men from
which the congregation was drawn was not rich, yet expected to keep up a respectable appearance on however small
a salary, the total of £245, 15s. 1½d. speaks well for their
liberality, and was sufficient for the support of the services,
though not for the provision of those vast sums which it
was the fashion of the day to say, "Stuck to the fingers
of the High Church clergy."

The Clothing Association made and distributed 184
garments, of which four were given to the poor of St.
Vedast, and the offertory gave £2, 10s. to the same persons.
The rest of the clothes were given to Homes and poor
parishes.

On the August Bank-holiday, the congregation went out
together for a day in the country, accompanied by the
Rector and Mrs. Dale. This yearly outing was continued for
some time, and was, no doubt, of great service both to the
girls, who might have lacked friends to go with or to look
after them on these crowded days, and to the young men,
who were furnished with a good excuse for refusing more
dangerous amusements.   Besides, they were all friends,
with common interests, and it was a bright cheerful picnic
for them, breaking into the dull routine of daily life.

The Rev. J. N. Nicholson left St. Vedast for other work
at the close of this year.   The offertory was neither large

nor reliable, being, of course, influenced by the prosperity of its contributors. But the Choral Celebration rendered a second priest a necessity, and the Rev. North Green Army-tage accepted the curacy for a nominal stipend.

So quiet was the work at St. Vedast, and so little did the Rector aim at being a representative man, that, in spite of his action with regard to St. Alban's, there was some diffi-culty in getting assistance in the payment of the costs in the faculty case. No one knew much about the church and its work, or understood its peculiar burden in the shape of four parish-elected churchwardens and unavailable funds. However, after a good deal of anxiety and delay, the Eng-lish Church Union gave a grant of £200 towards the costs, and Mr. Pelham Dale hoped to sink into the quiet routine of work and services.

The complainants had the charity trust funds to pay their law expenses, and voted £100 for that purpose.

CHAPTER VIII.

THE tone of the Pastoral for Advent 1875, like all such
papers written by Pelham Dale, clearly expresses his feelings with regard both to accusers and their accusation. He
wrote out of the fulness of his heart, and it was a generous
and sensitive heart. It may be confessed now that in many
ways the accusers had the best of it—certainly they wounded
the Rector far more deeply than he ever did them. He tried
to speak strongly as well as temperately at those most unpleasant vestry meetings, but his offence lay more in what
he did than said, in his refusal to sign fresh leases, and in
his demands for the accounts rather than in his expressions
of opinion.

He gave his opponents credit for being blinded by custom
and prejudice; he longed to argue and reason with them.
The character of his own mind and the nature of his judgment of others made it difficult for him to believe that any
one was ready to accept opinions without conviction, or
to commit himself to any action his conscience did not
approve. Never did he cease to regret his inability to convince and persuade his opponents, while they had certainly
no intention of being either convinced or persuaded of
what they did not choose to believe.

Their accusation against him was, as he acknowledges,
most painful to him, and their neglect of and indifference
to the ordinances of the Church not less so. Again and
again he made suggestions to meet them half-way; he

offered to give them a perfectly plain service *if* they would attend it; he would yield to their prejudices, but he could not think they wanted to drive away all who did not share them. But gradually he was forced to see that for the religious portion of the dispute they cared little or nothing; they had never attended the church, they were none of them communicants, but a new law had been made by which they could claim their pound of flesh, and they meant so to settle their disputes.

Thus began the struggle that lasted until 1881, and which with its anxieties and publicity wore away the strength of the Rector as none of the clerical work had done.

For six weeks the congregation of St. Alban's attended the services at St. Vedast, where, after the letter from the Bishop, the clergy of the church alone officiated. When Mr. Mackonochie came back from spending his enforced holiday, he preached at St. Vedast's before resuming the services at St. Alban's. It was the mid-day celebration, and the church was so tightly packed that those who had meant to communicate could not leave their seats. For the sake of legal protection it was usual at this period of the movement to ensure the legal number of communicants; it so happened on this occasion that there were some twelve people desirous of coming to the altar, but the cumbrous pews and the crowded aisles made moving so difficult that they kept their places. At this time it should be remembered that all rubrics capable of being read against the High Church party were strictly legal, but great would have been the outcry had the priests ministering the Sacrament ventured to refuse any one who had not sent in his name. They did not wish to do so, but the carrying out of one rubric without obedience to the other is an impossibility.

For this offence Mr. Pelham Dale was presented to the Bishop by three of his churchwardens, Messrs. Serjeant, Morley, and Horwood. It was a curious scene, and will always belong to a curious chapter in Church history. Already—so quickly do things change—it seems an impossibility for such incidents to occur, but the change is in the mode of attack; the declaration of peace is not yet. These three men, not resident parishioners, not attending the church, but, by virtue of their position as ratepayers, standing to accuse a scholar and a theologian of practices they as ratepayers disapproved; the Bishop acknowledging their status and generally advising peace; the accused urging the claims of those who had thronged the church, and who wanted to worship, as against those who cavilled and did not come. From notes made on the occasion, it appears that when the reason of the absence of communicants was explained, one of the churchwardens contradicted the statement flatly, and said that it was never intended there should be any communicants.

The Bishop said he thought it was a pity Mr. Pelham Dale had admitted the St. Alban's congregation, upon which the Rector, filled with a natural indignation at the thought of those despised but reverent worshippers, replied, "My Lord, I am proud that I have done it."

After this unsatisfactory interview matters went on as before. The St. Alban's congregation returned to their own church, and the St. Vedast services continued to be well attended. Mr. Pelham Dale thought at this time that the storm would blow over. He did not consider his work or his church of sufficient importance to be made a point of attack, especially in comparison with those other crowded and important churches served by those holding the same views. Law, more especially ecclesiastical law, always costs a great deal more than it is worth, and he did not imagine that force would be expended in closing St. Vedast. He thought also that the money disputes between himself and his vestry were so much more the foundation of the quarrel than any ritualistic observances, that those outside societies that promoted attacks would not care to be mixed up in such matters.

However, on April 6, 1876, the three churchwardens above mentioned filed a representation against the Rector under the Public Worship Regulation Act.

The appeal of the Ridsdale case was still pending, and the lawyers were rather annoyed at any further steps being taken until the decision of the Privy Council was given.

To those attacked, the intricacies of the law were a matter of indifference, a sort of juggling with Acts of Parliament that it was hardly worth while to understand ; what was very clear was that they could not, without dishonouring their office, their faith, and their Church, submit in matters spiritual to the judgments of a lay court, and the censure or praise of the unsuitable judge who presided over it. Not unsuitable because he was promoted from a divorce court to the Court of Arches, but because he had no claim either by position or office to take the functions of the Bishops on himself. It was a betrayal of the liberties of conscience, of the rights of the Church, to submit to this authority.

The principle was clear enough, but what was not so clear was how far the responsibility of this betrayal rested on each individual priest of the Church, or how far they were justified in consenting to the indifference of the Bishops. It is easy to say after events what course should be followed, and what is right and what is wrong, but in the din of the battle it is a different matter. Questions press for immediate decision, the step must be taken at once, and the dust and smoke of opposing arguments make the objects in view indistinct and doubtful, and their importance difficult to estimate.

On April 10th came the letter from the Bishop informing Mr. Pelham Dale of the fact that the churchwardens had found it their duty to lodge a representation against him.

I.

MY DEAR SIR,—I have been informed to-day, to
my great regret, that the three churchwardens of St.
Vedast and a churchwarden of St. Michael have found
it their duty to lodge in my Registry a representation
under the Public Worship Act, complaining of certain practices in the conduct of public worship in
your church, which they consider illegal. I observe
that seven of the practices—besides two respecting
which an appeal is now pending—have been defini-
tively pronounced to be contrary to law; and I
cannot help entertaining some hope, notwithstanding
the tone of your reply, that by discontinuing them at
once, you will spare me the pain of allowing proceedings against one whom I had learnt to respect for his
character and learning, as well as for his father's sake.
Should you be willing to see me on the subject, I shall
be at home on the morning of Thursday, having confirmations on Wednesday and on Thursday afternoon.
—I am, dear sir, faithfully yours,   J. LONDON.

This letter, showing how little value the Bishop set on
the work being done at St. Vedast. and offering, as the
only course, instant submission to the churchwardens' complaints, was a severe blow to the Rector. It cannot be too
much insisted upon (because in the renewed life and vigour
that this struggle has given to our Church we are apt to
forget past deadness), that all the labours and prayers and
praises that were the daily life of the leaders of the movement were regarded with indifference or irritation by the
authorities. The closed church or the absent Rector would
never have called forth rebuke or lost the Rector *prestige*
or respect, but let the same man throw heart and soul into
his work, and he was pulled up short by the dead wall of

coldness and indifference. It was not a question of law—
it was a question of peace: so long as no complaints were
made and popularity was won, the worker might be
smilingly acknowledged, and as soon as the matters in dispute became matters of custom, they were readily adopted
by those who were perfectly neutral before. The interview
with the Bishop took place on Maundy Thursday. At 7.15
A.M. there was a choral celebration of the Holy Eucharist
at St. Vedast, and from this the Rector went to London
House. He was able to put the Bishop in possession of
the facts of the case, but there was nothing gained by the
meeting. The Bishop's ultimatum was that Mr. Pelham
Dale must entirely submit himself to the decision of the
Privy Council, however the Ridsdale case might be decided. This was an impossibility; he could not, and he
said so, consider the Privy Council judgment as the law of
the Church, and as such submit to it. That being so, the case
would be allowed to go on. So he went back to his church,
where the choir, who were not ratepayers or parishioners, or
anything of legal consequence, were busy in their various
duties. One of the advantages, one of the beauties of a
ritualistic service, is that it is not for the priest only ; so many
faithful laymen can share in its responsibilities, and so the
interest widens and the love of the members deepen under
the influence of their voluntary service. On Good Friday
there was little time for brooding over troubles. The Rector had to leave his house at 7, to be at Matins and Medita-
tions at 8.30 ; at 10.30 there was Litany, Ante-Communion,
and the Reproaches ; from 12 to 3 the Three Hours ; 4 P.M.,
Children's Service ; at 7 Evensong with the 22nd Psalm,
Prayers and Sermon, so that he could not be home until ten.

It was a late Easter, the 16th of April. The Rector
preached at Evensong. The paper that reports his sermon
observes that "he was evidently suffering under severe
indisposition, caused, we understand, by exposure to cold on

Good Friday." It would probably be nearer the truth to say caused by mental worry since Holy Thursday. He was a man whose mind acted quickly on his health, a man of an excitable nervous disposition, who very seldom let either nervousness or excitability revenge themselves on his surroundings. The sermon, as briefly reported, was from the 19th verse of the 20th chapter of St. John:—

"Then the same day at evening, being the first day of the week, when the doors were shut where the disciples were assembled for fear of the Jews, came Jesus and stood in the midst, and saith unto them, Peace be unto you." After pointing out how the appearance of our Blessed Lord after His resurrection to His disciples might be considered symbolical of His dealings with the faithful Christian soul, he enlarged on the mysteriousness of these appearances as especially demonstrating a real but mysterious Presence with His disciples. He appears in mysterious Presence to Mary Magdalene, who at first mistakes Him for the gardener; to the two disciples, but their eyes are holden that they might not know Him; in the midst of the disciples gathered together for fear of the Jews.

The preacher then pointed out that this shadowed forth a great fact—that which now had become a central fact in the Church's controversial teaching—the Real Presence of the Blessed Lord in the Holy Eucharist. It was this Catholic doctrine of the Real Presence in the Blessed Eucharist that the elaborate ritual was intended to illustrate and set forth. The Rector then told his congregation that he had evil tidings for them, and informed them of the attack made upon him. It was, he said, the end of a controversy which had

been silently growing during the thirty years of his
incumbency. During the whole of that long period he
had scarcely allowed a single Palm Sunday to pass
without a special reminder of the Church's rule that
every parishioner communicate at least three times a
year, of which Easter is to be one, but sadly without
effect; none of those parishioners who promoted the
proceedings had ever received the Blessed Sacrament
at his hands. Unfortunately this was not an uncom-
mon case. Indeed, it was now quite usual for persons
to call themselves Christians and Churchmen, to expect all the consolations of Christians and Churchmen,
and yet live in systematic neglect of the Blessed Eucharist, and this with the words standing in their Prayer-
Book exhorting " Christians, as ye love your own
salvation, that ye will be partakers of this Holy Communion." Let it cost what it would, it was his duty, it
was the duty of every faithful priest, to lift up his voice
against so flagrant an abuse, against a practice so
utterly repugnant to the teaching of all Scripture and
of Primitive Christianity. It was not really a question
of a little ritual more or less which was now in dispute; it was the doctrine which lay beneath it. The
Calvinistic bias of modern Christianity might have
blinded many good and pious persons who had thus
learnt to undervalue Sacramental grace to the real
issue, but it was nothing less than this:—Is the Lord
with His Church ? Is He specially present at her
altars ? Does He manifest Himself to the faithful as
on that first Easter night of the Resurrection ?

In conclusion, the preacher asked for the earnest
prayers of the congregation that he might be enabled

to act courageously and faithfully yet prudently in a
matter of so grave importance to the Church; he said
also they must pray for her adversaries. Might they
be destroyed indeed! but by the force of Christ's love
bringing them to repentance and giving them grace to
discern the sweetness of that blessed food which as yet
they despised.   The continual reminder during Holy
Week of the sufferings of our dear Lord, who endured
the cross, despising the shame, had been a source of
great comfort during the anxiety of the past week.
Nor would those he addressed altogether regard the
announcement he had made as unsuitable to the day
when the great victory was achieved, and our Lord,
who had in our sight suffered, had also shown Himself
risen again for our justification.

As the first attacked in the London diocese under the
new Act, Mr. Pelham Dale's case attracted some attention.
The president and secretary of the English Church Union
wrote, advising him to resist for the sake of those others who
had fought in the same cause.   But having in mind that
the accusers were non-resident and non-attending, that at
that time disputes were continuing with regard to the disposal of the charity funds, they all expected a more promising result from the interview with the Bishop.   The friendly
parishioner sees the matter more correctly.   "I very much
fear," he writes, "that the people with whom you have to
deal do not attach the least importance to their not being
communicants, and they consequently will not dread at all
any exposure on this head.   Their law is the 'Privy Council,'
and they do not recognise any 'Law of the Church.'"

The sting of these attacks, now legalised by the Public
Worship Regulation Act, certainly lay in the fact that some
of the Bishops upheld them, supporting the complaints of

any three malcontents, against not the incumbents only, but in many cases churchwardens and congregation also. How little comprehension of the spiritual life of the centres attacked must the framers of the Bill have possessed when they imagined such a method would annihilate both doctrine and teachers. But what did hurt those attacked was that they "were wounded in the house of their friend."

It appears from the letters from Colonel Hardy, the able and kind-hearted secretary of the English Church Union, that from the very first Dr. Phillimore (now Sir Walter) hit on the legal weakness of the prosecution: he asks, "Is not the Bishop himself the patron of the living?" *

Mr. Pelham Dale's decision was to offer a passive resistance, letting matters take their course; he would not plead before a judge he did not acknowledge. The English Church Union undertook to watch the case, and the president, Mr. Wood (now Lord Halifax), wrote to congratulate the Rector of St. Vedast on his decision.

Meanwhile the question of the disposal of charity funds in general had been opened, for Mr. Pelham Dale being unable to obtain accounts or copies of the trusts, referred the matter to the Charity Commissioners. Hope of further persuasion or reconciliation there was none, and he gladly relieved himself of an unsatisfactory burden.

The movements of the Commissioners were, like those in most Government offices, very deliberate; for years this matter dragged on, the correspondence consisting largely of acknowledgments of letters received. They obtained, however, a statement of accounts, and recommended a proper banking account for the St. Vedast funds. That (with the mid-summer holidays) was the extent of their work this year; the matter was not concluded for some years more.

* The *requisition* was made in the Bishop's name, and there was a clause in the Act that prevented the *patron* of the living prosecuting the incumbent.

The success of the churchwardens with regard to the Bishop of London's acceptation of their presentation caused them to take a very high hand with the Rector in all business matters.

The following letter tells its own story :—

May 15th, 1876.

DEAR SIR,—A notice has been enclosed to me of a Joint Vestry to be held at the Vestry Room of St. Vedast on Thursday next at 11 o'clock. There will be service at that hour, and thus the Vestry cannot be held. I think you will recognize on consideration that courtesy requires that I should be consulted, even if I had not the right as chairman to appoint convenient times and hours of meeting for a Joint Vestry.—I am, dear sir, your obedient servant,

T. PELHAM DALE.

Here is an example of the correspondence on the other side, written May 30th, in answer to a letter of April 12th :—

DEAR SIR,—The Churchwardens of the United Parishes of St. Vedast Foster and St. Michael le Querne desire me to inform you, in reply to your letter to Mr. Horwood of the 12th April last, that until judgment has been given under the Public Worship Regulation Act, 1874, in regard to the charges preferred by the Churchwardens against you with reference to your practice in the performance of Divine service, the Joint Vestry of the two parishes will not sanction the Churchwardens entering into any negotiation with you for the use of the school-room for any purpose whatever.— Yours faithfully,   JOHN HOOPER, *Vestry Clerk.*

It would be well to insert here letters from the Rector of St. Vedast to the papers, written in the following year, because they put the facts plainly and clearly, and leave the readers in full possession of the story of the funds.

Sir,—The dispersion of the congregation of St. Ethelburga, in which several members of my own congregation found a refuge, induces me to ask for space for a few remarks on the present aspect of affairs. I do not intend to criticise the policy of my brother Rector, I feel sure that he has acted, in a most difficult position, in the way he thinks best for the interests of the Church; indeed it is clear that his policy entails one of considerable advantage. The Church of St. Ethelburga cannot be made a centre whence to disseminate Erastianism under the guise of Catholic moderation. What I wish to do now is to point out causes why in the City we should be furnished with such numerous and remarkable specimens of the aggrieved parishioner who never goes to church.

It seems that our opponents are particularly unfortunate in extracting damaging revelations to themselves at specially inopportune moments. Another instance of this has presented itself in the return of sums available for Church purposes, moved for by Mr. S. Morley, M.P., and published in the *City Press* of March 31st. By this return it appears that there is money enough, if properly applied, to furnish funds amply sufficient for the most sumptuous services in every City church, and leave a large margin, which could, and ought in justice to be applied to the poverty-stricken districts just outside, where the poorer City workers reside.

The City churches, however, are, with one or two exceptions, by no means magnificent in their ecclesiastical appointments; nor can the most practical eye detect the sign of this munificent endowment by any external indications whatever. In this return St. Vedast with St. Michael le Querne figures for a total of £1532, 7s. 1d. per annum; the sum available for church purposes in the case of St. Michael le Querne is not given in the return, nor am I myself able to state the exact figures, but the larger portion of the above sum is available for these purposes. This is about the average possessed generally by City churches. St. Ethelburga is comparatively badly off, possessing only £75, 13s. 4d. It is a curious fact that the heat of the opposition to full ritual in these two churches may, to a considerable extent, be measured by the magnitude of their respective endowments. At St. Vedast the persecution began before any ritual at all was introduced, and was continued in the face of offers to give in addition as plain services as the Church of England sanctions, if any really desired them, and which, in fact, were given.

At St. Ethelburga, on the other hand, a very advanced ritual was allowed to continue, happily for several years. This is not a mere coincidence. It is now no secret, notwithstanding the vapouring about English Protestant feeling, that a high ritual is daily becoming increasingly popular among that very class which but a few years ago were the chief supporters of Dissenting congregations. But high ritual and bright services are expensive, and though the offertories and incumbents have supported these, still inquiry is made as to what really becomes of those large sums available for "church" expenses. Now the answer in the case of St. Vedast is this: the surplus, which is large, is used to pay the poor-rates—in other words, divided among the parishioners; the difference is muddled away in excessive salaries, in ill-judged and costly repairs, cost of administration, and a parish dinner. Whether this is the case in other parishes, I have no knowledge, but if report speaks true, similar systems are adopted elsewhere. There is no doubt much honest though remarkably ignorant Puritanism in the City still surviving, yet it may be doubted if it would take the trouble to neglect its business and go and seek out Ritualism in the churches had not somebody a direct interest in putting it on the scent. As long as St. Ethelburga stood alone, it is easy to see that its large offertory relieved the parishioners of a burden, and threw it on the Rector and his congregation. When, however, others followed that good example, men began to wonder whereunto this would grow; Demetrius and his craftsmen became alarmed, and "No Popery" is the modern analogue of "Great is Diana of the Ephesians," and the church is closed.

T. PELHAM DALE,

Rector of St. Vedast and St. Michael le Querne.

With reference to a proposal about the use of these funds he writes as follows. The letter is headed " City Churches —Robbing from Peter to pay Paul."

SIR,—The proposal to apply some of the surplus funds of City churches to the needs of poor suburban parishes has been characterised as a proposal to rob Peter to pay Paul. That Paul is very much in need is evident from the accounts which reach us of suburban churches ready to fall for want of a few pounds' worth of necessary repairs; but what becomes of Peter's pence? Here is a specimen. Only last week the trustees of the parish of St. Michael le Querne voted £100 to pay their poor-rates, and authorised a dinner, which will not cost less than £30, possibly over £40. The excuse for doing this is "that the money is their own, to do what they please with it." That this plea is of doubtful validity appears from a case submitted to counsel by certain of the trustees in favour of this disposal of the trust moneys. But even granting the legality of such expenditure, is it not a crying abuse which needs instant remedy? There is surely a strong moral, if there be not absolute legal obligations, to apply these funds to the real intention of the donors, so far as it can now be ascertained, which was the beautification of the fabrics and of the worship of the Church. In times past this was always done; it is only of late years that the vicious custom of dividing the income amongst the trustees—for a vote in aid of poor-rate virtually amounts to this—has obtained. Nor can this vote be considered as surplus after other claims have been fully satisfied.

The Church of St. Vedast, to which parish St. Michael is united, is dirty and sordid and far inferior to the churches round it, though architecturally it is much superior. The excuse for this again is that the Rector is a Ritualist; it was no better when there was no ritual.

Nevertheless, this is supposed to justify arrangements which not only violate all good taste and true reverence, but are destructive to the comfort, and even prejudicial to the health, of clergy, choir, and congregation. The traditional robbery of St. Peter is a myth unknown to ancient Christianity, but it is on record on the very highest authority that St. Paul not only directed the observance of decency and order in the churches of the Gentiles, but had something over to spare for the poor saints, in whom St. Peter had special interest.

T. PELHAM DALE.

Here for the present we leave this subject, which has to be so far explained, since it was the origin of the animus which provoked the prosecution, and for that reason should have been the protection of the Rector from outside attack, at least until the matter was settled. Once again Mr. Pelham Dale laid this view before the Bishop and the public in the following published letter, written May 22nd.

MY LORD,—In the private interview on Maundy Thursday with which I was favoured by your Lordship, I expressed my willingness and desire to obey your Lordship to the utmost limit of my conscience. I had hoped, therefore, to have had, even after the interview, some expression of your wishes more definite than the direction to obey the law as contained in the Purchas judgment, with which you then favoured me. I would have either complied or else asked permission to state the reasons which compelled me to decline to do so. I trust you will allow me to do this now, although I cannot hope that such a statement will have any other effect than to absolve me from the charge of any wilful disrespect to my Bishop.

My difficulty then is this:—I am instructed by the Twentieth Article "that the Church," by which of course I understand the Church Catholic, for the word is without any limitation which might restrict it to the National Church, "hath power to decree rites and ceremonies and authority in controversies of faith." Yet it appears by the authority of a secular court, which, as far as I can see, will not even consider the question what the Church Catholic has decreed or practised, certain practices are condemned as illegal. These ceremonies have, it appears, the sanction of all Christendom, were practised in the most primitive antiquity; some of them, the unleavened bread, and very probably the mixed cup, are sanctioned by the acts of our Blessed Lord Himself. It seems to me, therefore, that to render obedience to such prohibitions is treason to the teaching of the Catholic Church. The Church clearly has determined the controversy between the Catholic and puritanising parties; the lawfulness or unlawfulness, the expediency or inexpediency, of such observances, and decided them emphatically in favour of the former. To give them up because a secular court has in an undefended case, and reversing a far more learned decision of an inferior court, decided against them, is an outrage against that fundamental principle of our Church, her appeal to Catholic antiquity, which every true son is, cost what it may, bound utterly to resist. Why not on the same principle give up, as has been proposed, the symbolic act of laying on

of hands in conferring holy orders, or deny to laity
or clergy, or both, the sacred chalice itself?

But I cannot consider the real matter in dispute a
matter of rites and ceremonies only; it also involves
doctrine, and that doctrine is this, viz., the necessity
of the Eucharist to the believing soul. You are aware
that the three delating parishioners are none of them
communicants in their parish church; one of them to
my knowledge is not a communicant at all. Now, my
Lord, this is an old grievance, and one which dates
back in our case at St. Vedast to time far anterior to
our present Church controversies. It seems to me
simply monstrous under any circumstances to allow
a voice in the regulation of services to those who
habitually take no part in them; but when these persons are by their own act excommunicate, what are we
to say then? I only know that it is an injustice which
no other religious body except the Church of England
permits at all. It was forced upon a reluctant and
remonstrating Church by an *omnipotent* (?) Parliament
legislating in the weakness of a panic. Yet a true son
of the Church is to be called disloyal because he protests and resists!

But bad as this is, it is not all; there is something
still deeper, and to my mind more pressing. This
implied recognition on the part of the Establishment of
the claim to be Churchmen without being communicants, lead those who are so to imagine they may do
that with impunity, which our Church tells them they
cannot do without peril to their souls—live in habitual
neglect of the Blessed Eucharist. I for my part will

never so act as to promote a soul-destroying delusion.
It would be treason against the life of those for whom
Christ died. To me it seems that the whole of the
faithful, clergy as well as laity, should protest against
such an error. It is because I perceive that a return
to the ancient ritual does, as a matter of fact, set forth
very plainly to those who can with difficulty be reached
by other means the value and importance of Sacramental grace, that I so earnestly desire its restoration
amongst us. It teaches both the eye and the ear in a
manner which the most unlearned and careless cannot
mistake, the great benefit of worthy, and the equally
great and awful danger of unworthy, participation, and
surely still greater danger of habitual neglect.

I must also point out to your Lordship that in my
own special case this delation comes from those with
whom I am at issue as to the expenditure of church
trust funds. It is no secret in the City, nor, I believe,
out of it, that the management of the large church fund
there is in a very unsatisfactory state. Any one who
attempts to do his duty as a trustee (and it has come
to my knowledge that the clergy have very pressing
responsibilities) must incur considerable odium. I
have simply asked, as yet in vain, to see the trust
accounts. I am advised that unless I enforce their
production, I may perhaps be guilty of a dereliction of
duty. Now I venture to think that there was here a
strong case for a stay of proceedings, at any rate for
a time (and you will remember I asked for no more)
under the special circumstances. It could hardly have
escaped the sagacity of our legislators that interested

representations were possible in some parishes, and I presume that the power of the Bishop to quash proceedings was given him to prevent an abuse that was very likely to occur. I mention these facts because I wish to put in the strongest light I am able what is likely to be the real character of proceedings under the Public Worship Regulation Act. If to stay these is out of your Lordship's power, you will perceive that you may expect ere long that so-called Ritualists will not be the only persons amenable to its provisions.

Your Lordship will permit me to observe that a City incumbent of a deserted City church is not exactly the person who might be expected to be the first to be in this great diocese to be proceeded against under the Act. If it were a case of a single individual guilty of disobedience to a well-ascertained law, the matter would be very different. But it is not so. The real question, as everybody knows, is not whether the Rector of St. Vedast shall be made to conform to the Purchas judgment, but whether this judgment shall be enjoined over the whole diocese before it is finally argued. Thus I am placed in a very painful position. I am unable to consider whether, for the sake of peace and as an act of obedience, I may not abandon my work amongst the young people of the City, but am compelled to resist, lest I should so act as to precipitate the solution of the present controversy by setting the example of surrender to that Erastianizing judgment, which is not even yet the law of the State, and I trust never will be. I cannot tell you the pain it gives me to write thus. Should matters come to

extremity, which God avert, to me it means the loss
of all. I am too old to begin life again, and the little
learning you spoke of so flatteringly is not likely to
afford more than the barest subsistence, if it do even
that. But only one honest course is open to me, that
is (if it must be so) to submit to be ejected from my
benefice and position; no State court can take away
my priesthood. I must obey the law, indeed, and, God
helping me, shall do so; but it must in this case be the
law of the Church, not of the State, the Divine in preference to the Human. If I have erred in the estimate
of my duty, I err with a clear conscience. I say, then,
with the Prophet, in all humility, "O Lord, Thou hast
deceived me, and I am deceived."

I reserve to myself the right to publish this letter,
with your Lordship's answer, should you favour me
with one.—I have the honour to remain, your Lordship's faithful and obedient servant,

T. PELHAM DALE.

The answer to this letter was the following :—

May 23rd.

MY DEAR SIR,—But for the intimation at the close of
your letter received to-day, I could not have contented
myself with a curt, and therefore apparently unsympathetic reply. But as it would be obviously unbecom-
ing to enter into a public correspondence on a matter
which is on its way to a judicial investigation, I can
only assure you again of the great pain with which I
have been compelled by your own decision, which,

however conscientious, I must hold entirely mistaken, to allow the law to take its course.—Believe me to be, my dear sir, very faithfully yours,

J. LONDON.

It was very evident that, in spite of the rough treatment the Public Worship Regulation Bill had received since it first left the hands of its originator, Archbishop Tait, it was to be supported. It is not putting the matter too harshly to say that seventeen years ago many of the Bishops were statesmen first and Churchmen afterwards. The law of the land was the object most reverenced ; the law of the Church and the dictates of conscience must be forced into compliance with it. Now, thank God, the spirit is so far different that Churchmen may look forward hopefully to being led and defended by their own rulers in those attacks upon Church and conscience that will never cease while the world lasts.

But we are now dealing with seventeen years ago, and the letters and papers of that date betray a very different spirit. Even those who counselled resistance foresaw defeat. They were prepared to adopt the strongest measures to ensure a retreat after a gallant but losing battle. Mr. Mackonochie and others advocated disestablishment in preference to the heavy yoke of State interference ; it was an open secret that the High Church party meditated leaving the Establishment rather than submit to such tyranny ; not, as they were constantly and scornfully advised, to join the Roman Communion, but continuing their orders by certain bishops who would have joined them, and having the Church of Scotland to fall back upon in case of need, to obtain freedom to minister according to Primitive Catholic use. With this in their minds as a last resort, they addressed themselves to the struggle, and, like many a forlorn hope, turned the defeat into victory.

The Rector of St. Vedast was forced into the foremost ranks. He hated publicity; he was not fond of fighting; he felt every act of injustice and unfair imputation keenly. His idea of happiness was work in Church services and priestly ministrations (and he never grumbled at the quantity or frequency of such duties), and for his leisure his scientific studies. His only escape from worries were these studies; he could forget everything in a discussion on the Darwinian theory of Evolution, or his pet discoveries on the refraction of light. He belonged to the Physical Society, and met men of all shades of opinion at various meetings without the differences doing more than add piquancy to the discussions. Once when returning from a scientific meeting, all those going by the Underground Railway travelled together, continuing their discussion. Professor Huxley and others of similar views were amongst his companions. Mr. Dale's station was then farthest west of them all—"An instance," he said out of the window as the train moved off, "of the survival of the fittest."

But, except for these recreations, the question of his position was always in his mind, giving him sleepless nights and forcing him to argue it out from a thousand different points. There were the various opinions of his friends, to whom, with his natural self-distrust, he listened with deference, but with whom he could not always, on reflection, bring himself to agree. To Mr. Mackonochie he listened with the respect that was due to the straightforward honesty of the Perpetual Curate of St. Albans. But there was a great difference in their position. Mr. Mackonochie was supported by churchwardens, congregation, and parish; he was doing a great work that none but the parish church could do. But the little outpost of St. Vedast had no such support. The congregation was of stray sheep from the wilderness of London, and might be passed on to other churches if that one were closed.

Then there were the legal advisers of the party, who, earnest and clear-headed, were indeed to be valued, but at times made those they defended fear lest they should be led into the paths of expediency. To suffer in silence was the Rector of St. Vedast's own idea of the best mode of procedure; to go steadily on, and to yield only to actual force in the end. But he was not fighting only for himself, but for the whole Church, and he recognised the right of those attacked through him to share in his defence.

The legal party knew that to crush the whole of the High Church movement by expensive legal proceedings would be a lengthy proceeding, lasting to the time of their children's children. Their plan was to hamper, oppose, and quibble until the wave of party feeling should flow in the other direction and the judgment be given on their side. Then the law would become a dead letter, for they had no wish to grasp such a weapon on their part; and indeed, when one side persecutes the other, may all honest men be found on the side of the persecuted, or their Christianity will be lost!

As early as the 1st of June 1876 Mr. Pelham Dale was informed that the Legal Committee of the English Church Union considered that "the *original requisition* of the Bishop being informal, and consequently illegal, it is probable that all preliminary proceedings adopted by the promoters are legally invalid."

Such a victory as this seemed hardly satisfactory to the defendant; it did not close the long vista of coming attacks and deprivations, but he signed the papers and requisitions as he was asked. However, Lord Penzance treated the suggestion of illegalities with great indifference, and, to the surprise of the Legal Committee, who were very sure of their facts, issued in July a monition to Mr. Pelham Dale warning him to desist from the practices proved against him. It had been so confidently believed that proceedings would be quashed, that this termination came unexpectedly.

Mr. Mackonochie hastened to write an urgent appeal to take this opportunity to disown the jurisdiction of the court. "Let me entreat you," he says, "for the love of God, not to recognise any decree of this court of the world below. Surely we are now on our trial whether we will confess CHRIST or no." The Rev. A. H. Stanton of St. Albans writes, after an interview with Mr. Pelham Dale, to tell him of the Hatcham case. "Mr. Tooth," he says, "is in the same boat, monitioned at the same time, and prepared to ignore all monitions." He was, however, supported by his churchwardens and a large congregation. The week before the issue of the monition there was an adult baptism at St. Vedast's. The Bishop's chaplain, in a letter of July 20th, curtly acknowledges the usual intimation of the fact.

It was nearing the midsummer holidays, and every one hoped for a little breathing space after the time of anxiety and suspense, but all through August the legal matters kept moving. The Legal Committee recommended the modification of certain minor points of ritual that were not connected with primitive doctrine, viz.—(1) Biretta; (2) Genuflexion during the prayer of consecration; (3) *Undue* elevation of the consecrated elements; (4) Singing of the *Agnus Dei;* (5) Kissing the book; (6) Processions with acolytes. With regard to No. 3, it was proposed to adopt the Sarum use, which permitted elevation as high as the breast; and with regard to No. 4, to substitute another hymn. It was hoped by these changes to narrow the struggle to those necessary points which could never be yielded. Mr. Pelham Dale was not, in one sense of the word, a Ritualist. That is to say, he had not that gift of regulation and order that make to many priests one of the great attractions of Ritualism. At St. Vedast points of detail were left to the

other priests and servers to carry out; the Rector was
content to be assured of their teaching, and to give his
permission.   The beauty to him of a High Celebration was
that all these minor details were in the hands of others;
for himself, content that all would be done decently and
in order, he gave himself up to the glorious devotion and
praise of his solemn duty.   In after days he often spoke
of these celebrations at St. Vedast as being the most soul-
satisfying and least physically exhausting of any.   It is a
trial to a priest who has not a natural gift of order to take
the responsibility on himself, and to feel that his mind
must not be given wholly to the higher part, lest by apparent carelessness he should seem irreverent.

On this occasion he agreed to the modifications proposed, and regretted afterwards that he had done so, since
it did not, as he had hoped, bring the essentials into
greater prominence, but was a cause of triumph for his
enemies and alarm to his friends.   Colonel Hardy writes
thus to him on the subject :—

I hear that Mackonochie and some others think that
you should have modified nothing. . . . Doubtless,
erring mortals may commit mistakes in serious matters
as well as trifling ones; but I believe God will overrule for good the mistakes made at this crisis of the
Church's history, if the governing motives are pure
and right in His sight; and God knows all the difficulties connected with your case, so different from that of
others, and will cause everything to work for His own
glory and the good of His Church.   Of the eight or
ten priests that have been either prosecuted or threatened with prosecutions during the last year or so, I
don't know one who *entirely* agreed with any of the
others as to the line of policy to be adopted in his own

case and those of the rest. (Here follows a description
of the various methods suggested, and the letter con-
cludes :) " I mention these matters by way of encouragement, as you may possibly have been taxed with
' time-serving,' ' capitulation,' and so on, and most
unjustly so."

At last the lawyers went out of town, and there was a
period of peace. The Rector of St. Vedast went with Mrs.
Pelham Dale to Scotland to see a son in Aberdeen, and
came back the richer by sketches and attendance at various
churches, both Episcopal and Presbyterian. He was back
again in October and arranging for his Advent sermons.
But his position pressed hardly upon him. He feared that
the weakness of the St. Vedast case in its want of parochial
support would damage the cause more than assist it : it
would naturally be seized upon eagerly as a typical case,
which, in truth, it was not, and the claims of the laity,
as represented by the various congregations of churches
attacked, would be ignored. He still clung to the belief
that justice would be done in every English law-court, but
in after years he heard the judges again and again talk of
the necessity of protecting the alienated laity when they
were proceeding to remove the leaders of large and personally devoted congregations, and learnt that in such cases
popular prejudice is stronger than justice.

About the end of October, Lord Penzance granted an
inhibition to be served on the Rector of St. Vedast. Again
the weakness of St. Vedast was discussed, but Mr. Mackonochie was firmly of opinion that yielding would make Mr.
Tooth's case harder rather than easier, and that God had
called upon Pelham Dale to witness for His Church, and
that it was by His will that the little outpost of St. Vedast
was chosen for attack.

The following extracts from a private letter by Mr. Pelham Dale, written October 24th, show how he himself felt :—

Things have gone too far to turn back now. We shall get from the puritanizing faction as much as we can extort and no more, and delay would be disastrous. If we do not take a decided stand for the truth— which is ancient historic Christianity—we shall see a large defection of the less instructed to the Archbishop of Westminster ; of this I am convinced.

I think it would be possible to meet an entirely adverse decision by the plan I spoke about when I saw you. We must see that the laity have reverent Eucharists ; we must see that the grossly irreverent and heathens are excluded. Just imagine yourself celebrating according to the judgment against us. Even the very limited compliance which I, in deference to the English Church Union, have adopted, is so painful, that were I not convinced that it is suffering for His sake Who is there present, I would never celebrate at all. Then think of Jenkins v. Cooke, and how it might be one's duty at any celebration to resist a profanation which one shudders to think of. Let us, then, adopt the oratory system as a body of Catholics, and in them let us have Eucharists as they ought to be, none but baptized, confirmed Christians admitted, no spies or mere gazers present, catechumens in their proper place as of old time. Let the ritual be fixed for us by Ritualists of real learning according to the ancient models of our Church. Let us have heads over us, men whom we can trust, and who

will know something of Christian antiquity, and decide
the questions referred to them accordingly. Let us
try somehow or other to get this principle into the
public mind : that when Christian men differ the
ancient precedent rules. Let us show them the kind
of services to which this leads, in our churches if we
can, if not in our oratories, and I think that before
very long we shall find that true Christian laymen will
demand, in a way which cannot be refused by even
such a ruler as our present Archbishop, something
better than the dull puritanized Erastianism he en-
deavours to force upon us.

There was at this time a talk of joining the parishes of
St. Vedast and St. Michael le Querne with that of another
City church, in which case Mr. Pelham Dale would have
been able to retire on his income and been free to take
work elsewhere. This was so tempting a project to one
wearied with conflict that he feared lest he should sacrifice
duty in obtaining it, and would not allow it to weigh with
him in the decision, and, after November 12th, he wrote to
decline further negotiations in the matter.

November 5th was the Sunday after the inhibition was
issued by Lord Penzance. As it carried with it a suspension
of three months, there was a slight pause before it was
served, as an opportunity for compliance.

The Rev. Dr. West, of St. Mary Magdalene, Paddington,
was from this time a most generous and fearless friend.
There were many who, from fear for their own work, and
bearing in mind how the help to St. Alban's had been
followed by an attack, shrank from openly supporting the
victims of the Public Worship Regulation Act ; but Mr.
West (for he never used his title of doctor) had no such

hesitation.   He writes on the Saturday the following
letter :—

DEAR MR. DALE,—Forgive a junior priest writing
to you, but I do trust you will not allow a lay ex-
divorce Judge to suspend you from your functions.
I have made up my mind entirely, and the cause is so
damaged by protesting and glozing.   Hold fast for the
love of the Church and truth.   We all support you.
Shall I come and preach, or do anything else ?—Yours
very truly in Christ,   R. T. WEST.

There were letters of anxious sympathy from Hatcham
and from Folkestone, but these were written after the
Sunday.

On Sunday there were the usual services, with the original
ritual restored as before the concessions recommended by
the lawyers.   The Rector celebrated, and thus solemnly
defied the inhibition.   The lessons for the day were most
appropriately from the Book of Daniel, and Mr. Armytage
preached on that subject.   He spoke of how the faithful
had opposed the almighty power of Nebuchadnezzar, and
how God had delivered those who trusted in Him.   From
that they ought to take comfort in their distress.   Speaking
of the Public Worship Regulation Act, he said there was a
religious party who would not relinquish the services of the
Church to the Government or the State.   With the help of
God, they were, for themselves, determined not to obey that
Act.   Nationality was a local thing, but religion was above
all nationalities.   It neither belonged to the Englishman
nor the foreigner exclusively, for there was one God and
Father of all.   Let them take courage.   The time of their
delivery was near ; and so sure as that day's sun would set,
so sure the faith would be accepted by the Church and

people, and the Public Worship Act would be only quoted to show the folly and wickedness of fighting with Almighty God.

The paper from which this brief *resumé* of the sermon is quoted adds :—"The service was then proceeded with and conducted after the very highest Ritualistic fashion."

So the week passed, and the notice of inhibition was not served.

With the remembrance of the riots at St. George's-in-the-East in their minds, the Government were always anxious at these crises lest the more important City—especially the General Post-Office and Cheapside—should be the scene of similar riots. It was probably under pressure of this fear that the Bishop of London sent his secretary to negotiate, if possible, a surrender. This was the most trying time of any to the sorely troubled Rector of St. Vedast. He disliked resistance to authority ecclesiastical; that he had received no help or sympathy did not lessen his obligations to obedience; but then in the Church the authority is restricted and defined; no Bishop is absolute beyond certain limits, and no priest is bound beyond what he has taken upon himself in his ordination vows. So far as the freedom of the Church was in his keeping, Pelham Dale refused to yield to the authority of the lay court. In that case the Bishop said he would come himself and take the service. To this the Rector replied, that if his Lordship came as his diocesan, he would submit to him in all things, but it must be understood that the submission was not under the Public Worship Regulation Act. The Bishop promised to act outside the Public Worship Regulation Act in his capacity as diocesan.

As the inhibition had not been served upon him, and his protest had been already made, it seemed to Mr. Pelham Dale that, under the promise of the Bishop, he would have sufficiently defied the court, and at the same time have

shown the world that to properly ordained authority he
was willing to submit.

When the Bishop arrived at St. Vedast on the Sunday
morning, an official from the Court of Arches served the
inhibition, and fastened it on the doors of the church. Mr.
Pelham Dale left the services to the Bishop, and he and
Mr. Armytage, though present, and in their cassocks and
surplices, took no part in the conduct of the services.

All the daily papers made two mistakes in their account
of the Sunday-morning service. First they said that the
official of the Court of Arches put on the door the notice
of the inhibition that had been served on Saturday, whereas
there had been no service of the inhibition until that Sunday
morning, and they added that Mr. Pelham Dale took a part
in the church service, which he did not do. The inhibition
fastened on the doors was to the following effect :—It was
obtained by the churchwardens under section 13 of the
Act, and prohibited the Rector from performing any service in the diocese for three months, and it went on, " The
inhibition is not to be released unless he shall in writing
undertake to pay due obedience to the monition ; but if such
inhibition shall remain in force for more than three years, or
if a second monition shall be issued, any benefice or other
ecclesiastical preferment shall thereupon become void, unless the Bishop shall for some special reason postpone it for
a period of three months. The patron of the living may
present another minister, but not the incumbent inhibited.
Further, it is provided that the Bishop may during such
inhibition, unless he is satisfied that due provision will be
made for the spiritual charge of the parish, make due provision for the service ; and it shall be lawful for the Bishop
to raise the sum required from time to time for such provision by sequestration of the profits of such benefice or
other ecclesiastical preferment."

" There was," says the *Daily Telegraph*, " a numerous

congregation, though the church was by no means inconveniently crowded, and the contrast between the demeanour of those who had come from motives of curiosity, and of those who, following the doctrines of their Rector, devoutly crossed themselves at particular parts of the service, was very marked."

The Bishop's sermon did not touch on the matter of dispute; all he said was, " The pulpit from which a dying man speaks to dying men of their souls—of God who is their Saviour—is far too solemn a place for topics, however exciting and important, belonging to another sphere of thought. When the world is receding from the lone soul, when the spirit looks back upon the life that is past, how utterly trivial appear the questions of controversy which have weighed upon the minds of people, divided parishes, convulsed churches."

Heavily must these words have fallen on the ears of the Rector of St. Vedast as he looked upon his choir, the young men whom he taught and with whom he worked, from whose ranks he had sent out one missionary priest, and who were to be scattered and discouraged for these "trivial" reasons. To preach of "God who is their Saviour" to an empty church, because the only divinely appointed service must take a secondary place to the compiled liturgy of the all-important morning prayer. The controversy might seem trivial to the "lone soul," but the strength of the Eucharists received and attended would give many a dying man that last strength he needed.

In his humility the Rector thought that these men and women, since he had no parochial claim to their attendance, might find better teaching in those other churches that were equally open to them, but yet they were of his flock, and he yearned after them, storm-tossed as he was with all the conflicting doubts and scruples that assailed his soul.

Mr. Mackonochie wrote to him on this Sunday :—

MY DEAR BROTHER,—I must write to say how much I sympathise with you in the mental torture to which, I fear, you have been subjected for the last few days.

I do not conceal from you that I think your conclusion a very fatal one for our work and your own peace of mind; but the more for all this I sympathise with your anxiety. You will, of course, still have my prayers for yourself, and that if you have made a mistake, Almighty Wisdom may still overrule it to His glory, and the building up of the work which seems likely to be hindered by it.—Yours most affectionately in Our Blessed Lord,   ALEX. HERIOT MACKONOCHIE.

Is it even now too late to reverse the engines? I did not the least agree with Colonel Hardy's theory of your being in honour bound to the Bishop. In some things a higher honour overrules such considerations, even if it was true of a matter of even worldly honour.

Colonel Hardy's letter is from one who takes another view.

"We shall be much interested," he writes, "to know how you got on in your most difficult position yesterday. I see by the papers that the Bishop and his chaplain took the Matins, &c., but nothing is said as to the Early Celebration or Evensong" (this is a mistake; many of the papers say that the Bishop's chaplain took Evensong). "If you continued your functions in those matters, you have practically disregarded Lord Penzance's inhibition, the Bishop's action being, as Mr. Lee said, *outside* the Public Worship Regulation Act."

It was disheartening to one who had yielded to his Bishop from a sense of duty to find it considered a submission to the Court. The Bishop himself withdrew from his promised neutrality, and spoke as an official of the Public Worship Regulation Act.

Mr. Pelham Dale made the following explanation of his position in two letters written to the *Times*. The first was dated Sunday, St. Vedast :—

SIR,—Three courses are open to a clergyman in my position—to submit, to secede, or to suffer. I cannot do the first, because I conscientiously object to the jurisdiction which has condemned me; I cannot do the second, because I am sure that the Church of England, notwithstanding the encroachments of the State upon her liberties, is the true Church in this land. I take, therefore, the last course, and suffer. The Bishop has, canonically or otherwise, assumed in person the charge of my benefice, and on him the responsibility must rest.—I am, sir, yours truly,   T. PELHAM DALE.

After the description of the service in Monday's issue he wrote :—

SIR,—Will you allow me to send you a statement of facts as to what occurred on Sunday last, as the account which appears in your journal is not quite accurate? The inhibition was served just as the Bishop arrived for morning service, who, at his own desire, not mine, came to exercise his spiritual authority and take the spiritual charge of my people.

I have not submitted to the new court, nor do I intend to do so, and the living must go into sequestration in consequence.

My presence at St. Vedast yesterday was an act of personal submission to the Bishop, and not to the court, and so I stated in terms to the Bishop. I considered that I was bound to take this course by my letter to the Bishop published in the *Church Times* and *Church Review* of the 2nd of June. The morning and evening services were entirely under the direction of the Bishop. This is but the commencement of a policy of persecution which must fail in the end. I am but as the soldier at the bridge-head—there are plenty more behind me who will fight the same battle. Acts of Parliament cannot control men's consciences; and I am persuaded that you will find, though a few more deprivations may follow, that in a short time the Public Worship Regulation Act will become, like other persecuting Acts, a dead letter on the Statute Book.— I remain, sir, yours truly, T. PELHAM DALE.

Mr. Armytage was forbidden by the Bishop to officiate at St. Vedast, and Mr. Ackland, of Kensington Grammar School, was appointed curate by the Bishop at a stipend of £100 a year. The Sunday was all that was provided for, though the curate agreed to take the Wednesday and Friday Evensong in that first week.

Mr. Armytage wrote the following letter to the *Church Times*:—

SIR,—Allow me to give your readers some information on the St. Vedast case. The Bishop's visit to St. Vedast last Sunday was not at Mr. Dale's suggestion, but was a move of the Bishop himself, made with the evident view of preventing a contempt of court being committed by the Rector.

The Rector has not submitted, and states that he will never submit, to the judgment of Lord Penzance. His conduct on Sunday must therefore be considered as an act of submission to the personal exercise of the Bishop's spiritual authority, as stated in his letter to the *Church Review* and *Church Times* of June 2nd.

As matters already stand, he will lose part of the income of the living, which is worth but £300 a year, without a house, and is at this moment practically deprived of his benefice, for the full use of its tempo- ralities can only be restored on his written submission to Lord Penzance's judgment.

We neither of us took any part in the Sunday's service, which, at the Bishop's desire, consisted of Matins, Litany, and Table Prayers.

We are all agreed in the righteousness of opposition to this judgment, but a divergence of opinion arises as to the treatment of the Bishop.

Some would have resisted his entry into the church, because practically he acted in the name of the court. Others, and among them Mr. Dale, would never resist their diocesan, whatever might be the reason or the object of his visit to their churches. The Rector, how- ever, still reserves to himself the liberty of action for the future.

For myself, I may add that I was deprived of the curacy of St. Vedast last Friday at a moment's notice by a letter from the Bishop.

This somewhat harsh step is still more harsh when taken in connection with the practical deprivation of the Rector, for summarily and at a blow it destroys all the minor spiritual work of the Church throughout the week in the way of confession, instruction classes, and other like work.

N. GREEN ARMYTAGE.

Mr. Pelham Dale having resolved to submit to the Bishop but not to the Court of Arches, decided to leave the Church of St. Vedast in the Bishop's charge, but to refuse to accept the suspension, and to preach and officiate in the diocese. His choir and congregation dispersed, and attended other ritualistic churches, keeping up by meetings and various means their interest with St. Vedast. If only they had been ratepayers, their claim to attend the church would have been strong enough to give them a voice on the subject in dispute. However, there was no law to protect those who were satisfied.

It was very difficult to make persons outside understand the peculiar circumstances of St. Vedast. Letters of all kinds poured in, many containing advice and suggestions that were impossible under the circumstances. That the Rector had no churchwardens of his appointment, and that he was fighting for the possession of his schools against heavy odds, was a position as unusual as it was unpleasant.

However, there were many letters and resolutions of sympathy, as well as many objecting to his submission to the Bishop; but those who knew Mr. Pelham Dale knew that he was not a man to act without careful reflection or perfect honesty. He could not have resisted his Bishop unless he had been perfectly assured that he was entirely in the right in doing so; and he was not certain that, after receiving the promise that his Lordship would act outside the Public Worship Regulation Act—a promise which, as seen by Colonel Hardy's letter, was made openly—he was any longer right in resisting if he made it public that he did not acknowledge the State court. He did, however, feel it bitterly when he found that the Bishop expected a compliance with the terms of Lord Penzance's inhibition.

That most staunch and fearless of friends, Mr. West, of St. Mary Magdalene's, Paddington, came forward, and at his invitation Mr. Pelham Dale worked at his church, celebrating, preaching, and taking part in the services, and so enjoying his priestly privileges, and showing openly that his motive for yielding to the Bishop was not fear of the court or for the safety of his living, which he knew would be sequestrated at the end of the three years. Very few men had the courage of the Vicar of St. Mary Magdalene's. He had, too, a fine work, that had grown up under his organisation. His personal fortune, his health and strength, were all expended on his church and parish. It was a new district, but had its fine church and two mission churches, its schools, sisterhoods, and all the classes and guilds for instruction and help that a large, and in some parts very poor parish requires for its complete organisation. In those days frequent early celebrations were much rarer than they are now ; and on Sunday Mr. West kept open table for friends from a distance, who otherwise would not have had time to return and attend Matins and the High Celebration, for the church was full to overflowing, and late-comers, if they got inside the building, often failed to find seats. It was a church with a position of its own, like All Saints, Margaret Street, a typical church. Attempts were made often to find the three malcontents that should be allowed to close the church against the crowded congregation, but public opinion in the district was too strong. Then three were once found—a milkman, a publican, and a freeholder—but they fell away, for the following reasons, when they were brought to the point. The milkman feared to offend his customers, the working-men threatened the publican with a row at his house, and the man of property reflected that he charged higher rents on account of the church being near.

So, though Mr. West never hesitated to say openly that he was every whit as guilty as the persecuted priests, in the matter of ritual and hearty contempt for the new courts, his work flourished unchecked.

Mr. Pelham Dale had been engaged since September to preach in November at St. Ethelburga, Bishopsgate, but Mr. Rodwell (who was himself threatened at this time) having informed the Bishop of the fact, wrote to say that the Bishop had expressed a wish that a substitute should be found. It was, of course, a matter for the Rector of St. Ethelburga to decide; a substitute was found, and the following notices distributed in the church :—

To the Congregation of S. Ethelburga.

MY DEAR FRIENDS,—I desire to say a few words in reference to the absence of Mr. Dale from the pulpit of this church.

In the first place, he wishes it to be known that he was ready to fulfil his engagement, notwithstanding his inhibition, and that though he defers to the spiritual authority of the Bishop, he does not acknowledge any spiritual authority in the court which has condemned him.

In the next place, I have to say that from the Bishop of London I have received a most kind and courteous letter expressing his wish that a substitute should be found for Mr. Dale, but breathing throughout a spirit of the greatest kindness and consideration for him. To a wish so expressed, I feel that I am bound by my ordination vows to yield obedience, but I have informed the Bishop that I obey *him* and not Lord Penzance's court. I trust, *therefore*, that every one

of you will see that Mr. Dale's non-appearance here
this evening is due not to the action of our Father in
GOD, the Bishop of the Diocese, but to a most unjust,
unconstitutional, and uncatholic law, whose avowed
object, as stated by the Archbishops in the House of
Lords, and the Prime Minister in the House of Com-
mons, is to put down and to stamp out the Catholic
party in the Church of England.   They, however, are
determined neither to be silenced nor to be crushed,
God helping them.   J. M. RODWELL, *Rector*.

The publication of this paper brought this letter from
the Rev. Edward Stuart, of St. Mary Magdalene's, Munster
Square :—

MY DEAR MR. PELHAM DALE,—I have just read in
this evening's *Standard* about yourself and St. Ethelburga's Church.   I have been so sorry to read it.

I do sincerely hope you will come and preach at St.
Mary Magdalene's, Munster Square, soon.   My house
is your house, and my Church is your Church, and
my heart is your heart under present circumstances.

Please do let me know when you will come; the
sooner the better.—I remain, yours most sincerely,

EDWARD STUART.

Mr. Stuart's invitation was accepted as frankly as it was
given, and the Rector of St. Vedast preached there on
December 3rd.

Mr. Stuart was ill at the time, suffering from a disease of
the brain that eventually killed him.   He insisted, however,
on being present on the occasion and showing every affectionate attention to his guest.   His illness left him clear-
headed, except for momentary forgetfulness, but made him

extremely nervous and excitable. But if it increased his eccentricity, it did not lessen his sense of humour. An amusing correspondence took place between him and Mr. Dale's churchwardens. These letters are not given here, as they are not fair representations of Mr. Stuart's style and humour, owing no doubt to the disease then attacking him. He was by nature a fearless, kind-hearted man, and his work was well founded and permanent.

The churchwardens of St. Vedast, who very likely knew no more of Mr. Stuart than that he was a well-known and popular High Churchman, resented his letter, and, by their reply, provoked a still more irritating piece of mockery. They then printed the whole correspondence as a leaflet, and forwarded a copy to the Bishop with a complaint of their treatment, and of Mr. Dale for preaching in the diocese. The paper was given, according to the note at the end, "With the churchwardens' (of St. Vedast and St. Michael-le-Querne) compliments to their fellow ratepayers and parishioners. 12th December 1876."

So ends this curious paper, which was actually printed for distribution and duly sent to the Bishop, who, no doubt, was sufficiently puzzled and annoyed by this new development of the dispute.

This description of the eventful year 1876 shall be closed with extracts from a letter written in answer to a friendly critic by Mr. Pelham Dale :—

"It appears to me that I am by no means compelled in conscience to resist him" (the Bishop, whom his correspondent considers to have acted as an officer of Lord Penzance's court) "if I believe, as I do, that to suffer wrong is the best course for the Church. I accept your parallel from the history of St. Paul. He and Silas did not *resist* the *stripes* or the stocks.

" I act as I do for the following reasons :—

"(1.) That in an Erastianized Church it is unreasonable to expect that bishops should suddenly act strictly according to Canon law.

"(2.) That the course I take does not precipitate a virtual schism, but gives time to act.

"(3.) That it puts before the unbelieving our desire to obey if we can do so.

"(4.) That in my case, the work being essentially missionary, those to whom I ministered are not strictly my own people. I *could* not have put forth to them such an address as Mr. Tooth has most properly done.

"(5.) That having no congregation to support me, and the churchwardens and parish against me, the appearance of inhibition enabled them to shut the church against me, law or no law, and I was quite aware that they would do it. Nevertheless I would have risked a street row had not the Bishop come in person.

"(6.) Last of all, I believe that I shall most effectually show my disregard of the court by openly but unobtrusively ministering as I am now doing in the diocese.

"Disobedience is a necessity, but defiance of the law, even when usurped, is to my mind not to be resorted to until all other methods have failed. Let the world see that we are victims to a persecuting clique, not rebels against any lawful authority."

CHAPTER IX.

FIRST IMPRISONMENT UNDER THE NEW ACT—CURATE'S
STIPEND AND PARISH BUSINESS—DECISION OF QUEEN'S
BENCH—RETURN TO ST. VEDAST—PASTORAL, 1877.

JANUARY 1877 saw the committal of Mr. Tooth to Horse-
monger Gaol. The first imprisonment of a clergyman
of pure and industrious life for matters of ritual created
some excitement. It was thus announced in the *Church
Review :*—

"A minister of Christ has been put in prison in England
for his religion in the reign of Queen Victoria. No amount
of special pleading can explain away this fact, or qualify it,
or put it in another guise."

Up to this the public had regarded this climax as an
impossibility; the kinder-hearted thought that the prosecutors would never wish to carry matters so far; the more
scornful thought that the clergy would yield first.

After the first shock of an action of this kind the public
mind grows accustomed to arguments in favour of such
strong measures. No doubt if the much-talked-of Smithfield fires had been relighted for this occasion, they would
have been argued into respectable necessity by their promoters. The spirit of intolerance, especially religious intolerance, is as much alive and as bigoted as ever; let those
who have tasted of its bitterness beware of ever putting forth
their hands to use it as a weapon. It carries with it more
than the actual wrong to one's neighbour, the cruelty to
the individual. It was not only Arthur Tooth's bodily

sufferings, and he left the prison broken in health; there were those under his care who, deprived of his instruction, and thoroughly disgusted with the teaching offered to them by persecutors of their faithful priest, fell away into unbelief and immorality. The clouds at this time were thick and dark around the Church; to many it seemed as if the end were come, as if wrong were victorious, as if religion were dead. Some of these souls crept back in the end, wounded and wearied, and longing for the old peace and comfort that was not dead after all; but others—they have fallen back, and been swept away as far as man can tell, and those who struck them back into the whirlpool have a responsibility that may weigh heavier than offences against the men attacked.

The final release of Mr. Tooth was attributed at the time to the tender-heartedness of the Queen; it was really a clever escape from an awkward position by the Prime Minister, Lord Beaconsfield. It was found that under a Liberal Government, who disowned the responsibility of the Bill, the Queen had no such power.

The following letter from the Bishop of London to Mr. Pelham Dale has ceased to be private and confidential, since lapse of time has made the subject a matter of history. It explains the attitude which Bishop Jackson held between the conflicting parties :—

MY DEAR SIR,—May I write to you privately on two points, not officially as Bishop, but simply as a brother clergyman, offering suggestions which may save you loss and inconvenience.

The first has reference to your *preaching* in the diocese. There seems little doubt that this would be held to be included among the "any services of the Church," and that thus, without any obligation of duty or any strong reason, you place yourself at the mercy of any one who may choose to bring you within the penalties of disobedience. Only lately Mr. Stuart wrote to your churchwardens to tell them that you had preached for him; and they were doubtful whether it might not be their duty to repeat the fact. I recommended them to take no notice of Mr. Stuart's letter, and they complied; but it might be difficult to avert the consequences if the act were repeated.

The other matter is the curate's stipend. Mr. Ackland, as I told you, is licensed to the curacy at a stipend of £100 per annum. He expressed a wish to take no stipend, but I did not think this right, nor do I suppose that you yourself would like it. The Bishop has the power of sequestrating the benefice in order to pay the stipend, but it would be a pity to have to do it. In a sequestration much of the income is necessarily wasted in sequestrator's charges and court fees, which had much better go into your pocket. I would suggest, therefore, that you should simply tell your clerk or collector to pay Mr. Ackland out of the moneys in his hands at the rate of £100 per annum, and that thus you and I should have no further concern in it. The whole matter has been sufficiently painful to us both, and the less we have to do with the legal proceedings the better.

You will, I am sure, take the suggestions as they are meant, as prompted by a strong desire to spare you as far as possible from any further loss or annoyance.

That this letter was kindly meant there can be no doubt, but that there was no appreciation of the Rector of St. Vedast's point of view was also very apparent. Mr. Pelham Dale thanked him for his kindness in reply, but explained that as he himself was ready to take the services of his church, he would not consider himself in any way responsible for the appointment or payment of the curate forced upon him. Nor could he do anything to avert the penalties of a court he did not acknowledge. The Bishop's letter is dated January 4. There the matter rested. On February 15, Mr. Ackland writes to Mr. Dale on the subject of his stipend. The three months for which he undertook the charge are over, but he considers himself responsible during the continuance of the inhibition, which the Rector has taken no steps to conclude. He wants the Rector to authorise the parish clerk to pay him out of the tithes ; he also wants the keys of the chest the registers are in, as there will be, he understands, a child to be baptized on Sunday next.

Mr. Pelham Dale had many times explained his views ; he now writes briefly :—

DEAR SIR,—I have already written twice to the Bishop distinctly declining to pay his substitute. You will also remember that I told you that I could not in conscience recognise you as curate of St. Vedast. I must also remind you that I told you I should attend whenever registers were required.

There again the matter rested until the 25th of March, when there was an announcement in the *Times* that the living of St. Vedast was sequestrated to pay this stipend.

All this time, from last year until now (1877), the leases of the properties of the two parishes were waiting for the signature of the Rector, and the correspondence was more constant than satisfactory. The Rector was now acting under legal advice.

A letter from him to a churchwarden, written March 17, 1877, shows how matters were standing at that date :—

DEAR SIR,—The solicitors of Messrs. Welch and Son have written to me to complete their lease; this I have promised to do, and to arrange matters according to their satisfaction, although I reminded them that their uncourteous and improper occupation of the school and churchyard during the rebuilding of their premises did not entitle them to apply to me as persons aggrieved. I think the matter should be settled forthwith; indeed you are aware that I am not the real cause of the delay. I shall, however, require that due security be given for the safe custody of the rent by the opening of a proper banker's account; that no *rights* to ancient lights be surrendered, and that the Rector has a room suitable to the holding of classes, as unanimously agreed to at the Vestry when terms were settled.

You are aware that I am dissatisfied with the way in which the parish accounts are kept, and that the parish has already suffered considerable loss. As long as this was a question of the custody of the rates, in which I had no interest, it appeared to me, especially consider- ing the number of commercial men in the parish, that I did my duty sufficiently by pointing this out in Vestry. As a trustee, however, and with a large balance in hand, I see the very strongest reasons why I must insist that matters may be so arranged that I may be able to do my duty with regard to custody of moneys, of which it appears I am the chief trustee.

The other side, while very anxious to obtain their lease, were determined to secure the school-room as ordinary parish property, and so the correspondence went on—legally con- ducted on both sides—while the Charity Commissioners were still acknowledging the receipt of letters on foolscap paper.

The errors in the procedure, that had been so autocratically put aside by Lord Penzance, were still kept in sight by the lawyers of the English Church Union. April and May were passed in preparation, and in June the case was argued in the Court of Queen's Bench, and this time the whole suit was declared void, as the Bishop was the patron of the living. An appeal was lodged, but in July was abandoned, so that Mr. Pelham Dale was once more in possession of his church, and there seemed a prospect of peace. Peace was what he most wished for; he hated publicity, law, and the disagreeables of an ecclesiastical suit, aggravated in his case by the difficulty of his unusual position.

He decided, therefore, not to resume the former services, as his congregation had been scattered, but to have an early celebration, with, of course, lights and vestments, and to return to the classes and instructions, especially the 1.15 services. One of the principal reasons for this decision was that he hoped to bring the dispute about the trust funds to a conclusion, when that would cease to be an element in the dispute. Hitherto the Vestry had shielded themselves by condemning him as a law-breaker, while they ignored his trusteeship. Once or twice the Rector had been warned that this same dragon, Law, would hold him responsible for the funds in case misappropriation was proved. It was to be a case of "heads I win, tails you lose," anyhow, and a more tiresome, worrying complication of affairs could hardly have been invented. However, a Commission was promised, and he hoped to get rid of the responsibility of the funds he could not control. Till then he was anxious to keep quiet and unnoticed so far as he conscientiously could.

His choir and fellow-workers agreed with him on the matter being put before them, and so once more the work went on.

This Advent the Pastoral was put out as usual. The account of 1877 shall close with it, as giving a full description of the position and feelings of the worshippers and their priest.

MY DEAR FRIENDS,—In addressing you again, at the beginning of the Christian year, I must in the first place put on record my deep sense of thankfulness to our Heavenly Father, that He has permitted me, when I had least expectation of such an event, to resume my ministrations amongst you. Last Advent I had in silence to suffer with you for what I believe was our Master's honour. Now, with the more confidence, we may rejoice together.

I need not disguise from you that the two years which have passed since we last kept our Advent has been to me a time of supreme anxiety and distress. It was, as I then told you, no light matter to me to find myself in opposition on points of vital importance to some of my parishioners, even when I felt sure that wider and deeper information in matters little understood would certainly show that I was at least honest and loyal, even if I were mistaken. I had hoped that this difference would be confined, so far as I was personally concerned, to the very narrow limits of our own small parishes and humble little church. But this was not to be. I was compelled, much against my wish, to take a position of public antagonism to those for whose opinion and authority I had the greatest respect and veneration. But when conviction has reached a certain point, one's own conscience becomes the supreme arbiter. Truth is truth, and

however painful it may be to differ from those with
whom for long years one has been accustomed to act,
any compromise which involves sacrifice of principle
is clearly inadmissible, and to this point my conscience
told me I had myself arrived. I could not submit to
a jurisdiction which was practically to decide articles
of faith by processes utterly unknown to the Catholic
Church since its foundation. I was quite aware of the
consequences of not submitting, but there was but one
force that I could adopt—that was to suffer either
silently or under protest. I elected to suffer in silence.
The result you know. Our work amongst the young
in the City was broken up. My living went into
sequestration. I was branded as a law-breaker, doubly
guilty because from my position I ought to have set
an example of obedience. Yet, to do more than I did
in the way of resistance and protest on the one side,
seemed to me, under my peculiar circumstances, to
involve a certain disregard of my obligations of canonical obedience. To save myself by submission, on the
other, would have burdened my conscience with the
conviction that I had betrayed those liberties of the
Church which, as her ordained priest, I was before all
things bound to preserve.

The way in which deliverance from this painful
position came to me is now patent to all the world. I
may well be excused, then, if I say nothing on this
point ; the more so as I desire especially to utter no
single word which shall unnecessarily wound the feelings of those whom I am bound to regard—though I
think them fatally in error—as earnest in the cause of

what they regard as Scripture truth as I can possibly
be. This much is evident, that the progress of so-
called Ritualistic—I deem them Catholic—principles
has never been more rapid than since the prosecution
of them by process of law was inaugurated. But what
wonder ? If our principles are Scriptural and Catholic,
nothing will advance them quicker than suffering for
them.

I must not, however, forbear an expression of thanks
to those who stood by me in my trouble, and foremost
amongst these I must place the Vicar of St. Mary
Magdalene, Paddington. Though I was not at that
time personally known to Dr. West, he nevertheless
received me with fullest sympathy, and treated me
with a brotherly kindness so true and disinterested,
that my way was lightened and cheered beyond what
I could possibly have expected. To him, to his fellow-
priests, and to his congregation generally, I owe a
debt of gratitude which no act or service of mine can
ever adequately repay. The Lord grant him, and
them also, mercy in that day when He will recom-
pense to them that loving service of theirs to the weak
and suffering, in which (in so many ways) they show
a conspicuous example. To many others also who
gave me advice and counsel in the difficult position in
which I was placed, must I take this opportunity of
expressing my obligations : especially my old college
friend, the Vicar of St. Cyprian's, Marylebone.* Nor
can any of us forget the kindness of the Vicar of St.
Michael's, Shoreditch, at whose church the choir and

* Rev. Charles Gutch.

many of the congregation found true Christian sympathy and a home.*

But I gladly turn from these personal matters to topics connected with our work.

The mid-day services at 1.15 were the first to be resumed on my return. In hopes of making these yet more useful, the church has been opened at 12 noon, to afford opportunity, to those who desire it, for private prayer. An address, usually in the form of a conference, has also been added on the Friday, besides the usual sermon on Saints' days; and attendance in the vestry has been resumed by myself, to hear Confessions, and to give advice to those who might apply to me for it. I cannot, of course, here enter into the burning question of "Confession in the Church of England," but I must say that the Exhortation in the Communion Service seems to me to cover practically the whole ground. In it our Church advises resort to her priest, not simply in case of very heinous transgression and heavily burdened conscience, but generally for the avoiding of *all* scruple and doubtfulness. I can only say that I, for my part, shall be ready to do my office to the best of my power, as God shall give me grace.

I wish to draw the attention of my congregation to an alteration in our Wednesday Evening Service. A League, of which the object is the advance of the spiritual life, called St. Martin's League, has been formed amongst the officials in the Post-Office (part of whose buildings is situate in the parish), under the

* Rev. H. D. Nihill.

Presidency of the Rev. A. H. Stanton. Many members of this League, as opportunity offers, are attendants at the services and Bible-classes. On consulting together, it appeared that it would be especially desirable to have an independent service between the hours of eight and nine P.M. During Advent then—in addition to his other numerous calls—the President of the League has promised to give the address. I do not know any event that has given me greater satisfaction during my whole incumbency than to be thus able to receive workers within the limits of my own parish, who from the very nature of their labour are often deprived of the ordinary opportunities of religious instruction. God prosper with His blessing both the League and its indefatigable President!

The Working Association has already commenced its labours, and has a considerable stock of garments made up. Several large subscriptions have been given by persons unconnected with the City, having been induced to subscribe by the proved usefulness of the work. Already some of the clothing has been distributed. We need, however, more material as well as workers to continue this agency, and I shall be glad, therefore, of contributions. Any ladies desirous of enrolling their names, and receiving material to work up into garments, should apply at the vestry before Evensong on Monday evening. They will be most heartily welcomed.

The Offertories account is appended. It will be seen that they show a very considerable deficiency. This will necessitate my working single-handed for at least some time to come. The services of my valued friend and coadjutor, Mr. Armytage, Assistant-Priest, came to an end by the withdrawal of his permission to officiate, and he has thus been obliged to seek another sphere of duty. His loss is very great, the more that, working for an inadequate stipend, we must consider that what he did for us was in the nature of a labour of love. I trust then that those who attend the church, at occasional services and sermons especially, will see that the exigencies of the case demand a liberal offering. Not only would the assistance of another priest render the mission work amongst the young of the city more efficient, but beside, our own services could be made especially attractive to them. Further, there ought to be something over and above for outlying necessitous districts; such, for example, as our mission only just opened in Cowheel Alley, the claims of which I hope speedily to bring before my congregation. Our rich, well-endowed City parishes *ought* to have *nothing* over, so long as the poor outlying districts, whence the working bees of our commercial hive are drawn, have so great a lack.

To you, my fellow-labourers in the choir and in our Guilds of St. Lawrence and St. Agatha, I will say no more than this. Continue to me those prayers which in the time of our partial separation you gave me. Then you agreed together—"as touching what you should ask of our Heavenly Father"—that it might please Him in His own good time to restore me to my ministry. He has, according to the tenor of our petitions, answered our prayers. Continue then, I say, this theme of supplication, and especially at our Eucharist, that now the Word of the Lord may have free course and be glorified with us. The knowledge that you did this bore me up when all things seemed (it was but seeming, we know) to be against us. It shall bear us up still: so shall we be able to say with the Psalmist, "In the Lord put I my trust: I will not fear what man can do unto me."

In conclusion let me—reminded by this sacred Season —exhort all to a holy looking for and waiting for His appearance who shall come to judge the world. A time of religious zeal, if it may sometimes beget controversy, should at least be marked by increased holiness in the spiritual life and work of all. Otherwise surely we are self-condemned, and must, if we deal honestly with our own consciences, trace our imagined earnestness to the form without the power. A religion without love, however it may vaunt itself, will never be accepted by the Lord of Love, but is poor, and miserable, and blind, and naked. Let us then, while contending earnestly for the faith once delivered to the saints, contend in the spirit of meekness, desiring above all the things which make for peace; and may the God of peace keep your hearts and minds in Jesus Christ.—Your faithful priest and servant,

T. PELHAM DALE.

This concluding paragraph contains the lesson he was always impressing on himself and those around him. He did not believe that his fellow-trustees were wantonly dishonest; he never said so—he never allowed it to be said. He considered that they were blinded by prejudice and custom, and indignant with him for disturbing "what had always been." He was very anxious to separate the two causes of dispute—the trust-money and the ritual. He wanted to meet those objecting to the ritual face to face, to argue, to persuade, even to yield so far as conscience permitted if they wished to attend the church. He could not bear to believe that they struck at him because they were angry, and so naturally seized the weapon curiously provided for the use of men in their position. He preferred to believe them tempted by the members of the Church Association—an indefinite body that one need not individualise; but for his fellows to hate him without a cause was positive pain to him. It was a weakness, perhaps, but it was the weakness of a loving and sensitive soul. Even when in one's affection for him one waxed indignant at his defence of his opponents, one knew that it was an outcome of that humility and width of love that very few of us attain to, with our quickly-roused anger and ready contempt for our fellows.

CHAPTER X.

CHARITY COMMISSION AND THE TRUST FUNDS—DONATION
FROM TRUST FUNDS TO THE CHURCH ASSOCIATION—
THE DEFENCE AND REPLY—PRESS ON EXPENDITURE
OF TRUST MONEY — VOTE OF THANKS TO CHURCH
ASSOCIATION.

ALL through 1878 the correspondence between the Charity
Commissioners and the Rector of St. Vedast dragged on.
A letter of his, written in 1876, is alluded to and answered.
He is also informed, first, that as a trustee he has a right
to see every trust document and all the accounts, but that
the Commissioners have no direct power to enforce compliance in this respect. Towards the end of the year the
accounts demanded by the Commissioners are sent in
without being submitted to the Rector. The correspondence would be instructive to any one entering into negotiations with a Government office—would inform them of the
necessity of patience at least—but it is neither brilliant nor
amusing. Mr. Pelham Dale saw the accounts at the office,
and writes the following criticisms on December 6th :—

(1.) *St. Michael contribution in aid of poor-rates,*
£100. I have already expressed my opinion as to
items of this character, especially in respect to counsel's
opinion, as I understand, of its doubtful legality.

(2.) *Churchwardens' account of costs at St. Michael,*

215

£30. *St. Vedast accounts, St. Michael to Church Association*, £25. I feel it my duty to protest against an expenditure so wholly indefensible.

(3.) *Share of church expenses: St. Michael*, £51, 19s. 11d. The items are detailed not very clearly in the St. Vedast accounts. Considering the present state of the church, I am at a loss to see how this sum can have been expended. Much less judiciously laid out would provide for at least the comfort of the congregation, who now complain of cold and dirt.

The want of a proper banking account and the withholding of the school-room from its proper uses are also commented on.

The delays, wilful procrastinations, and misunderstandings in the correspondence with churchwardens and vestry clerks are too tedious to be interesting. After many inquiries for the deed of the Sir John Johnstone's School-room, and a positive denial of its existence, it is acknowledged this October to be in a safe in the vestry. The inquiries after it from the Rector stretch over some years. After seeing it, he made a demand for the use of the room, which was refused.

The separation of the ritual disputes from those about the charity funds by no means recommended itself to the vestry. The Public Worship Regulation Act was an instrument of torture, especially devised for troublesome parsons; and there was no doubt the Rector's conscience annoyed them, so they determined that theirs, carefully guarded (by law), should retaliate. In February the churchwardens, no doubt at great inconvenience to themselves, for they lived in the suburbs, attended the eight o'clock celebration, and having thus qualified themselves for protesting against the illegalities they witnessed, took steps for a fresh prosecution.

In order to obviate the patronage difficulty the Bishop of Exeter made the requisition.

Still bent on postponing such attacks until after the Royal Commission should have settled the parish funds dispute, the Rector adopted the plan of taking a private oratory, and there he and his choir had their reverent services safe from the painful presence of those who attended the Holy Eucharist as legal spies—a practice which led in one case to so gross a sacrilege that even the promoters of the Act were staggered. In spite of this withdrawal the case was continued, and again Mr. Pelham Dale was monitioned to abstain from practices which were already discontinued. In the meantime he had given his evidence before the Commissioners. The trust in a Royal Commission to relieve him of a part of his troubles was vain. They moved so very slowly, and took so long to digest the information they received, that, though personally they were all that could be desired, as a body their action was almost imperceptible.

Of all the years of Mr. Pelham Dale's life, 1879 was the most trying and wearing, every day bringing fresh trouble and complication. His attempts to gain peace were productive of attack, the trust funds were far from a settlement, the lawyers were full of activity, the vestry meetings were peculiarly aggressive, the ratepayers' consciences were very tender on ritual points, and much respected by the authorities. As the least interesting, the trust funds shall be disposed of first—not that the business ever was concluded as far as the Rector was concerned; it may be still undecided, and in its languid old age afford a gentle exercise for the pens at the Charity Commissioners' office.

The following correspondence contains Mr. Pelham Dale's remonstrance with the chairman of the Church Association in January :—

DEAR SIR,—It appears from the accounts of St. Vedast parish charities rendered to the Charity Com-

missioners that there stands an item, " St. Michael
Church Association, £25," and I am informed that this
represents a sum contributed to the Association of
which you are president.   On making inquiry into the
matter, I find that such an item would probably be dis-
allowed by the authorities, in which case the trustees,
of whom I am one, would be personally responsible for
the amount.   I believe also that in the same way
another sum of £50 appears as a contribution from
the funds of another similar trust.   As it is obviously
improper that a religious society should accept public
moneys from the guardians of trust funds without the
clearest possible title, it is my duty to ask your attention to the matter, and for an explanation of the circumstances under which the money was received.—I
remain, dear sir, yours truly,   T. PELHAM DALE.

This was briefly answered on January 20th.

DEAR SIR,—I have received your letter, which shall
have due attention.—I am, dear sir, truly yours,

THOMAS R. ANDREWS.

As nothing further was heard, Mr. Pelham Dale wrote
on the 29th of January :—

DEAR SIR,—Allow me to remind you that my letter
of the 17th, to which, in your acknowledgment of the
20th inst., you promised due attention, remains unan-
swered.   I am at a loss to understand how so long a
period should be required to reply to so very simple an
inquiry as I there make, seeing that the sum referred
to appears in the accounts submitted to the Charity

Commissioners in August last. Since I wrote to you
I have accidentally lighted on the April number of the
Church Association Intelligencer for 1878. On the
cover of this number a donation is announced of £50
from the churchwardens of St. Michael-le-Querne.
This sum tallies with an entry in the accounts of that
parish sent in (if I remember rightly) in April last to
the Commissioners. It also appears in a report of the
Association for 1878, contained in the same number of
the *Intelligencer*, that the St. Vedast case (which, it
seems, had already formed the subject of a portion of
the previous year's report) was referred to as having
proved abortive, and the reasons of the result detailed.
Thus, then, I am compelled to conclude that a donation
was accepted by this Society out of public funds from
a section of a body of trustees, who were attempting,
from whatever cause, to prosecute a co-trustee, and
who were proved by the result to have acted illegally
in doing so. I must submit that such a proceeding on
the part of a professedly religious society is most un-
precedented, and I must therefore request an immediate
explanation. I also reserve to myself the right to publish our correspondence.—I remain, dear sir, yours
truly,   T. PELHAM DALE.

Thus pressed, Mr. Andrews writes on the 31st of
January:—

DEAR SIR,—In answer to your letters, I beg to
inform you that the sums of money received by our
Association were sent by Mr. Horwood, to whom I
refer you for further information.—I remain, yours
truly,   THOMAS R. ANDREWS.

A scrap of information being at last elicited, Mr. Pelham Dale writes to acknowledge it on Friday 4th :—

DEAR SIR,—Allow me to acknowledge your letter of January 31st, from which I conclude you were aware of the doubtful character of the moneys you received. I must also inform you that the gentleman to whom you refer me for information is not a member of the St. Vedast Trust, and has no right whatever to meddle with its funds; and further, that the whole matter being now before the Commissioners, I must simply await their decision.—Truly yours,

T. PELHAM DALE.

February 6th.

DEAR SIR,—I notice in yours of the 4th you say " I conclude you were aware of the doubtful character of the moneys you received." This conclusion is not true, and not warranted by any communication from me.—Yours truly, THOMAS R. ANDREWS.

February 7th.

DEAR SIR,—I am unable to admit that my conclusion was not warranted by any communication from yourself. You promised "due attention," and at length referred me to a trustee of St. Michael-le-Querne. I naturally concluded, therefore, that your Society, after communication with the person indicated in my letters, was prepared to give its countenance and support to this doubtful appropriation of trust funds.—I am, sir, yours truly, T. PELHAM DALE.

The churchwarden alluded to, Mr. Horwood, wrote his explanation to the *Times* of February the 8th :—

SIR,—The correspondence between the Rev. T. Pelham Dale and Mr. T. R. Andrews, which appeared in the *Times* of yesterday, demands some reply from me. It is asserted that the sum of £50 was paid by me to the Church Association from the trust funds of the parish of St. Michael-le-Querne, and the legality of this payment the Rev. T. Pelham Dale contests. Will you permit me to state that this was a contribution towards the heavy law charges incurred by the Association in fighting the battles of the parishioners of these united parishes, the aid of the Association having been solicited by the churchwardens on public grounds, the vestry having, long prior to the payment, requested the trustees, of whom I am one, by a resolution unanimously carried, to expend any amount necessary to fight the battle, and we are now grateful to the Association for the aid so afforded. The efforts made by the united parishes to restrain the Rector from an indulgence in illegal ritualistic practices having now been crowned with success, Lord Penzance having to-day given judgment in the case, and "admonished" Mr. Dale to abstain from all the illegalities, save one, charged against him. As to the accusation, which is not now made for the first time, against myself and co-trustees by Mr. Dale, and hitherto treated by us with contempt, viz., that of misapplying our parish funds, or, as that gentleman puts it, "that a donation was accepted by the society out of public funds from a section of a body of trustees who were attempting, from whatever cause, to prosecute a co-trustee," &c., the fact is that the trustees, churchwardens, and parishioners, almost without exception, were endeavouring to "prosecute" the Rector of their parish for known illegal practices, the Rector happening also to be a trustee. Allow me to say, in conclusion, that the trustees have throughout acted upon the opinion of eminent counsel, one of them being the Attorney-General, Sir John Karslake, in expending the moneys intrusted to them in accordance with the original deed of conveyance to the "parishioners" of St. Michael-le-Querne, viz., "for the benefit and behoof of the said parish and public uses," and "good of the same." I and the majority, *i.e.*, all except the Rector and one other of my co-trustees, have been, and are still, of the opinion that it was for the "good of the parish" to endeavour to prevent "illegal practices" in our parish church, and the result of to-day's proceedings seems to us to be a justification of the course we have adopted.—Yours faithfully (for self and colleagues),

JAMES HORWOOD,
*Senior Churchwarden, and a Trustee
of St. Michael-le-Querne.*

On this letter the Rector makes the following comment in writing to the *Church Times* on February 11th :—

Mr. Horwood's letter of explanation shows that the Church Association are the real prosecutors, and that they did receive the trust moneys to pay abortive costs, but that the chairman was not aware that they were paid out of the trust. The transaction must have been most irregular. The money could only be properly paid by a cheque countersigned by the clerk of the trustees. The unanimous vote alluded to is simply Mr. Horwood and his friends. The parishioners seldom, the representatives of the large firms never, appear at the vestries. I have also reason to believe that a large number of our more thinking parishioners are becoming heartily sick of the whole system of conducting the prosecution, even though opposed on religious grounds to myself. The opinion of counsel, so confidently appealed to, pronounced a contribution from trust funds to poor-rates as of doubtful legality; but were the legality of such a contribution undoubted, it would certainly determine nothing as to the propriety or lawfulness of prosecuting a co-trustee out of trust funds. I proposed with regard to the questions which had long been discussed between us, especially the matter of paying poor's-rates out of trust funds, to ask the advice of the Charity Commissioners.

I reiterated this proposal at several successive half-yearly meetings of trustees, but in vain. At length I put the whole matter before the Charity Commissioners, who have the case in hand. As I am awaiting their decision, I can add nothing more on these points except to say that I have expressed to them an opinion that the expenditure is wasteful and the accounts lax.

It is well known that the representants have no real interest in the services of St. Vedast, as they never communicated even when present.

Though I certainly was not under any obligation to do so, I did, after my return, what in other cases was, we know, considered satisfactory by bishops and others, —had simply an early celebration, making Matins perfectly plain. I may say generally that I have many times offered every possible concession to the persons who complained, provided no surrender of principle was involved in it. They said openly that they never intended themselves to attend any services, and except for the purposes of prosecution they have kept their word. Since August last, to the no small loss of myself and congregation, I have abstained from celebrating at St. Vedast; this was done after free consultation with all my communicants, and was unanimously assented to by them, as we felt that it would not be advisable that a mere money dispute should be complicated with questions of vital interest to the Church at large. They felt that I was unfairly weighted, if the representants were able to pay costs out of funds for which I might be made personally liable.

The daily papers commented on this correspondence. The public were not in favour of charity funds being used for the benefit of the trustees, though, regardless of the long struggle and the small power of one against a body, they asked what the chairman had been doing to allow such a thing.

The *Times* in a leader says, "The 'love feast' at Richmond, even at the cost of £60 a year, becomes a blameless and even praiseworthy destination of charity in comparison with the case of the united parishes of St. Vedast and St. Michael-le-Querne, where it is stated that the expense of the prosecution of the Rector has been defrayed out of the parochial charities."

The *Echo*, after describing the case, says—

"The charity funds of city parishes are sufficiently misused when they are applied in the provision of rich dinners for those who fare sumptuously every day, and in relieving wealthy city traders from paying their proper proportion of poor-rates; but to rob the poor for the support of the Association for hunting down Ritualists is beyond endurance. And this from the very people who are always mouthing about pious founders!

"There is a very ludicrous side to this dispute. Mr. Dale himself is a trustee of the St. Vedast charities, and he is advised that he, like the other trustees, is liable for the restoration of the amount that has been misappropriated. It would certainly be hard for a man to be compelled indirectly to subscribe to the costs of his own prosecution; but apparently, from his letter, Mr. Dale only knew of the matter through perusing the accounts. Possibly, if he had attended to his duties as a trustee, the trouble might have been prevented."

This most unfortunate trustee had, as we know, expostulated in vain. The actual vote of money to the Church Association must have taken place when he was away. His holiday was always a signal for a vestry meeting to be called; sometimes he returned for them at the expense of time and money. He went back one summer from Northumberland for this purpose. The meetings were not legal if, as often happened, he had no voice in arranging them, and no care was taken that he received notice; but *not legal* is a very empty phrase. Who is to put the cumbrous machinery of the law in motion, and who is to be sure that it will work when started? Law is made for millionaires; it would

VOL. I.   P

probably have been cheaper to pay a portion of his own costs than to prosecute his co-trustees.

Finally, the Commissioners pronounced such use of the funds to be illegal, and the churchwardens were ordered to refund it. In spite of this, the Church Association received a donation in February 1880 from the St. Vedast Vestry. The trustees refused to refund the money, and never did so. For the other matters, the Commission seemed powerless to take any measure less drastic than confiscation, or stronger than giving orders which they could not enforce.

The vestry meetings that have so often been mentioned were at this time a modern substitute for the rack. If the Rector did not go, then all sorts of votes for which he was considered responsible were passed; if he did, all the aggrieved ratepayers took their turn at insulting him. Now and then their eloquence gave him a little amusement, as on one occasion when the Advent services were commented on, and one member took great objection to anything so Popish as the " Miserere." " Who ever," he asked, " heard of the Miserere, and in the joyful season of Advent too?" But still one needs a companion in one's adversity to enjoy such incidents. The quieter men did not attend the vestries, and some of those who would have otherwise supported the Rector were afraid of incurring the enmity of their fellows. The Rector was told to " hold his tongue," that " he had some Guy Fawkes plot in his head." " If he had not married he would have been a Popish priest long ago." " In the grand old days of his fathers they would have made short work of him." Such amenities make discussion or explanation difficult, and Mr. Pelham Dale was not fond of fighting or disputes, though a religious or scientific discussion with an equal who could keep his temper was a great delight to him.

At the last Easter vestry he attended he was more amused than hurt at a resolution proposed by the senior churchwarden: " That the hearty thanks of this Vestry, on behalf of parishioners, are eminently due, and are hereby tendered, to the Council of the Church Association for the further valuable aid and assistance rendered by the Association to this parish and that of St. Vedast, at the solicitation of the four churchwardens in connection with the last 'representation' of numerous illegal Ritualistic practices in the performance of Divine service in the parish by the Rector, the Rev. T. Pelham Dale, resulting, on the 19th inst., in the issuing of an inhibition by the official Principal of the Arches Court of the Province of Canterbury, notifying to the said Thomas Pelham Dale, and all others whom it may concern, that he is inhibited for the term of three months, and thereafter until the same shall have been duly relaxed, from performing any service in the church, or otherwise exercising the care of souls in the diocese of London, and ordering him, the Rev. Thomas Pelham Dale, to pay the costs."

At the end of proposing this resolution, of which no notice had been given, the speaker said he would hand the Rector a copy.

"Am I to have the pleasure of keeping it?" the Rector asked with a smile.

"The inhibited Rector of this parish has no right to question me. I know the Jesuitical way of putting things," was the retort.

After pointing out that no notice had been given of the motion—which was not, therefore, regular—the Rector, having of course been outvoted, put it in the following form : "That the thanks of the Vestry be given to the Church Association for their kindness in prosecuting the Rector."

That there was something rather ludicrous in the Retors putting such a vote smilingly to the meeting, struck some of those present; they protested against the form of words, and he accepted the following form, which was carried : "That the sincere thanks of the Vestry, on behalf of the

parishioners, are greatly due, and are hereby tendered, to
the Council of the Church Association for the further
important aid rendered by the Association to the parish of
St. Vedast *alias* Foster."

The original resolution was published in the form of
an advertisement in the *Times*, headed "St. Michael-le-
Querne," and signed by the vestry clerk, the charity funds
paying for the insertion.

CHAPTER XI.

MONITION OF FEBRUARY 1879—THE ROMANCE OF THE CELLAR AND OPINIONS OF THE PRESS—PRESENTMENT OF CHURCHWARDENS, NOVEMBER — DEFENCE AND CORRESPONDENCE.

THE result of the proceedings against Mr. Dale, begun in February 1878, was the issuing of a monition from the Arches Court on February 21, 1879.

After August 1878 all the celebrations had been either at the little Oratory, or some church, where the members of the St. Vedast congregation preferred to meet.

But the prosecutors did not enter into the Rector's wish that the dispute about the charity funds should be first brought to a legal settlement, and that then their ritual disagreements should be fought out. They continued the prosecution in spite of the absence of an object of dispute, until, finding that they were steadily ignored, they tried a fresh change of attack.

This system of ignoring the new courts raised a tremendous storm of indignation. A great amount of rhetoric was expended in defence of the rights of the State and the omnipotence of Parliament in all matters. " In all matters temporal " was the retort of the attacked.

Excepting the *Morning Post*, there was not a single London daily paper that did not resent and decry the conduct of the High Church party. These papers all comment solemnly, indignantly, or sarcastically on a story told by the officer of the court who served the monition, of how Mr. Pelham Dale had flung up his hands at the sight of him, and rushed down the stairs to hide in the cellar. The judge was naturally glad to deliver a judicial reproof on such undignified conduct, not, indeed, directly to the accused, for he was not there to hear it, but to the reporters and those present. To no one was the story more of a surprise than to the "gentleman and clergyman of the Church of England" so solemnly admonished. What really happened was this. Ladbroke Gardens stand upon a hill. The room at the back of the kitchen is therefore above-ground, and has two French windows overlooking the gardens. This room was Mr. Dale's study; he refused, as he always did refuse, to accept legal papers from the hand of an officer, waved the man away, and went down to his study.

It was in this room that Elsie lived. Poor Elsie! a beautiful collie, with but one devotion, of which her master was the object. It was his custom to say that he did not like pets, but Elsie proved this to be an error. She belonged at first to one of his daughters, and the study being the quietest room, Elsie was put there from time to time to be out of the way of visitors and children. It was done with apologies to the owner of the study, who grumbled a little at her constant visits, until Elsie's mistress, thinking her too timid and nervous a dog for a family or town life, offered to sell her, to put a stop to intrusions on the quiet of the study. This proposal was not received so gratefully as was expected; he thought it would be cruel to send away so nervous and affectionate a creature. No one else thought the dog affectionate, but now it appeared she had chosen her master, and he could not repel the devotion. So Elsie became his dog, and spent her life in expectation of his return, with short periods of bliss when he was at home. During his imprisonment poor Elsie watched and waited in that room

with patient wistfulness. If she were coaxed upstairs, she
escaped again, ignoring pity and endearment, preferring to
wait and listen, cocking her ears from time to time with
momentary hopefulness, only to let them fall again with a
deep sigh at the disappointment.

The papers by no means paused at the " Romance of
the Cellar " as a subject of abuse. On looking over extracts
from journals of that date, 1879-81, their virulence seems
astonishing. What has happened once may happen again,
and no doubt the next struggle between Faith and Erastianism will be every whit as bitter.

The Fountain went so far as to state that ' Dale and
Peace" (the murderer) "stand on the same level." The
extract was sent by a friend with kindest regards. *The
Fountain* is, of course, a paper with a bias, and evidently a
strong one, but almost as severe comments might be found
in the dailies, only less pithily expressed. They all agree
in speaking of the Rector of St. Vedast as if he stood alone,
and in ignoring the large and rapidly growing party of
which he was the representative. They narrow their attack
by considering only those clergy as Ritualists whose three
aggrieved parishioners are produced.

This was a time of great triumph for the prosecuting
party. The Bishops themselves were shown to be unable
to resist their power. The Bishop of Oxford, Dr. Mackar-
ness, having, as the *Rock* put it, "rushed to the rescue
the moment his dear friend the arch-Jesuit of Clewer was
assailed," and tried to prevent the prosecution of Canon
Carter, was also brought before the courts.

Canon Carter resigned his living rather than be the cause
of proceedings against his Bishop. The Bishop of Oxford
did not agree on ritual points with Canon Carter, but refused to hand over his episcopal powers to Lord Penzance.

It was a foregone conclusion at this period that every
decision would be against the Ritualistic party, but if they

were to be "stamped out," such extinction must be represented as desirable.

No attention was paid to the monition of February. It was understood that, unless Mr. Pelham Dale chose to plead before the judge that the practices complained of were discontinued, the judge chose to take it for granted that the acts were committed. It was laid down as a rule by this court that acts of commission were far worse than those of omission, so that offences of neglect sank into insignificance by comparison with the offence of over-zeal. Nevertheless when one point failed the other could be tried, if the offender were a High Churchman. As the alterations in the conduct of the services had not been made out of respect to the Arches Court, but with the view of separating the dispute of the trust funds from the shelter of an aggrieved parishioner's tender conscience, they were not affected by the monition. The newspapers say—

" Yesterday some thirty persons were present at morning service in this church, and about twice that number in the evening. Mr. Dale conducted morning and evening prayer in the usual way, which is quite free from any extravagance, and made no allusion to the judgment, which in no way will practically affect him, as since August there has been no celebration of Holy Communion, in which service all the ritual objected to was introduced.

" It is understood that Mr. Dale will decline to pay the costs, and leave to the prosecution the option of applying for his commitment for his contempt of court."

On August 11, Mr. Pelham Dale found it necessary to write to the Charity Commissioners, pointing out that his vestry and co-trustees were acting without him, calling meetings without consulting him, and ignoring the decisions of the Commissioners.

On August 25 he received the following letter from the Bishop of London :—

My Dear Sir,—I find that at the Archdeacon's visitation the Churchwardens of your two parishes presented that the Holy Communion had not been administered in the Church of St. Vedast since August 1878; that on no Sunday or Festival, not even on Easter Day, has any preparation been made or any notice given; and that not even "all that is appointed at the Communion until the end of the " Church Militant prayer, &c., has upon any Sunday or other Holy day been said. This presentment will no doubt be repeated at my visitation in October; and if so, with the 21st Canon, and the first and eighth Rubric at the end of the Communion Office before me, I could not refuse to receive and act upon it.

Let me hope, therefore, that in the interval the ground of complaint (which I certainly heard of with astonishment) may be removed, and that I may be spared the painful duty of animadverting on an omission which it must be difficult, I should think, to defend.— Believe me to be, faithfully yours,

J. LONDON.

To this Mr. Pelham Dale replied :—

My Lord,—Your letter has just reached me while away from London for a short vacation. I hasten to reply, lest I should be wanting in personal respect to yourself.

As the churchwardens are plaintiffs in an ecclesiastical suit, any action of theirs must necessarily be regarded by me from its legal aspect, and I must act as I am advised.

I have had no communication of any kind from the Archdeacon.

Your Lordship will, I feel sure, under these circumstances, excuse me from entering further into the matter at present.

A little later on he wrote the following fuller explanation :—

MY LORD,—After very carefully considering your letter of August 25th, I have come to the conclusion that it will probably be my duty at no distant period to resume the celebrations at St. Vedast.

I mentioned in my former letter to you that I could only regard the presentment, should it be made, as an incident in the suit, made under advice, and with the possible legal consequences of any action I might take clearly before the minds of those who suggested it.

I do not, however, at all shrink from such a presentment. I should rather hail it as an opportunity to state my case before my Bishop, surrounded by his presbyters, feeling that I am fully justified in acting as I have done, and that I have consulted the true interests both of my own people and the Church at large. I do not at all wish to impute motives, but I imagine that I can hardly be expected to believe that such presentment could be made with a simple desire to obtain the full privileges of the Church at her Easter Festival, seeing that none of the representants have ever been communicated at the church, or even attended, except for the purpose of obtaining evidence for the prosecution. If I desired to do so, I could no doubt

legally justify myself under the discretion given me by
the third Rubric after the Communion Service, but this
is not my object.   I have to show your Lordship that
I have used my discretion well, and that the method I
have adopted is the best, notwithstanding its obvious
objections, to protect the consciences of my people
and to avoid scandal.

My real prosecutors are, it is well known, a powerful Association, which has been publicly thanked for
its assistance and subsidised out of parish funds.   This
Association, whose action appears to me entirely to
defeat its own objects, has endeavoured to force upon
me personally (and taken funds of which I am the
guardian as the reward of doing so) the Puritan view
of the Blessed Eucharist.   This view I hold to be
unscriptural; moreover, this is attempted to be enforced by means of doubtful law.   You will remember
that the first representation was filed before the Ridsdale judgment was given.   I was distinctly advised,
when considering the course I ought then to take, that
the vestments were certainly permitted if not enjoined.

The Ridsdale judgment has since been pronounced
by very high authority bad law.   It is no secret that
it is a judgment of policy.   This being so, it is futile
to anticipate obedience to it as settled law, or to accuse
those who resist such tactics as these of being law-
breakers.   We know that if we are sufficiently pertinacious we shall at length obtain from civil courts
substantial justice, and in the interests of doctrine,
attacked under the guise of Ritual, we are, whatever be
the personal consequences, bound to be pertinacious.

That my present course has thrown difficulties in the way of my opponents, this threat of appealing to you shows; for after having ousted your canonical juris-diction, then to resort to it appears as if party victory, *not* the determination of the law, was the object in view. I think also that you can scarcely blame me if I have refrained from giving such opponents facilities for getting up evidence, or that I should feel very great reluctance to do that which would almost certainly lead to the most solemn act of our worship being used for such a purpose.

As to my own communicants, they are altogether with me, and, with an affectionate appreciation of my difficulties, have determined to seek Celebrations else-where. The daily Eucharists at the Cathedral supply in this respect all that we can want. As to myself, the privation is indeed great, but I had far rather never exercise my ministry again than betray my trust in sacrificing what I know to be the lawful heritage of my Church. Nevertheless, I feel that a church without a Eucharistic sacrifice at its Altar is a thing so anomalous that nothing but a higher interest which demands that self-sacrifice of the congregation can justify it, and then only for a time. Notwithstanding, therefore, the probability that acts of irreverence such as I have already alluded to may occur—and recent events show that this fear is not imaginary—I must shortly resume the Celebrations at my church. The exact time I must leave indefinite, for it is our misfortune that we who are attacked are compelled to regard the legal aspect of these things and determine our course, not by Church festivals, as others can, but above all to take care that no action of ours impedes or hinders the cause we have in hand, or indirectly complicates the difficulty of others persecuted like ourselves.

It is, my Lord, with deep pain that I write thus. I can, however, hardly think that you will allow your high office to be made a handle to administer a reproof such as your letter seems to imply, if you will only inquire into all the surrounding circumstances. Could you be placed in the situation I am, you would, I feel sure, sympathise with the difficulties entailed upon a priest who has had to administer the holiest rites of our faith Sunday after Sunday in the presence of hired spies, on the watch for some action on which to found a complaint, or out of which evidence can be made to support a case.

I have already sufficiently placed before you in the letters I wrote when the proceedings three years ago were commenced against me what my convictions as to my duty were, and nothing that has occurred since has weakened—rather much has strengthened—that view of my duty which I then set forth to you.

To your Lordship as my Bishop I shall always listen with the utmost respect and deference, and—unless I feel that a higher duty compels me—with obedience. More than this I cannot promise.—I remain, my Lord, your faithful servant,   T. PELHAM DALE.

To this letter he received no answer, and there the matter rested until after the Bishop's visitation on the 29th of October.

The holidays that were broken and disturbed by these

threats of a fresh attack were being spent in Lincolnshire. It was his first visit to that county, and he was staying with his son Arthur at Aswardby Rectory, near Spilsby.

It was a trial to return to town and plunge at once into the old troubles. They began with a vestry meeting, in which the senior churchwarden angrily denied that £50 had been contributed out of the charity estates to the Church Association. The Rector wrote a very gently-worded letter, asking him if there had been any mistake, and offering to correct it if it were so. The answer came through the solicitor, to the effect that the churchwarden was prevented by domestic affliction from attending to business, but declined to enter into a correspondence on the subject.

DEAR SIR,—writes Mr. Pelham Dale in reply,—I am exceedingly sorry to hear of Mr. Horwood's domestic affliction, and am quite prepared under the circumstances to excuse a display of irritation and excitement at the vestry meeting, which doubtless he would, if under less anxiety, have avoided. I do not know that it is at all necessary that I should enter into any correspondence with him on the subject, all I wished for being a correction of any error I might possibly have fallen into with regard to the payment of money contributed out of the estates to the Church Association.

This letter was so sincere in its gentleness and restraint, though doubtless it was not so understood, that in after years he would often urge in explanation of Mr. Horwood's attitude towards himself this domestic affliction, the particulars of which he heard later.

There was also the quarterly dispute on the subject of

the leases, which on this occasion the Rector referred to
the Charity Commissioners for decision.

As usual after a tussle of this kind there came a Ritual
attack, and the threatened presentment was made at the
Bishop's visitation.

The letter from the Bishop having been headed private,
was, Mr. Dale considered, written from a kindly desire to
warn him. Being fairly certain that the presentment would
be proceeded with, and not displeased at the opportunity of
public defence which it gave him, he attended at the visitation with a carefully prepared statement to read in reply.

It seemed all through this period as if misfortune and
annoyance defeated all the actions he resolved upon. A
visitation is a lengthy affair. Mr. Dale was present all the
morning. He went to take his mid-day service, and was
away from one to two. He had, however, written to explain
this necessity, and to ask that his name might not be called
then. He returned to the Cathedral, and waited to the
end, without even hearing his name. He came home, believing that the presentment had not been made, and
decidedly disappointed at losing his opportunity of defence.
The form of the presentment made an accusation which
he was naturally desirous of explaining and refuting.

The defence shall be given here in the form in which it
was prepared, as the best explanation that can be given of
the line of action taken by him, and the reasons that led
him to take it. It must be remembered that the sacrilege
constantly referred to at this period was the disgraceful act
of profanation in the stealing of the Consecrated Wafer,
and exhibiting It in court.

MY LORD,—I feel happy that I have to defend myself against this charge in the presence of my Bishop,
surrounded by his clergy, because I can set aside all

question of statute-law, and proceed at once to the
real root of the matter, which is to answer the question: Have I acted as a faithful priest, caring for the
souls of his people, ought to have done in this respect,
or no? I will not then touch upon mere technical and
legal considerations, for I might, had I chosen, have
avoided the presentment altogether. It would have
been easy in my case to have colourably complied with
the Rubric, and given notice of a Celebration, with the
probability, almost certainty, that four persons of discretion, parishioners, would not have presented themselves. I might now, if I were so disposed, appeal to
the Rubrics at the end of the Communion Service, and
show that on various grounds I had a right to exercise
the discretion as to Celebration of the Blessed Eucharist
given by them to the parish priest. But I do not intend
to do this, such tactics and such pleas as these savour
of mere evasion, inconsistent with the solemnity which
ought to surround every accessory connected with the
Celebration of the Blessed Eucharist. If under the circumstances it were right that I should have celebrated
this Sacrament three times during the past year, it
would have been equally right to have celebrated
continually. For, if it is to be a real Communion,
a meeting of faithful worshippers all united together
in the spirit of brotherly love, then even a daily
Eucharist could not be considered too frequent; but
if otherwise, if in a spirit of strife and party warfare,
then even to announce a Celebration of a single Communion would be at best but a painful unreality, and
might involve something very much worse. It is then

on this ground alone I base my reply. If this presentment were a mere legal incident in the progress of a
suit, I should decline to make any answer here. It is
only too probable that, according to State law, your
Lordship has no jurisdiction to decide at all. What I
urge, therefore, I say without prejudice to any legal
proceedings I might be advised to take. I am answering to you as to my Father in God, a Bishop with
canonical jurisdiction over me, and so restrict myself
entirely to the religious side of the question, and on
that ground alone I shall show that I have acted as a
God-fearing priest, looking upon the interests of the
souls of his people, ought to have acted.

Now, I need not remind you that during thirty-three
years of my incumbency I have been increasingly desirous to give opportunities to my people of receiving
the Holy Eucharist. These have never been less frequent than a monthly Celebration, with the greater
festivals in addition. Of late years I have celebrated
twice on Sunday, once every red-letter Holy-day, and
once in the week besides. Had I been able to do all
I desired, I would have given opportunities even more
frequent than these. Yet never during all this long
period have any of those who present me once communicated with me at St. Vedast. Thus, then, it is
clear the presentment cannot be made with a sincere
desire for increased Eucharistic opportunities. You
will not, I am sure, wish me to bring evidence to
support this. Painful facts, sufficiently notorious,
speak for themselves. Nor, again, can this presentment be regarded as made officially in the interests

of the communicants and at the suggestion of any of
them.   On the contrary, they are much aggrieved at
the proceedings.   You will, indeed, perceive from the
entries in our books that the number of communicants
continually increased up to the time of my inhibition,
numbering over eighty at the Easter Festival.   The
result of these proceedings was that this flock (for a
City church a large one) was dispersed, and in consequence our missionary work among the young broken
up.   I do not wish to say that this was the result
really desired, but was clearly such as in all probability
was likely to occur.   It surely, then, is most unjust for
persons to complain of what they must have known
would be the certain result of their own acts.   After
all, my Lord, it amounts to this : that persons who
have been for years self-excommunicated complain to
you because they cannot now compel a devout congregation to receive the Blessed Sacrament in a way that
congregation regard as irreverent, and urged on them
in the interests of what they believe to be heretical
doctrine, and who, rather than do this, seek Celebrations elsewhere.   For I must point out to you that these
acts of mine have been with the concurrence of my
communicants and after repeated consultation with
them.   We are quite aware that we are involved,
against our will, in a controversy which affects not,
simply our own congregation but the Church at large.
St. Vedast has been singled out as a focus about which
is to rage a controversy which seems to us to involve
not the ritual, but the doctrine of the Blessed Sacrament.   We are fully aware also that any action we

may take may not be without its effect on the general
progress of the litigation now unfortunately proceeding. We can easily understand that our legal opponents may have very special reasons for wishing to
commit us to some course of action, and we, on our
side, are equally convinced that it is desirable in the
interests of the Church not to precipitate any action
at all. Hence we determined that it was better, for
a time at least, to hold back and allow other cases,
involving the same principles as those for which we
contend, to make some progress before we did anything
which, either legally or otherwise, might prematurely
bring matters to an issue. If the principal result of
celebrating the Holy Mysteries is to be either a party
triumph or a legal victory—and this appears the probable alternative—no one can blame us for proceeding
with a caution and deliberation involving consequences
which might in other and happier circumstances be
altogether reprehensible.

Then again, my Lord, I cannot look upon the persons presenting me as really acting of their own minds.
It is a matter of very common notoriety that my real
prosecutors are a powerful Association, who have been
not only publicly thanked for their assistance, both
moral and material, but have been subsidised out of
parish estates of which I am the trustee. Now, as
guardian of the trust funds, I have had for many years
past to protest against what I consider an injudicious
expenditure and lax accounts. This duty, always
painful enough, has been complicated with a theological
dispute, and that by the action of this society. They

have thus compelled me to take the, naturally, very
unpopular course of appealing to the proper authorities,
under the penalty of being otherwise made personally
responsible for the moneys illegally contributed to
assist in my own prosecution. Again, another great
wrong has been done me. The professed object of the
society is "to uphold the doctrines and principles of
the Church of England, and to counteract the efforts
now made to subvert her teaching on essential points
of Christian faith, or assimilate her services to those of
Rome." Those who present me do so at the instance
of this Association. They are naturally not theologians,
and unable to judge of the real point at issue. Yet
this society, without a morsel of evidence, assumes that
I wish to pervert the doctrines of the Church and
assimilate her services to that of the Church of Rome,
a charge I most indignantly deny. That is, my
Lord, this irresponsible and self-constituted body have
branded me publicly as a dishonest heretic. This
society has, moreover, stirred up repeated prosecutions
against me—has encouraged the malcontents by afford-
ing special prominence to these prosecutions in their
organ ; and when all this fails, have accepted a donation from public funds to mitigate the loss incurred in
urging and promoting proceedings. These, my Lord,
are facts which have one by one come to light in the
course of these proceedings. I may also state that
I am at this moment acting under the advice of the
proper authorities to recover the money unlawfully
contributed, that, therefore, to say the least, it would
have been more decent to have delayed the present-

ment until their judgment should be made known. Thus, at least, the solemn responsibility which surrounds the Blessed Eucharist would cease to be complicated with the baser issues of expenditure of charity accounts and the legal responsibility of public trustees. On this ground alone, if there were no other, I should court the strictest investigation, and be only too thankful that my Bishop should examine the whole matter. You will then know how much I have borne in what I believe—you may think me mistaken—the cause of Catholic Truth in that Church whose priest I am, and whose scriptural doctrine and ritual I am bound to maintain with all my power of body and soul. One word in conclusion. By no means think that in ceasing to celebrate the Blessed Sacrament at St. Vedast I have any desire of saving myself. God helping, I will maintain what I hold to be the faith, doctrines, and ritual pure and undefiled at whatever personal loss to myself.

This paper was not read at the Cathedral on the 29th of October, for the reasons given ; it was, however, afterwards submitted in all its arguments to the Bishop, as a clear account of Mr. Pelham Dale's line of defence.

It may be imagined that, having been frustrated in his desire to make his public defence before the Bishop and clergy, Mr. Dale was disagreeably surprised at receiving the following official letter from the Bishop :—

FULHAM PALACE, S.W., *November* 18, 1879.

REV. AND DEAR SIR,—At my visitation at St. Paul's, the Churchwardens of your two parishes made the presentments of which I had previously given you intimation.

They were to this effect :—

First, that since August 1878, the Holy Communion has not been administered at the Church of St. Vedast, not even on Easter Sunday, and that no notice has been given of Communion.

Secondly, that during the same period the first part of the Communion Office, viz., the Commandments, Collect, Epistle, and Gospel for the day, &c., have been entirely omitted.

With respect to this second point the Rubric is precise :—" Upon the Sundays and other Holy Days (if there be no Communion) shall be said all that is appointed at the Communion until the end of the general prayer [for the whole state of Christ's Church militant here on earth], together with one or more of these Collects last before rehearsed, concluding with the Blessing." The Act of Uniformity Amendment Act authorises the separation of the several prescribed services, but not the omission of any.

I have, therefore, as your Ordinary, to direct you to comply in future with the Rubric above quoted.

With respect to the former presentment, it is ordered " that every parishioner shall communicate at the least three times in the year, of which Easter to be one." Hence it has been reasonably inferred that every parish priest is bound to provide for his parishioners opportunities of communicating at the least three times in the year, of which Easter is to be one. Nor is he exempted from the duty by the belief, however supported by experience, that his parishioners will not come. No one can foresee the future. They who have not come, may come. If they do not, the fault and loss will be theirs. We shall have done our duty towards them, and obeyed our Church's law.

I must therefore direct you to give warning for the celebration of the Holy Communion at least three times in the year, of which Easter shall be one, and to celebrate it on the days and hours named; if there be four (or three at the least) to communicate with the priest.

I need hardly add my hope that the opportunities will not be limited to three times in the year.—I am, dear sir, your faithful servant,   J. LONDON.

In addition to this formal letter, a copy of which was sent to the churchwardens, and printed by them with the monition, the following letter was enclosed :—

DEAR SIR,—On examining the presentment of your Churchwardens, I found that there were other complaints besides those to which the accompanying admonition refers; but I am advised by my Chancellor, as indeed I had concluded myself, that they relate to matters which cannot be dealt with in Visitation, and as such I am referring them back to the Churchwardens.

The matters are additions or alterations stated to have been made in the church without the leave of the Ordinary ; and certain practices presumed by the Churchwardens to be illegal, such as kissing and putting on a stole, and coming into the church at

Baptisms and other times with a procession headed by a cross-bearer with a lofty mounted cross.—I am, dear sir, faithfully yours,   J. LONDON.

It was not only that he was not aware of the presentment, and had lost his opportunity of defence, that troubled Mr. Pelham Dale; it was that this reproof and curt information should be the only reply to his full and confidential letter written to the Bishop from Lincolnshire. He had not regarded the first letter from the Bishop in any other light than that of friendly warning, and he considered himself both unjustly and unkindly treated by this action. It was then, as always in this case, as if he could never obtain a hearing. He wrote in reply :—

MY LORD,—I enclose a printed paper which fills me with surprise. I was at the Cathedral on the 29th. My name was never called in my hearing, nor was any presentment made. The admonition which I received from your Lordship I had, under the circumstances, regarded as private, and so you can imagine that to find it printed made me feel the injustice with which I had been treated. I had in my letter to your Lordship expressed my willingness to defend myself, and state my reasons for the course I have thought right to take, and accordingly I had a written defence in my pocket at the Cathedral. Moreover, I had written to you on Thursday, asking if you had any commands for me on Friday the 29th. To neither of my letters have I received any reply.

In reading the printed paper, you will see that there is a desire to interfere again with the altar. I have received from my people a request that I should resume

my Celebrations without those Catholic adjuncts, which
we all hold dear, rather than give up my work. I
shall be glad to know, in case of my acceding to their
request, if I can look to your Lordship for protection
against the encroachments and interference of my
Churchwardens.

The wish expressed by his people was that he should be
contented with actual necessities, the Eastward Position
and mixed chalice, until the fund question had been settled.
Rightly or wrongly, it was generally believed that, if the
Royal Commission ended with the usual wholesale confiscation, the interest in vestries and parish affairs would
die out, and the mission work at St. Vedast would go on
steadily, attracting no attention from the ratepayers; but
the Rector was convinced that the enmity would not be so
easily calmed, and that the Bishop could not be relied upon
for any support. The question at the end of the letter was
put to prove this, and it was proved by its being ignored in
the reply, which was as follows :—

December 3, 1879.

MY DEAR SIR,—I do not rightly understand your
letter, in which you express your surprise that you
"did not receive some sort of intimation of the presentment of your Churchwardens."

It was in answer to my intimation to that effect that
you wrote the two letters which you refer to. The
clergy are not cited at my Visitation till the last day;
but whenever I observe in their Churchwardens' duplicate presentment anything which affects them, or in
which I think they would be interested, I give them
privately notice, as I did to you, in order that they
may attend if they please. This is all I do, or ought

to do, as I have no right to *require* them to be then present.

I rather gathered from your second letter that you intended to be in the court; but a note received on the day, and which I have not kept, informed me that you would be engaged at church in your services till twelve, at which hour the Visitation is over. When your Churchwardens were called, however, some one said that he had seen you in the Cathedral, and I sent over to inquire, but you were not found.

I have again looked over your letter, and I do not find anything now—nor did I then—which appeared to require or invite any reply from me. The Churchwardens had lodged this presentment in my Registry; they were not at all willing to withdraw or modify it; nor indeed could they, as it only stated facts. You yourself did not seem to wish it withdrawn, but said that you did not shrink from it. There was nothing more for me to say.—I am, dear sir, faithfully yours,

J. LONDON.

This letter seemed neither just nor kind to the much-harassed Rector of St. Vedast. He had, he felt, taken every precaution; he had not left the Cathedral until one, and neither he nor the friends with him knew that the presentment had been made. He was now single-handed, so was compelled to take the service himself. He wrote the following explanation on December 4th, the day he received the above letter :—

MY LORD,—I took care to be at the Cathedral in ample time before the hour mentioned in the citation. I was present the whole time to the end of the charge, except between the hours of 1 and 2 P.M., the time of my service. I was so near a gangway amongst the seats that I could have been very easily found. It was therefore no fault of mine if I were not in attendance at the exact spot, but the neglect was due to the arrangement of the Visitation.

As to the presentment itself, I wish to observe that the mere fact of there being no Communion does not imply necessarily any fault in the priest—the rubric directs that there shall be, &c., a sufficient number to communicate with the priest, at his discretion.

I have only to show, therefore, that I exercised a sound discretion in the matter. My letter to you made no admission of any kind; it was impossible it should, as when I wrote it no charge had been made, and I cannot accept an admonition which has been heard *ex parte* but as a mere private document, expressing a wish on your part, which in the case of the Table-prayers had been already complied with.

I feel this the more as the Churchwardens have none of them attended the church as communicants, and, with one exception, not at all. Besides which, I have taken especial pains that no one who really desired any services, public or private, from the Rector but should have ample opportunities of expressing the wish. I can assure you I should have only been too glad to have met these wishes to the utmost of my power.—I am, my Lord, your obedient servant,

T. PELHAM DALE.

To this letter he received the following curt reply, written by the hand of a secretary and signed by the Bishop. It put an end to all hopes of explaining his position, and to any belief that the Bishop wished to enter into it :—

MY DEAR SIR,— I am in receipt of your letter of the 4th inst. Let me first remind you that you have never given me any intimation that you had resumed reading the "table prayers," meaning, I assume, that part of the Communion Office which is directed to be said on Sundays and other holy-days if there is no Communion. Had you done so, I should not, of course, have included this matter in my admonition.

I must also point out that no clergyman can possibly tell whether there will or will not be a sufficient number to communicate with the priest, unless he has given "warning for the Celebration of the Holy Communion, which he shall always do upon the Sunday or some holiday immediately preceding." Without this no one could be expected either to come for the purpose of communicating, or to signify his name to the curate at least the day before.

I am a good deal surprised at your calling my admonition "a mere private document expressing a wish on my part." The terms I used, "I have, as your Ordinary, to direct you," are not those of a private letter expressing a wish: they are the words of the Bishop directing certain things to be done, which are undoubtedly lawful and honest, in virtue of the oath of canonical obedience which you have taken. And I purposely avoided the use of any more formal document ; because it has been often said that if the Bishops would deal with their clergy more in accordance with the *forum domesticum*, without the interposition of

legal deeds and legal officers, they would meet with
more cheerful obedience.

If, however, you wish for an admonition under hand
and seal, you may have it. Should this not suffice, I
should have no resource, being alternate patron of the
benefice, but to send, most unwillingly, the complaint
to be dealt with by the Archbishop under the Church
Discipline Act. A Churchwarden's presentment at
Visitation touching matters of omission so serious
cannot be neglected.—I am, dear sir, faithfully yours,

J. LONDON.

This letter decided the matter. To be rebuked and admonished on such a subject, he who never let either Sunday or Saint's Day pass without a celebration of the Holy
Eucharist, was more than painful—it was at once humiliating
and absurd. He had himself been shocked at the profanity to which such trials had already led, a profanity that
was continuing at that moment, to the shame and sorrow of
all reverent Churchmen. He had imagined that the fear of
a repetition of such an act would influence not Ritualists
alone, but all devout men; he found that the desire to
please the State came far before the dread of any insult
for the Church. He thought that the misappropriation of
charity funds would be considered a serious evil; he learnt
that to preach the Gospel to those who were not ratepayers
was a greater offence. However, his road was now plain,
he was forced into the front of the battle; in spite of himself his position had become a prominent one, and so his
resolution was taken.

If every weapon were to be allowed against a Ritualist,
he would suffer for his convictions. He would resume his
services, gather his people around him, and be attacked for

what it was an honour to defend. On December 16th he wrote to the Bishop as follows:—

MY LORD,—The time is now come when I must speak quite plainly. You are perfectly well aware that the presentment is a mere incident in the suit, and has no religious significance whatever, except as it bears upon present party controversies. My duty is quite plain, however. I hold that the legal (so-called) Cele-bration of the blessed Eucharist is irreverent, and I had rather brave a loss of all than do a conscious dis-honour to my Present Lord. I hold the Eucharist to be the true Christian sacrifice, where God meets with us to speak to *me* there (Exod. xxix. 42). I must, therefore, simply decline to offer the sacrifice without the usual adjuncts, especially the mixed chalice, only forbidden, as I believe, in the interests of a doctrine more false and unscriptural than that it professes to oppose. I shall therefore celebrate at an early oppor-tunity with these adjuncts, and take the consequences, whatever they may be.

As I write this only after the most careful considera-tion and earnest prayer, the final result of many months' deliberation, I do so, not acting in any spirit of defiance, but as a final appeal to that *forum domesticum* to which you allude in your letter; that is, to the Bishop, not to the State officer, but the Father in God, and by episcopal consecration over me in the Lord. I must, therefore, ask you to treat this as confidential, as I will your reply. I can assure you that I do not allow a day to pass without special supplication for my Bishop; and I truly feel, whatever may be the event, that I may hope for the Divine guidance and blessing in this most painful crisis.—I remain, my Lord, your faithful servant,   T. PELHAM DALE.

After waiting ten days, on December 27th he received a letter, this time written by the Bishop:—

MY DEAR SIR,—You must pardon my silence; but the whole of last week was occupied by the examination and services of a large Ordination.

I look with respect on all conscientious conviction; but I confess myself at a loss to understand how rites can be held to be irreverent which satisfied such men as Hooker and Bull, Beveridge and Cosen, with many others, whose high-toned devoutness I for one am accustomed to look up to with a kind of admiring envy. Surely a Ritual which was sufficient for them may suffice for me; and at any rate those adjuncts can hardly be held to be *essential* which they were content to do without. And non-essentials, however much we ourselves may be disposed to value them, can never be pleaded before the Divine tribunal in justification of disobedience to lawful authority, or even, it would seem (Rom. xiii. 1, 2) to *de facto* authority, " the powers that be."

Nor indeed is it a light thing to break the traditions of our own branch of the Church Catholic, which have been in use for three centuries, and were adopted, not in carelessness nor in irreverence, but on grounds of fitness and reason. The unmixed chalice, *e.g.*, was the retrenchment of a custom which had become an unreality, and which had even to be defended on grounds of which the primitive Church knew nothing. "They" (*i.e.*, Tertullian and the ancients), writes Dean Field, the friend of Hooker, "mingled water with that wine which they consecrated in the Blessed Sacrament, because even in ordinary use their wines, being hot, were wont to be so allayed; we, not having the like reason of mixture, mingle not water with wine in the Sacrament, as likewise the Armenians do not; yet are we not contrary to the ancient Christian use continuous of old observations." [1]

This reason for our Church's custom has at least much weight, while to hold the necessity of using the mixed cup because it was so used at the first institution (which is not certain), is to concede the primary argument of those who refuse to kneel at the Lord's Supper.

In the matter then of the mixed chalice and the other disused accessories of the Celebration of the Holy Communion, such as the Eucharistic vestments, incense, and lights, we are assuredly safe in following the use of our own branch of the Church Catholic, and the practices of her holiest and ablest divines; while we are not safe in disobeying lawful authority. I venture, therefore, to believe that your Ordinary will be "reverently obeyed" when he "admonishes" you, as I do now, to abstain from all these additions, and to celebrate the Holy Communion as was formerly your wont, as it was that of your wise and venerated Father.

Praying for you in this and all things the guidance of God's Holy Spirit, I remain, very faithfully yours,

J. LONDON.

[1] The writing here is difficult. The Editor has no means of verifying the quotation.

Most unfortunately the copy of the answer to this letter has been lost; but it might not be difficult to guess the reply to the Bishop's arguments. On the difficult subject of the new court and its usurpation of episcopal power he could not be persuaded to formulate an opinion. It was this, however, that prevented Mr. Pelham Dale's submission to him as his Bishop, that in the former case he had found that the Bishop had withdrawn and left Lord Penzance in his stead.

Notice was given at St. Vedast on Christmas-day that the Celebrations would be resumed. The Bishop writes again on December 30th :—

MY DEAR MR. DALE,—Has not conscience a right to put in a plea on the other side ? Or has the lapse of thirty-four years worn out the obligation of those solemn words, "I will endeavour myself, the Lord being my helper, reverently to obey my Ordinary, . . . and them to whom the charge and government of the Church is committed, following with a glad mind and will their godly admonitions"? Are you *quite sure* that this vow may not stand to witness against you ? I write anxiously, because it is the feature of the present day which most of all alarms and distresses me— the apparently light ground on which the obligation of solemn vows, and even oaths, is minimised, or even disregarded.—Very faithfully yours,

J. LONDON.

In this letter of exhortation, as in others, allusion both to the officials of the Public Worship Regulation Act, and to the opinions of the party forcing their doctrines on the Church by the use of these courts, is avoided. The conscience of the churchwardens was spoken of with invariable

respect, but the Rector's difficulties were of no moment.
Looking back to this time of persecution and officialism,
let us not underrate the struggles and burden of anxiety
suffered by those who won us our present freedom. Let
us remember the apathy and dulness that was creeping
over services and parishes unrebuked, even honoured ; and
let us thank God for those who, amidst all the coldness,
sneers, and indifference, found courage to stand firm. We
are very far from perfection still ; we have time-servers,
expediency-worshippers, promotion-hunters with us as of
old, but we have learned to respect a single-hearted, conscientious worker. We have learnt to regret the scorn and
want of sympathy that drove out Newman ; that left the loyal
scholar Dr. Pusey to die without receiving a single honour
from the Church he served so well ; that added to the
burden and shortened the lives of Charles Lowder and
Alexander Heriot Mackonochie.

But in 1879 it was the fashion to scorn and revile these
men ; their motive for hard work and self-sacrifice was
traced to a secret connection with Rome, or to an enjoyment of the offertories.

"Don't tell me, sir ! It sticks to their fingers — it
sticks to their fingers !" was the exclamation of a business
man, who considered the alms-bag the only motive of the
service.

The case of Perkins v. Enraght was usually heard at the
same time and in the same manner (i.e., no appearance of
defendant) as Sergeant v. Dale. It was in the prosecution
of Mr. Enraght that there was the disgraceful scandal of the
theft of the consecrated wafer, afterwards produced and exhibited in court. Neither the Archbishop of Canterbury or
the Bishop of Worcester could refuse to notice so grave an
act of sacrilege.

On the 12th of December 1879 the Archbishop of Canterbury obtained a surrender of the consecrated wafer, and

it was reverently consumed by him in the chapel at Addington, in presence of the President of the English Church Union and a Mr. Douglas, representing the Bishop of Worcester.

Mr. Dale and other members of the High Church party were informed of this; but the reparation went no farther at that moment; no steps were taken to prevent a repetition of the sacrilege.

On December 12th a decree was applied for, pronouncing the Rev. Thomas Pelham Dale in contempt for his refusal to pay the costs. "The judge," writes a friend who was present, "said 'Be it so,' and the matter was done."

CHAPTER XII.

IN 1880 it seemed to many that the Church of England
was doomed. The violence of her internal disputes, the
official aloofness of her rulers, who, Gallio-like, "cared for
none of these things," the high price set on peace and
respectability, the cool indifference to hard work and self-
denial, were all so prominent, so forced upon the attention,
that they appeared more universal than they were. Over
and over again those of the High Church party were repulsed
and insulted; their work was ignored; it could be dispensed
with, and they were urged to go and leave the Church to
that moderation of everything to which she had attained.

The Rector of St. Vedast found himself brought, as it
were. to bay. He did not consider either his work or his
services the fittest representatives for his party; he had
tried to withdraw from the prominent position into which
he had been forced; he had tried in vain to separate the
ritual dispute from the parochial funds dispute. He had
made the facts of his case public; he had brought it before
the Bishop, with the most certain expectations that the concessions he had made would be gladly accepted and used
in his protection until the cases were disentangled. But the

weakness of his position, his four opposing churchwardens, his non-resident parishioners, recommended him as a subject for attack. There were the alienated laity. True, they never had come to the parish church of their business houses; but then the services had been held for the benefit of others, and no one in those days considered clerks who paid no rates of any value.

It is not every one who can credit the sincerity of an opinion he does not share. But when, like the Rector of St. Vedast, he himself does do so, it is the more bitter to find the confidence is not returned, that concession is counted weakness. But it has probably always been that the sting of persecution lies not in the mere battle between religion and the world, the Christian and the heathen, but in those more subtle differences that cause a man's own familiar friend to draw back from him in doubt and hesitation, and because of that familiar friendship communicates the thrill of doubt and hesitation, making him question, "Who am I, that I should be right and he wrong?"

The Early Celebration was begun again on December 28th, and it was now decided to resume the High Celebration with full ritual.

On January 7th he wrote to the Bishop in answer to his letter of December 30th:—

MY LORD,—I do indeed regard obedience to my Ordinary as a very solemn obligation, only to be set aside by that still more solemn one of "driving away erroneous and strange doctrine." This in my case has, it seems to me, really occurred. I have been singled out by a Puritan society, notoriously my real prosecutors, to enforce a doctrine which I believe to be unscriptural, and which is certainly not that of our Church, nor of the Catholic Church at large. This is the Zwinglian doctrine that the Eucharist is simply a commemoration, not a mystic sacrifice, as the ancient Church taught. If, then, at their bidding I should surrender the position of protest into which I have been forced altogether against my will, I should do that which is equivalent to placing the pinch of incense of old time on the idol altar. No doubt, in themselves, the matters in dispute are non-essential, but not in a *test* case; and you will remember that I was taken even before Mr. Tooth, and when the law was yet undetermined even by a decision so questionable as that of the Ridsdale case. I would willingly have made concessions to the scruples of any who think differently to myself, and to this end intimated to the presentants my desire for peace; to no purpose, however, for no names were sent in as wishing to attend the Celebration. I feel, therefore, that the whole transaction connected with the presentment was simply another attempt to force upon the Church of England false doctrine, and that *non-possumus* was my only answer. Had it been otherwise, your wish would have been enough, and it is plain that my own personal interest is altogether on the side of compliance as things are.

Excuse this delay in answering your letter, but I did not wish to reply without careful consideration, such as, indeed, your kind letter deserves at my hand.—I remain, your faithful servant,   T. PELHAM DALE.

What thought and anxiety went to make up these decisions, only those can imagine who can also conceive the sensitive, conscientious, large-minded nature of the man thus beset. Here the very width of his sympathies and anxiety to see all sides of a truth were against him; he must, as his custom was in all questions, take the arguments of all sides into consideration and be certain of each fact for its own sake. His hatred of publicity was balanced by his dread lest the dislike should over-influence him. He slept but little for the working of his anxious active mind, often spending half the night in discussions on the subject. His wife was his *confidante* and sympathiser, less inclined than he for argument and more easily convinced, but ready with him to make any sacrifice for the sake of his conscience.

So the services were resumed as fully as the fact of his being single-handed permitted. At the first Celebration only one parishioner was present, so that he need not legally have held the service, especially as he was aware that the attendance was more for observation than worship. But the members of the Guilds of St. Lawrence and St. Agatha, who were not ratepayers, came to the church, instead of going to their little oratory, which was henceforth disused.

Having taken this step, Mr. Pelham Dale dismissed all further idea of conciliation or compromise. He went steadily on, ignoring the proceedings of his opponents. To his surprise, the order against him was allowed to run out, and he was not, as he expected, arrested at once. That public opinion would prevent imprisonment being resorted to, was generally written and said at this time.

There was some idea that the Commissioners would institute a prosecution for recovery of the £75, 13s. 6d. accredited to the Church Association in the accounts of the parish charities. On February the 10th a friend writes that "much curiosity exists in legal circles as to the upshot of the Attorney-General's action against churchwardens. It is rumoured that the Church Association have decided to refund."

The vestry clerk wrote to the Commissioners on 4th of March :—

DEAR SIR,—The contents of your letter of the 26th ult. have been communicated to my clients, and I am desired to assure you that no further sums shall be paid or applied out of the funds of the charities in aid of the funds of the Church Association. This assurance I hope you will consider sufficient.

The £75, 13s. 6d. will be found credited in the current year's accounts of the charities, and I trust that I may now consider the matter settled. I will do so unless I hear from you to the contrary.

The secretary of the Charity Commissioners did not accept this cool assurance as sufficient redress. The money was ordered to be refunded. The last subscription of £85 was returned, but the churchwardens refused to pay back the remainder, and the Association profited by it, as no further steps were taken.

On the 13th of March a fresh inhibition was applied for, and promptly issued by the official principal of the Arches Court of Canterbury on the 19th, and executed on the 21st.

On the 15th the Bishop wrote to say that he had just seen in the newspapers, with surprise and regret, that Mr. Pelham Dale had again been proceeded against under the Public Worship Regulation Act. " Can nothing," he writes, " be done to prevent this ?" and desires him to call at the Palace on the morrow, the Tuesday in Passion Week.

The only expedient the Bishop had to propose was resignation or surrender; but the time for these had gone by. The Rector of St. Vedast would not again surrender his rights to Lord Penzance, even through the medium of his Bishop.

On March the 18th he wrote to the Bishop :—

MY LORD,—I have very earnestly considered what you said in our conversation of last Tuesday.

I acknowledge not only its great weight and importance, but the kind and fatherly way in which it was urged. I can, however, come to no other conclusion than that which I then expressed. I must therefore act in the matter as my brother Mackonochie has done in like case—receive with all courtesy any gentleman you may choose to appoint during the inhibition, but must refuse to recognise him as my substitute in any way.

I trust, therefore, it may be possible so to arrange as to avoid any open scandal in the matter, it being my intention to dispute the position.—I remain, my Lord, your faithful servant,   T. PELHAM DALE.

The same appointment was made as at the last inhibition. The Rev. Charles Tabor Ackland being licensed as curate to St. Vedast, Mr. Ackland wrote to Mr. Pelham Dale on March 19th :—

MY DEAR MR. DALE,—The Bishop has again laid on me the unpleasant duty of taking charge of the services at St. Vedast's. He tells me that you will not recognise my position, but that you desire that matters shall be so arranged as to avoid any open scandal. To carry out that desire I write this letter. I propose to be at St. Vedast's on Sunday next at 9.45 A.M., prepared to take the services. Mr. J. B. Lee, the Bishop's secretary, will accompany me. In the event of your refusal to allow me to perform the duty laid upon me, to avoid scandal I shall retire.

For the better avoidance of scandal, will it not be well that no one shall be in the vestry save our two selves, the Bishop's secretary, the Churchwardens, and such friend or legal adviser as you may think it desirable to have with you. If this suggestion shall meet your wishes, will you kindly give the directions necessary to carry it out ?

With the like object, I have requested the Churchwardens to make in writing, not by word of mouth, any protest they may wish to make against your course or mine.

If I shall not be venturing too far, may I ask that you too will give your reason in writing, if it be your intention to assign any reason for refusing to allow me to take the services.

I think the course suggested in this letter will remove all chance of open scandal, and the time of the interview will not interfere with the arrangements for the services.

It will be my duty to report the result of our interview to the Bishop, and to ask his directions as to what further steps, if any, shall be taken.

I trust very earnestly and believe that the same kindly feeling will remain between us that governed our relations with one another when I was before compelled to obtrude myself upon your notice.

Believe me to be yours very faithfully,

C. T. ACKLAND.

The Rector had prepared his protest, and the programme given in the above letter was closely carried out. With regard to his friendly relations with Mr. Ackland, though he had no desire to behave uncourteously, he never understood why Mr. Ackland considered himself bound to interfere in the matter, and to accept the curacy of St. Vedast against the Rector's wishes, nor does the letter offer any explanation. The 21st was Palm Sunday; the first inhibition had been resisted at the same season four years ago. A copy of the inhibition was fastened to the door of the church, and a similar document served on the Rector. The Bishop's secretary, Mr. John B. Lee, accompanied by Mr. Ackland, arrived at the church shortly before ten o'clock.

Mr. Pelham Dale received them in the vestry-room of the church, where were assembled three of the church-wardens, Messrs. Sergeant, Horwood, and Bengough, and four members of the choir.

Mr. Lee made a statement of the circumstances under which he appeared there, presented the curate-in-charge, and exhibited the license, giving a copy to Mr. Pelham Dale. The Rector then read the following statement :—

REVEREND SIR,—Though willing and desirous to obey the Bishop in all lawful commands, I must, notwithstanding the document read to me, refuse to allow you or any other priest to supersede me even for a time in my ministrations at St. Vedast. I am urged to this course for the following reasons :—That the charge of souls of this parish was committed to me on the 23rd day of April 1847 by Charles James, then Bishop of this diocese ; that, therefore, as one who has been canonically instituted to such a charge, conferred by the Bishop in his office as a successor of the Apostles, and according to the order instituted in His

Church by our Lord Jesus Christ, I should be guilty
of grievous sin, and great unfaithfulness to the Church
I serve, were I to cease to exercise my mission at the
bidding of any authority of a less divine character than
that by which I was appointed.

Now, I have not been suspended from the office
thus conferred upon me by any court which has like
authority from God to deprive me of what He has
given, or thereby to release me from the responsibility
of holding it and using it for Him to the best of my
power, He being my Helper, till He shall take it from
me or call me to my account.   Therefore, I hereby
declare that no priest has, or can have, any right or
power to minister in this Church during my occupancy
of the charge save myself, and any others whom I may
authorise to officiate in my stead.

Dated at the Vestry of St. Vedast, this 21st day of
March 1880.   T. PELHAM DALE,

Rector of St. Vedast and St. Michael-le Querne.

Mr. Lee warned the Rector of the consequences of his
refusal to obey the Inhibition of the Court of Arches, and
to recognise the license of the Bishop; to which Mr.
Pelham Dale replied that he was aware of the consequences,
and prepared to submit to them.

The curate-in-charge then read his statement as follows :—

To the Reverend Thomas Pelham Dale, Clerk, Master of
   Arts, Rector of the United Parishes of St. Vedast,
   Foster Lane, and St. Michael-le-Querne.

Whereas you have been Inhibited from performing
any Service of the Church, or otherwise exercising the

Cure of Souls within the Diocese of London; and
whereas the Bishop of London has given to me, Charles
Tabor Ackland, Clerk, Master of Arts, his Episcopal
License and authority to perform the office of Stipen-
diary Curate in the Parishes of St. Vedast, Foster
Lane, and St. Michael-le-Querne during the continuance of the said Inhibition; and whereas, in discharge
of my duty, I have presented myself to take charge of
the Services and perform the Ecclesiastical duties belonging to my office; and whereas you have declared
that you will not recognise the License of the Bishop,
whereof a copy has been given to you. Now I, deem-
ing that any further attempt to-day to discharge the
duties of my office, in the face of your expressed determination to dispute my position, may give rise to
scandal, do for the present retire, under protest, to
report to the Bishop the circumstances which have
prevented me from obeying his directions, and ask his
instructions as to what further steps, if any, shall be
taken.   CHARLES TABOR ACKLAND.

March 21st, 1880.

With which legally-worded statement the interview ter-
minated, the only expression of feeling being the indignant
protest of one of the churchwardens when Mr. Ackland
shook hands with the Rector.

The churchwardens printed the proceedings in the Court
of Arches, the inhibition, and the description of the interview and statements read, adding as a footnote: " Mr. Dale
subsequently proceeded with the services as announced,
viz., the ' *Litany* at 10.15 A.M.; *Matins* at 10.30 A.M., and
Celebration (Choral),' the latter in the ILLEGAL and INHI-
BITED *manner*," and presented the whole account, nicely

printed on good paper, "With the Churchwardens' compliments to their fellow-ratepayers and parishioners, 23rd March 1880."

There had also been an Early Celebration, and in the evening there were Evensong and Sermon; all of the services, four in number, were taken by the Rector.

The Monday papers gave an account of the proceedings, adding that the Rector in resisting Lord Penzance's monition was taking the same course as that pursued by Mr. Mackonochie. In the sermon no allusion was made to the proceedings; the services for Holy Week were given out, with the list of preachers for the week and Good Friday. The services on Good Friday began at nine in the morning and ended at nine at night, the three hours being taken by Mr. Rhodes Bristow, of St. Stephen's, Lewisham.

The *Record* for that week announced that application would shortly be made to the Dean of Arches to signify the contempt in the usual manner, with a view to the committal of Mr. Pelham Dale to prison.

This was what the Rector of St. Vedast expected; he imagined that it was the object of his opponents in forcing him to take this course.

Day by day his friends opened their morning papers expecting to read the news of his arrest and imprisonment, but for the present the step was delayed, though constant attacks and annoyances prevented the pause being a peaceful one.

He was warned of an attempt on the part of the churchwardens to lock him out of the church, and to prevent this he took the keys into his own keeping, being determined not to be driven into legal proceedings to regain possession, if it could be avoided. The churchwardens had duplicate keys, but these they would not allow to be used, so the Rector had to be at church some time before the service began, to ensure proper lighting and warming. At the Easter Vestry the comments on this action were loud and noisy. The organist had been kept waiting outside the church; the church was like an ice-house; if the sexton could not get in when he wanted, he had a right to refuse to go at all; finally, they (the churchwardens) had been advised not to allow their keys to be used, and they should not be.

It being very evident that these annoyances were not likely to decrease, Mr. Pelham Dale prepared to submit to the inevitable, and went patiently on his way, sparing himself in nothing, and gathering a congregation once more into the little church.

On the 28th of April he received notice that the Court of Chancery had appointed the vestry clerk and three others as commissioners "to sequester your real and personal estate" to pay the costs.

The sequestration was delayed until July, when once more the slow moving Charity Commissioners demanded the annual accounts.

The Rector had, as usual, to complain of letters written in the name of the trustees without his knowledge or permission. He had ceased to expect any definite result from these annual revelations, but made them as advised.

Meanwhile, the sexton, with whom the Rector had always been on friendly terms, had begged possession of the keys for his own convenience, promising not to let them go out of his possession; so for some time the petty inconveniences had been lessened. The senior churchwarden discovered this alteration, and came down upon the man with a threat of dismissal if he opened the church. On the 30th of July Mr. Pelham Dale found the church locked. The reason for this betrayal of trust was not far to seek; the appointment was a good one; the servant was at the mercy of the churchwardens. He went with the man to the office of the churchwarden and remonstrated at such a use of his power. The remonstrance was useless as far as removing the penalty

from the servant in case of disobedience to the churchwardens, but it made them hesitate about keeping the church
closed at the time service was announced.   It was a Friday,
and at the time of the usual Evensong the Rector found
the doors open and everything prepared.   The choir were
there, and also several members of the Church of England
Working Men's Society, all anxious to do their best to
support the Rector.   Such a mode of attack was not likely
to drive away supporters.   It rather raised the spirit of
resistance and indignation.   They considered, whatever the
authorities might say, that it was their rights against the
tyranny of the ratepayers that were being defended by Mr.
Pelham Dale and those like-minded.   There was an eager,
excited group in the vestry after the service.   The Rector
remonstrating with the sexton, who, very white and nervous,
could not risk disobeying those in power, while the younger
men crowding round were longing, many of them, to capture
the keys by force.   However easy and final such a method
might be, it was not likely to be permitted by the Rector,
who at last sent for a policeman and went with the sexton
to Bow Street.   The case, he was told, must be dealt with
by a summons, not, as he had hoped, by an order to the man
to return the keys to their owner.   There was no doubt
that anything done by the attacking party would, if declared
illegal, be punished by a nominal fine ; it had always been
so.   If Mr. Pelham Dale lost the church, it might be very
difficult, however strong his position appeared, to capture
it again : so he was advised.   He determined to hold it.
The vestry was a separate room, as has been elsewhere
explained ; the Rector and one or two of the choir remained
there all night ; the working-men relieved guard and brought
food.

The matter was not so quickly arranged as was at first
expected ; the summons appeared useless, and Saturday and
Sunday nothing could be done.   It was not until Tuesday

afternoon, by putting fresh locks on the doors—of which the churchwardens no longer had duplicate keys—that they were able to retire from their stronghold. After this a series of petty annoyances was still continued. The church was lighted by a gaslight in the centre of the ceiling, and the lighting-rod was taken away; when a substitute for that was made, the crank for turning on the gas was carried off, and so on.

Again, in August the case was brought before Lord Penzance, with the view, it was supposed, of getting an order for imprisonment before the mid-summer vacation, but decision was postponed in all three cases—viz., of Mr. Pelham Dale, Mr. Green of Miles Platting, and Mr. Enraght of Bordesley—until the 28th of October, so that they too had a vacation free from fresh legal troubles. The sequestration and attendant worries form the greater part of the correspondence of the months of August and September. The committee of the English Church Union took upon themselves the repayment of sequestered money as well as all law expenses; so, though Mr. Pelham Dale was far from making his fortune, as many declared, he did not actually lose by the proceedings against him.

CHAPTER XIII.

AT this time party feeling ran very high. On the one side
those that were attacked were drawn together by a common cause. The knowledge that their privileges and their
churches might be taken from them made them prize and
reverence them the more. It gave a greater meaning to
the prayers, the daily psalms, and the Gospels. Every
attack that was made, seemed to fall on some day specially
rich in promises or comfort for those persecuted. In many
of the offices and warehouses men found it expedient to
conceal any leaning towards Ritualism, and this outside
antagonism strengthened the sympathy and brotherhood of
the worshippers. The church became the centre of interest
and affection. There was a certain risk, a certain amount
of sacrifice, implied in each man's attendance there. As for
the priest, promotion and reward in this world had already
been given up, and sequestration, imprisonment, suspension,
were threatening him. It was the fashion to deny that the
working-classes were attracted by Ritualism, but there was
not one of the attacked clergy who was not the object of
affection and respect to a large body of working-men ; and
these feelings were fostered by the persecution, which was
so far beneficial. It gave a reality, a sincerity, a vitality to

their religious life. It roused, to be sure, a certain fighting spirit; but yet, how well that spirit was kept in check! Again and again they refrained from retaliation, and from that desire to "have a row" which is so natural to the healthy young Englishman when insulted.

On the 28th of October Lord Penzance sat in the Arches Court, the Arches Court being a dressing-room—described in the *Times* as "The inconveniently small room which the authorities of the Palace of Westminster are pleased to appoint." *Punch* had a little sketch of the difficulties of the reporters in obtaining seats on the washing-stand, the boot-jack, or the mantelpiece. The secretary of the English Church Union secured standing-room, and telegraphed to Mr. Pelham Dale that the *writ of significavit* was granted against him, decision in Mr. Enraght's case being postponed to November 20th. The explanation was added in a letter, that if the writ were not used within ten days of being issued, it lapsed.

One reason against using the writ was the attention imprisonment was sure to attract. It was urged by the promoters of the Bill that if the law was left to run its course, it ended by heaping every possible penalty on the head of the person prosecuted—sequestration, suspension, deprivation followed inhibition and monition. This course of forbidding the priest to exercise his office and taking from him his living was the crueller and quieter penalty; but it was lengthy, and the prosecutors wished to feel their power at once.

The 28th of October is the festival of St. Simon and St. Jude. Mr. and Mrs. Pelham Dale went together to St. Vedast in the early morning, and at the Early Celebration they made a special intention that the mission work might be allowed to continue. How rapidly this work had grown since the resumption of the ritual was shown by the service held on the 26th. This was the Harvest Thanksgiving. The choir and their friends had done their best to make the service particularly beautiful. "The altar," says an account in the *Citizen*, "was the chief feature. Vested in white, and embellished with numberless vases of flowers, choice fruit, and about forty candles, it presented a very striking appearance." On these occasions the dark wood-work, with the rich carving at the east end, made a most effective background for the white frontal, flowers, and candles; and that everything was the gift or the handiwork of the worshippers there, added not a little to its value. At half-past seven in the morning most of the regular members of the congregation were present and received the Blessed Sacrament. At a quarter past one the Te Deum was sung, and a sermon on the harvest preached by the Rev. C. E. Brooke of St. John the Divine, Kennington, to a large congregation, composed chiefly of business men.

By the evening the rain was pouring down, but in spite of the weather the church was thronged, and upwards of two hundred people were unable to get standing-room. The choir was assisted by members of other choirs, many from Fast-End churches, and an instrumental band, which, like the organ, was played by men who gave their services freely. After the sermon by the Rev. R. H. Clutterbuck of St. Philip's, Clerkenwell, there was a procession, the banners and white-surpliced choir passing down the middle aisle, and up the south aisle by the oak-wainscoted wall, singing, "Come, ye thankful people, come;" "Praise, O praise our God and King;" and finally, with a depth of meaning that thrilled all present, "Faith of our fathers" was sung before the altar.

This service was the climax of the mission at St. Vedast. In it the Rector saw the fulfilment of his wish. No longer silent and deserted, the quaint, dark, little City church was a centre of life and religion for those workers in the great city to whom he had from the first longed to minister, and who now crowded into the high pews and along the ill-paved aisles.

It was the prayer that this work might be continued that

the Rector and his wife offered in the church in the morning
of the 28th. There was to be another such service on All
Saints' Day, but the preparations were in vain; from that
day to this no such sounds and no such worship have ever
echoed within the walls of St. Vedast.

While he was taking the 1.15 service on the 28th the news
from the court was telegraphed to his house, and he received
it on his return. His wife was not sorry to have the suspense so far over; she was beginning to be anxious for his
health, upon which the want of rest and excessive worry
were telling. Many still said that the writ would never be
served, and no one doubted that All Saints and All Souls
would be kept before the end came. On Saturday the
30th Mr. Pelham Dale went down to St. Vedast. On his
way home he called upon a friend and was begged to stay
to dinner. He accepted, but said he would go home and
tell his wife of his engagement. Meanwhile a man had
called at Ladbroke Gardens to see Mr. Pelham Dale. Mrs.
Dale offered to deliver any message, and her suspicions
were roused by a refusal, polite enough, but followed by an
urgent inquiry as to when he could be seen. She could
not say, but she and her daughter noticed the man about
the street the rest of the afternoon. Unfortunately she
did not know where her husband was, or would have sent
to warn him and so postponed arrest until Monday. They
watched for him from the window, but the officer was too
quick for them, and the Rector of St. Vedast was arrested
as he came up his door-step. He, the tipstaff, and a clerk
from the lawyer of the prosecutors, entered together. The
clerk settled his hat firmly on his head and sat down in the
hall. The tipstaff, on the contrary, was as civil and obliging
as it was in his power to be. The arrest was complete, he
said; there would, he supposed, be no resistance.

"Of course I shall not resist, but I protest against the
arrest as illegal," Mr. Pelham Dale answered.

"In that case, sir, I am sorry to say it will be my duty not to let you out of my sight," was the reply.

There was a little delay, first that Mr. Pelham Dale might have something to eat, since it was out of the question that he could keep his engagement to his friend, and then while a few necessary things were put together. Meanwhile his daughter went out and telegraphed the news to their friends, passing the little clerk, who stared at her with his hat on. The idea that the Pelham Dales had of prison were chiefly drawn from Mr. Pickwick's experiences, and they were glad of the advice of the friendly tipstaff. A cab was called, and the prisoner's daughter came back from the post-office in time to kiss him and take the church keys which he gave her as he said good-bye. Mrs. Pelham Dale went with him, hoping that she might be allowed to see him in his rooms.

The sheriff's officer gave Mrs. Pelham Dale his card on the way, asking as he gave it that he might be allowed to assist in any subscriptions or demonstration against the imprisonment. It is a long drive from Notting Hill to Holloway; it became a very familiar one to Mr. Dale's family in the next two months. On a Saturday night the thoroughfares at the Camden Town end are crowded. The flaming gaslights over cheap stalls, the shouts of the vendors, the swinging of the doors of the gin-palaces, the throng of men and women and the children (who never seem to be put to bed), were a commentary on the imprisonment of one who had made a centre of religion and refinement in the great city.

The streets became quieter near the prison, and the cab stopped in front of a great archway, the gates were opened, and they drove into the outside yard. Here a second court, surrounded by buildings and ornamented by the City griffin, is entered between two small porter's lodges, where flaring uncovered gas-lights show whitewashed walls with printed

rules and regulations hanging on them, a few seats and a
desk in one, and a few seats and a table in the other. Two
warders came out and received them, inviting Mrs. Pelham
Dale to accompany her husband into the lodge. The
luggage was taken to be searched. Some papers were
signed, and the affair was complete. A warder holding a
heavy bunch of keys requested Mr. Pelham Dale to follow
him, adding that the luggage would be brought to his rooms
after it had been examined. Very anxiously Mrs. Pelham
Dale asked the official if she might not be allowed to see
her husband's quarters and stay with him a short time.

The man was respectful, even considerate in his manner,
and explained that he could not admit any one without
an order; but added, seeing her disappointment, that she
would not probably find much difficulty in getting one;
meanwhile he would look after Mr. Pelham Dale, and anything that was wanted could be sent the next day. She was
allowed to cross the inner court, where at another door
they had to separate. They said farewell, and she watched
him enter, and heard the echoing clang of the iron-bound
door down the stone passages as it shut between them.
Her pang of anxiety, helplessness, and loneliness was a
sensation not easily forgotten. It remained in her recollection as the most painful moment of all. She was, moreover,
anxious about her husband's health, and he had an abscess
on his right hand, a sign of weakness and debility that
alarmed her.

The porter directed her to the governor's house, but
both he and the deputy-governor were said to be out.
Unable to gain any information there, she drove to St.
Alban's, Holborn, where she found the news had already
been received. From thence she went to Mr. West, of St.
Mary Magdalene's, Paddington, where she met with that
perfect sympathy and kindness which he showed throughout the whole time of trouble.

Being far too restless and anxious to think of sleep, she and her daughter were sitting up talking after the rest of the household had gone to bed, when the bell rang. The late visitors were some six or seven working-men, who stood hesitating, full of sympathy, but afraid of the sight of a wife's grief. Their relief was great when they were eagerly welcomed by Mrs. Dale, who was thankful to have friends with whom to discuss the best means of getting access to her husband. The men had already drawn up bills to be printed, announcing their indignation at the imprisonment, and they declared their intention of going to Holloway that night, late as it was, to try and see the prisoner, and learn his wishes for their conduct on Sunday. So they started on their errand, leaving Mrs. Pelham Dale much comforted by their sympathy and energy, for half the pain of her position lay in the consciousness that she was doing nothing, and could do nothing, to help her husband. They were so far successful that their representative, Mr. Powell, obtained an interview with the governor, who, while refusing to allow him to see his prisoner, assured him that Mr. Pelham Dale should be treated with the consideration due to his character and position.

That the arrest took place on a Saturday was a great hardship to the prisoner's family and friends. Nothing could be done on Sunday ; offices were closed, officials were absent. After the Early Celebration at St. Mary Magdalene's and breakfast at Mr. West's house, Mrs. Pelham Dale went again to the prison, but was told she could not see her husband. Again she went to the house of the governor, Colonel Milman, who was still not to be seen. Mrs. Milman, however, came out, and assured her that Mr. Pelham Dale was quite well and comfortable, and that she would be allowed to see him at eleven on Monday ; and with this she was forced to be satisfied.

There was a crowd of the usual worshippers outside the

closed church of St. Vedast that morning. The choir-master fastened a notice on the door—

" In consequence of the Rector of this parish, the Rev. T. Pelham Dale, being confined in prison for conscience-sake, there will be no service in this church until further notice."

One of the prosecuting churchwardens read the notice, and stated that there soon would be a service, an incident noted in the *Times*.

The Bishop's legal secretary came and looked at the closed church, and in the evening Mr. Ackland paid an equally legal visit, to show that he would have taken the service if he could.

The Archdeacon was surprised at the speedy process of the writ, and, preaching at St. Paul's in the afternoon, recommended a quiet submission to the law.

The *Times* and *Guardian* add to their account that Messrs. Moore and Currey having refused to proceed with the case if it entailed the incarceration of a clergyman, another soli-citor applied for the necessary writ.

At St. Mary Magdalene's Mr. West went into the pulpit after the Nicene Creed, not to preach—the sermon had been given at Matins—but to deliver an emphatic protest against the imprisonment of the Rev. T. Pelham Dale.

On Saturday evening the prisoner had been taken to his rooms on the ground-floor and shown the prison rules, the one bearing hardest upon him just then being that the gas was to be extinguished at half-past eight at night. The long dark night, without the accustomed relief of light and books, seemed endless to his excited but weary brain. But six o'clock, the time to rise, came at last. The rooms were far from luxurious, nor were they capable of being made so. They were two cells knocked into one, with a little bed-room, just large enough to hold a bed and a washing-stand. The small pointed windows were closely barred, and looked out on the cabbage-sown exercising ground, where the prisoners took the air, under the superintendence of the warders. The first room had a small window in the wall, through which the prison authorities could inspect the prisoner—not that they ever did so in Mr. Pelham Dale's case. A small round table and two chairs were as much as the first room with the fireplace could hold, a cupboard and a deal table furnished the second division. The floors and wooden furniture were clean enough, but the walls and paint were well-worn and shabby.

The question had been asked on coming into the prison whether he would take prison fare or have his food supplied from without; he chose the latter, and owing to the refusal of admittance to Sunday visitors, he found it difficult to get anything.

For breakfast he had some prison bread, which was excellent, and cocoa, which, being sweetened, he could not drink. About one, a dinner was sent from a public-house opposite—a dish of highly-flavoured Irish stew. But the smell in the small close rooms turned him faint and giddy, and he begged the warder to take it away again, preferring the bread-and-water diet to any more attempts at the public-house cooking.

By Monday he was in the doctor's hands, and profited by more suitable food and proper attention to his right hand, which he was forbidden to use.

On Monday Mrs. Pelham Dale was told she could see her husband for half an hour every day, or for an hour every other day. She chose the daily visits without hesitation, and spent the short time in noting down what was necessary for his comfort.

By Monday morning an account of the arrest was in all the papers, and the news brought with it a general expression of surprise and indignation. Most persons, whatever their opinions, had come to the conclusion that imprisonment being a most unsuitable punishment, it would never be resorted to. Mr. Pelham Dale's standing, his scholarship, his age, were declared to be sufficient protection, and those prophets of peace found their good-hearted prophecies falsified by the action of the prosecuting party. Many of the ecclesiastical authorities, disagreeably surprised at the result of the Public Worship Regulation Act, betrayed an irritable impatience. Persecution in the nineteenth century was impossible; therefore either imprisonment was not persecution or Mr. Pelham Dale was there by his own wish. The whole thing was ridiculous and absurd, and they wanted it put a stop to. They blamed the fanaticism which had used the weapon they themselves had forged, but most they fumed at and blamed the inconvenient conscience that objected to have any civil judge rule in spiritual matters. Others, more generous, lifted their voices in defence of the prisoner. From the moment he entered Holloway Gaol, Mr. Pelham Dale received sympathetic letters and messages from persons of various opinions, as well as those of love and gratitude from his own party.

On Monday Arthur Dale came up from Lincolnshire, and set to work at once to gain all possible relaxation of prison rules, and went with the working-men from office to office for that purpose. In these cases the rulers, like the unjust judge in the parable, yield to a sufficient amount of pressure, "lest they be wearied." Mrs. Pelham Dale and her son went together to London House and succeeded in seeing the Bishop, who, however, stood carefully aside, and made them understand that he had no interest or influence in the matter.

Mr. Gladstone, then Prime Minister, was not to be seen; his secretary, Mr. Liddell, gave them an interview, but could do nothing except bestow upon them the characteristic party advice, " If you want anything you must agitate."

This they had every intention of doing, and by Wednesday the order for severity in Mr. Pelham Dale's case was withdrawn, and permission was granted for his wife and one member of the family to visit him daily, at first for an hour, but finally the time allowed was from nine till four. His son obtained leave at once to be with him from twelve till four, to write the letters which his maimed hand prevented his writing himself.

On the first Monday, before any of these concessions were made, Mrs. Dale was with him for a short half hour, made shorter by the anxious fear that something important for business or comfort should be forgotten in the hurried interview.

"'To every other caller," says the *Times*, "a refusal had to be given, and these numbered over thirty before midday; but their cards were sent in, and also the fruit and flowers which many of them brought." *

The prison officials were from the first most kind and attentive. "Don't you mind, miss," said one of the warders to his daughter, who was waiting in the white-washed office with some parcels; "it ain't as if he was in for anything wrong."

It was not only these men who expressed their sympathy, but policemen, guards, cabmen, and men of like position took opportunities of showing their kindly feelings for Mr. Pelham Dale and his family. The prisoner's health had suffered considerably from the strain and suspense. He was unable at first to take advantage of the permission to walk alone in the exercising ground, as he suffered from attacks of giddiness, and, with many apologies to the good-hearted warder, he requested him to accompany him for his constitutionals. He thought himself that his heart was affected, and though neither then nor eleven years later could

* Among the rest was a beautiful bouquet from Mr. Spurgeon's congregation.

THE EXERCISE GROUND, HOLLOWAY PRISON

the doctor find any sign of disease, his death from heart-attack showed that the weakness he believed in was there.

The sisters working in the parish of St. Mary Magdalene —a branch from Wantage—brought him his dinner every day from the houses of different members of the congregation. He had a small appetite and preferred plain food to dainties—nor would he ever have anything hot on account of his dislike to the smell of cooking in his own room. He was allowed a great luxury—from a prison point of view: a tea-kettle, and afternoon-tea was the most cheerful meal of the day.

Mr. Ackland having conferred with the Bishop of London, called at the prison to see if he could obtain from the Rector the means of getting an entrance into the church, but at first no one was allowed to see Mr. Dale except those whose names had been submitted to the authorities as connected with legal business. Colonel Hardy of the English Church Union and Mr. Powell of the Church of England Working-Men's Society could come daily. The latter brought with him all the newspaper extracts bearing on the case.

Failing an interview, Mr. Ackland sent in the following letter, written on Monday, November 1 :—

MY DEAR SIR,—The Bishop of London is informed officially that the Church of St. Vedast was throughout yesterday closed against public worship and so remains. His Lordship is, of course, aware of the steps which led to this, and they gave him much pain. But he considers it absolutely necessary that the Church should be available for public worship on Sunday next, and as the Churchwardens state that they have no means of access, the only keys of the door being in your possession or custody, I am instructed by the Bishop to inquire whether he may rely upon the church being open to the public for Divine Service at the accustomed hours on Sunday next—and I am to inform you that Mr. Ackland, who, as you are aware, holds the Bishop's license for the purpose, will be quite prepared to take charge of the services.

The Bishop would prefer that during your enforced absence you committed the care of the church key to his Lordship, but it will be sufficient if he has your assurance that all needful arrangements will be made for the holding of the public services on the next and all succeeding Sundays.

The bearer of this letter will wait to bring back your answer.—I am, my dear sir, yours faithfully,

JOHN B. LEE.

No answer could be sent, since on that Monday Mr. Dale was alone, and was unable to use his hand.

About a week later the Bishop sent his footman to the prison with orders to bring back the keys of the safes. The man did his best to carry out the command, and the officials were rather indignant at the messenger and his pertinacity. He could not of course penetrate farther than the lodge, but imagined that the keys would be taken from Mr. Dale's keeping by a warder and handed over to him. The keys were really in the hands of the legal advisers, to be used or not as they thought fit; but had they been with Mr. Dale in prison, the officials would have taken no steps in the matter, and would certainly have permitted no one who was not in authority to command them or their prisoner.

Mr. Pelham Dale felt the insult of this incident acutely. He was a man whose manner and position had hitherto secured him from indignities. But now this was one of many such pangs—never inflicted by those in whose custody he was—but coming from that outside world which protested loudly that martyrdom of any sort was impossible and absurd in this century. However, if the prisoner were not a good fighter, and could neither oppose retaliation nor indifference, he was a good sufferer, for he bore neither malice nor hatred, and was often in after days the one to excuse or explain the actions of his opponents.

The Church of England Working-Men's Society took up the defence of the attacked clergy with energy and enthusiasm. They made preparations for a mass meeting of their society, as the best refutation of the constant denial of their existence in the papers. They placarded walls with appeals and notices published by them. One of their posters ran as follows :—

ENGLISHMEN!

The Reverend

THOMAS PELHAM DALE,

Rector of St. Vedast, Foster Lane,

Now lies in Holloway Jail,

A Prisoner

For Conscience Sake.

Is it to be tolerated that a man like him, who has for a quarter of a century served the Church well and faithfully, shall be incarcerated in a common prison. And for what ?

For doing that which his conscience believes to be right, and in strict accordance with the Prayer-Book.

If Mr. Dale is put in prison for conscientious

disobedience to so-called law (on which judges and
other high legal authorities differ in opinion), why are
those clergy who openly break the plain rules of the
Prayer-Book to be let alone ?

FAIR PLAY FOR ALL

An Englishman's Motto!

— · — · · —

Issued by the
CHURCH OF ENGLAND WORKING MEN'S SOCIETY,
69 HIGH HOLBORN, W.C.

C. POWELL, *Secretary.*

Besides a good many bills of this description, the Society
issued many excellent little tracts and leaflets explanatory
of Mr. Pelham Dale's position.

The choir-master wrote to the Bishop of Lincoln, Dr.
Pusey, Canon Liddon, and the Bishop of Bedford.

Canon Liddon replied on Monday, November 1st, as
follows :—

MY DEAR SIR,—On the subject of Mr. Dale's imprisonment, if my sympathies were with the persons who
have promoted it, I should regard such an event as a
very great misfortune.   For, unless all history is to be
distrusted, persecution is, in the long-run, much more
fatal to the cause of the persecutors than to the cause
of the persecuted.   Mr. Dale will not forfeit the consideration and affection which his life and character
deservedly command on account of an incident which,
in all probability, the more far-sighted as well as the
more considerate of his opponents already regard with

very great regret. Certainly they have good reason to do so. Once more thanking you for your letter, I am, my dear sir, yours very truly,   H. P. LIDDON.

Dr. Pusey answered almost as promptly from Christ Church, Oxford, November 2 :—

MY DEAR SIR,—I thank you for your early information that your pastor, Mr. Dale, has been sent to gaol like an ordinary felon, although, of course, he will receive whatever courtesy prison rules will allow. At his age (I am told about sixty), I suppose that it may gravely affect his health, if not his life. It will be a blot hereafter upon the administration of English law in this our nineteenth century that, while our Supreme Court of Appeal has informally interpreted the law most rigidly in favour of any one accused of heresy, it has used special pleading to condemn the use of a vestment and any one who should wear it.

No Church Court could have pronounced that to act in conformity to a direction contained in the Prayer-Book, which is put into the hands of us, the clergy, as our guide in our ministration to our people, should be a venal act. No words could be plainer than those prefixed to the order for morning and evening prayer : " Such ornaments of the church, and of the ministers thereof at all times of their ministrations, shall be retained and be in use as were in the Church of England by the authority of Parliament in the second year of King Edward VI." No one doubts that the vestment, for wearing which your clergyman has been sent to gaol, was one of those ornaments. English

VOL. I.   T

common sense will prevail against the special pleading of lawyers. You are probably aware that a minority of the members of the Privy Council, among them the Chief-Justice Kelly, whose sound judgments were esteemed so highly, did not concur in the judgment for contravening which Mr. Dale has been sent to gaol. It is not the law (which all Englishmen respect), but a misinterpretation of the law, which your clergyman has contravened. But the remedy is in your own hands. If you and the parishioners of the two other parishes, whose ministers Lord Penzance speaks of sending to jail, petition her Majesty to exercise her prerogative and to restore you your clergy (although I, who am not acquainted with any who have access to her Majesty, have no right to form any opinion), I could scarcely doubt that her Majesty would graciously listen to a request so reasonable.

I write this as not belonging to those who are called Ritualists. I may, therefore, be held impartial when I say, that no one of those who are now recognised as having done good service to the Church nearly fifty years ago, in awakening her when half asleep, had the slightest doubt about the meaning of the Rubric, for obeying which your minister has been sent to gaol.— Yours very faithfully,   E. B. PUSEY.

Once again Arthur Dale wrote to the *Times*, and endeavoured to put the real state of the case before the public. This obtained more success than previous attempts, since public attention was fixed on the matter.

SIR,—Allow me to make a few remarks with regard to the imprisonment of my father. Is it not a disgrace

to the boasted toleration of the nineteenth century that
an old man of blameless life and untiring activity
should be imprisoned for conscience-sake ? But the
case is really far worse than appears on the face of it.
Through the migration of the citizens of London west-
ward, my father found himself with an empty church.
Undaunted by this, he determined, if possible, to gather
a congregation round him. He was enabled to do this
the more easily by the energetic support he received
from several young men connected with the City. The
services commenced with a very moderate ritual. But
whether the ritual were moderate or the reverse, the
opposition was always the same. Perhaps it was
natural from their point of view that the churchwardens
should object to the services; but it was perfectly unnecessary that they should descend to petty annoyances
and little meannesses. But never once was retaliation
even thought of. Those who know my father will
agree with me that such a thing was impossible. After
seven years of ceaseless worry and endless vexation,
the dispute has culminated by my father being incarcerated in Holloway Gaol; and this has happened in
spite of constant overtures of peace made by my father.
In appealing to the public through your columns, I
would refer them to the able article that appeared in
the *Times* newspaper concerning the misappropriation
of the charity funds of St. Vedast. Also, it must never
be forgotten that the Church Association has received
£75 from the charity funds towards paying abortive
costs. Perhaps this has more to do with the rancour
of these gentlemen against my father than religion ;

but, whatever the reason, the fact remains that it is a
scandal to all concerned that an old man of great learning and long service in the Church should be ruthlessly
torn from his family and thrown into prison. But not
only have his family suffered, but also his united congregation in being deprived of his much-prized ministrations.—Yours, &c.,   ARTHUR MURRAY DALE.

But though the *Times* and the *Standard* both had leaders
on this letter, they still held that the consciences of the
churchwardens were to be held in reverence, passing lightly
over the Rector's difficulties and ignoring the most important altogether. Excepting the *Morning Post*, no single
London daily paper ever acknowledged a clergyman's right
to a conscience. At this time the *Morning Post* was a
threepenny paper, and consequently little read by any but
rich or fashionable people—by what Jeames calls the
"upper suckles;" but its championship of the High Church
cause brought it so many willing supporters, that it de-
scended from its fashionable height to become the popular
daily paper which it now is.

As soon as he had an amanuensis Mr. Pelham Dale
wrote to the Bishop in answer to the letter from Mr. Lee,
appointing his son as curate to St. Vedast. No answer
was received in time to do anything before Sunday, and the
legal advisers were of opinion that no service should be
taken until the Bishop's acceptation of the Rector's nominee.
Before Sunday the churchwardens broke into the church
and took possession ; but somewhat alarmed at the illegality
of the act, they announced that their reason for doing so
was the urgent need of repairs. The church was indeed,
as the Rector had said again and again in discussion on the
expenditure of the funds, in a disgraceful condition. The
floor was sinking, and the rats from the vaults below invaded

the building. The rats, said the churchwardens, were attracted by the candles, and had nothing to do with the vaults ; but now they suddenly discovered the real state of matters. They kept commissionaires in the church to prevent the Rector's friends gaining admittance ; they locked and padlocked the doors on the inside and entered only through the vestry by Priest's Court. On Sunday the doors were not opened. Mr. Ackland came. Mr. Arthur Dale with the choir and working-men came also, expecting that there would be a service, which Mr. Ackland was prepared to take, and Arthur Dale intended to make the necessary protest on his father's behalf against the breaking open the church. The Rector in his prison cell at Holloway spent an anxious Sunday, in the fear lest his friends should be led into any violence by the unexpected action of the other side. No collision however occurred ; there was a unanimous opinion that the churchwardens had gone beyond their powers, but those acting for the Rector contented themselves with keeping a man to watch the proceedings of all who entered the church. The man reported that possession was kept night and day, the watches being relieved. The men on guard, he said, complained of the swarms of rats— one had run up under the coat of a man, who flung himself on his back and killed it. Perhaps some of the long threatening subsidences had made a fresh opening for these creatures.

CHAPTER XIV.

MR. PELHAM DALE needed an amanuensis in Holloway;
even then it was impossible, especially as he could not
write himself, to answer all the letters during the hours
spent with him in prison; and often one or two hundred
were brought back to Ladbroke Gardens to be acknowledged from thence. Most of these letters were expressions
of sympathy from individuals, and votes and resolutions
from Church Societies. But there were some very curious
effusions amongst them. There was a note from a gentleman pointing out the extraordinary fact that Mr. Dale had
been taken to prison on the writer's birthday. There was
a lady, a poetess by her own account, who wrote on foolscap
paper, and filled many sheets. She began by charging
Mr. Dale, on his honour as a gentleman, not to try and
find out who she was. Then, after a sketch of her parent-
age, childhood, and girlhood, she showed how in maturer
life she had reconciled her clergyman and churchwardens,
when they disagreed about the cross as a church decora-
tion, by the happy suggestion that it should be put up, but
where no one would see it! A remarkable fact was that
persons of all sorts and descriptions felt themselves capable
of giving advice, warning, or rebuke. Some of these were
black sheep, open and acknowledged sinners, who wrote to

remonstrate with the Rector of St. Vedast in letters that were grave and serious, without an intentional touch of humour in them. It is perhaps only a repentant sinner who can feel himself incapable of deciding a theological question. Then, there were the anonymous letter writers, some of whom expressed their opinions by foul words, which, though unpleasant to read, were far from convincing the recipient that his opinions were faulty because they were not to the mind of the writer. Scurrilous post-cards and unstamped letters (to try and make the prisoner pay a penny for a sheet of bad language was a very favourite trick) never reached Mr. Dale at Holloway. The governor protected the prisoner from such insults by returning them to the post-office, and the reporters, who were constantly at the gaol for news, were told that he did so. According to prison rules, every letter taken to Mr. Pelham Dale was initialed on the envelope by the governor. There were amongst these some honest expostulations; but entreaties not to light the fires at Smithfield, and suggestions that he might, like St. Paul, be persecuting the Church from mistaken zeal, were hardly logical when addressed to Holloway Gaol.

But the letters of sympathy far outnumbered the others. They came from all quarters—words of comfort and cheer from fellow-priests, congratulations and expressions of respect from old friends and from friends hitherto unknown; letters from working men and women of various occupations; letters from barracks and ports, manufactories, shops, and warehouses. One, to whom writing is evidently an unaccustomed labour, says at the end of his letter, "I am only a poor working-man. I know I cannot come to London on the 18th to raise my voice with those thousands who will do so then, but I can raise my voice when I kneel night and morning to say my prayers. Yes; I will pray that God will give you a speedy deliverance, and that He will forgive all your persecutors." "God is with you, and

takes care of you," writes another; "I always remember
you in my prayers. I trust in God that you will soon be
released from such an awful place. We must leave it to
God. God will punish." Another says, also a working-
man, "I think from my heart it is a disgraceful thing to
place you where you are. Let us fight together for our cross
till death." "We pray," writes one, "that the time is not far
distant when you will come out of your tribulation shining
like a bright and glorious star, as did the saintly men of
old who had washed their robes in the blood of the Lamb."

It was after a mass meeting of working-men that Mr.
Tooth had been released, and much was hoped from the
coming demonstration. The large hall of the Cannon Street
Hotel was taken for the purpose, and proved much too
small. The meeting was for men only. Many came from
the Midlands and returned by a night-express, so as to be
at their work again in the morning. The street outside
was blocked by the crowds that could not gain admittance,
and for a while traffic was stopped. The authorities were
not a little anxious, and appealed to the secretaries for
assistance in clearing the street. As it was certainly not a
fit place for an overflow meeting, the resolutions to be proposed in the hall were read and received with cheers, after
which the crowd dispersed.

Mrs. Pelham Dale had been offered by the secretary the
use of a small gallery from whence she could hear the
speeches. When she and her daughters came in, they were
both embarrassed and pleased at the mass of men rising to
their feet with cheers. The pleasure was for their prisoner's
sake. When they left him alone for the long evening and
sleepless night, they felt restless from sympathy, and anxious
to be doing some work for him. To see this crowded
meeting full of enthusiasm and affection for him and his
cause was a solace and comfort.

He had now been eleven days in prison, but the previous

strain and worry, followed by the unusual quiet and restraint
of prison life, affected his nerves, so that if by any chance
his wife was a minute or two late, he was full of anxious
imaginings of what might have happened while he was
powerless to help or assist her.

His son read the following letter to the meeting after the
Office had been said :—

*To the Members of the Church of England
Working-Men's Society.*

MY DEAR FRIENDS IN CHRIST,—I cannot forbear
a few lines to thank you for the interest you are taking
in my behalf. As one who has had the great privilege
afforded me in early life of seeing what work and
working-men really are, the dearest wish of my heart
has ever been that in some sort, since I have been
called to the priesthood, I might specially be called to
minister to working-men the Gospel of the grace of
God. I am, as you know, able to write but little, but
that is of the less importance, because I write to members of the Church of England. I will only say be
true sons of that Church which appeals to Holy Scripture and ancient doctors to establish her doctrine and
regulate the interest by which that doctrine is to be
impressed upon her people. Above all, remember that
we must in all our efforts not lean upon an arm of
flesh, and least of all condescend to handle weapons
of this world's warfare. Be temperate, therefore, in
speech, cool and calm in action, and as you work
harbour no feelings of resentment or anger against
those who differ from us. Rather let us try and speak
the truth in love, for it is not by might, not by power,

but by My spirit, saith the Lord of Hosts, that the
temple of the Lord will be rebuilt, and the tabernacle
which has fallen down be restored to its beauty and
loveliness.—Your faithful friend and servant in Jesus
Christ,   T. PELHAM DALE (Priest).

The announcement of this letter, written to them from
a prison-cell, was received with a burst of enthusiasm, the
whole mass rising to their feet and cheering and waving
hats and handkerchiefs. And the tone of the letter, which
is so characteristic that it recalls to those who knew him
the very sound of his voice, brought back the solemn feeling that the silence for prayer, and the thrilling sound of all
these men's voices thundering out "The Church's one
Foundation" had roused at the opening of the meeting.

The speeches were eloquent and wonderfully temperate,
considering the excitement and enthusiasm that animated
the meeting.

" We are here to-night," said the chairman, " not as
disloyal citizens to plot against the State, but as loyal
Churchmen, with hearts burning with zeal for the
Church of God. We are not filled with ardent rebellion,
but our loyalty to the law-makers brings us here to
prevent the one being prostituted, and the other from
doing acts that can only bring shame upon themselves.
We are all here as true subjects of Queen Victoria,
and we can all say heartily God bless her ! We are
also here to protest against all treason against Christ,
whose minister she is. May each speaker then to-
night speak plainly, for now is the time to speak, but
respectfully. Let there be no evil-speaking, no railing,
no threatening, but in the face of our enemies let us

show that we are Christians and communicants. While
stirred by a righteous indignation, yet are we subject
to the law of charity." Then further on he said, " We
are here to seek in every loyal manner to obtain the
release of the Rev. Thomas Pelham Dale ('So we will!'
called out his hearers); to prevent others from sharing
his fate, and to testify to the world our complete sympathy with him and those who are threatened, and to
urge others who are wavering, but whose congregations
may wish to advance, to cast away all doubts, and
boldly to proclaim themselves on the side of so-called
lawlessness. Oh, these moderate men! what a stumbling-block they are in every movement, and the
Church has a fair share of them—good, quiet, peaceable
souls, who will play at Ritualism so long as it is safe
and the Bishop does not frown ; but when a time like
this arrives, they tremblingly hold aloof, and whisper
dubiously about 'those extreme men,' and 'what a
trouble they are.' It is these 'extreme men,' your
Mackonochies, your Tooths, your Dales, your Enraghts,
and the like, that form a mighty breakwater, against
which the troubled and angry waves of Protestantism
expend their fury, so that those peace-loving, law-
abiding clergy may ride in smooth water, and enjoy
the comforts of their cosy parsonages amidst the happy
family circle. Let the extreme men be put away, and
see where the moderate men will be. He must be
blind who cannot see what is gradually creeping upon
the Church. Part of her patrimony has already been
confiscated by their legislative enactments in the cause
of promoting religious equality. Our churches will be

required next for Nonconformist services, and to-night we find an imprisoned clergyman as one outcome of religious liberty. What an anomaly is the Government, trembling and anxious one day lest they should offend the conscience of an unbeliever, and next throwing a priest into prison because he will not perjure his."

Later on the speaker alluded to Father Lowder of St. Peter's, London Docks, "who with his dying breath left a testimony to his loyalty to the Church." A good many more extracts might be made from the speeches of the evening, which were certainly above the common platform eloquence. Such an audience was enough to rouse oratorical talent, which always needs warmth and sympathy if it is to flow freely, but these examples will suffice to show the frame of mind of the speakers.

The City authorities were not a little alarmed at the crowd and the block in so important a thoroughfare, and the passage to the Hall was lined with police. The National Anthem was sung at the end of the meeting, and as Mrs. Pelham Dale came out of the Hall and down the passage, every policeman removed his helmet and stood bareheaded.

None of the daily papers noticed this token of respect ; only one local weekly demanded the punishment of the men, but it gained no attention.

Those who were present expected a good result from this meeting, but the Government took no notice of it.

In accordance with Dr. Pusey's advice, a petition to the Queen was set on foot and very largely signed. It was suggested that a direct appeal from Mrs. Dale was likely to gain attention. She wrote, therefore, as follows :—

MADAM,—I am venturing to appeal to your Majesty to right a grievous wrong that, committed in the name of the law, blots one of the purest reigns in our history. My husband is at this moment in Holloway Gaol, imprisoned for conscience-sake. That in this age a man should be classed with criminals for no act of immorality, for no wilful breaking of social laws, but simply for holding to those religious principles that seem to him to be taught by our Bible and Prayer-book, is surely a step back to those persecutions under which England groaned of old.

Madam, I appeal to you as a Queen to use the power that you have, and that it is known you will graciously use in a good cause, to rescue my husband from prison, and the most glorious and free reign of all English—nay, the world's—history from the accusation of oppression and religious persecution.

Madam, as a Christian, you would not desire my husband to hold his ordination vow of loyalty to a Heavenly King more lightly than that to his earthly sovereign, or to commit the sin of doing what his conscience and religion forbid him. Not even his worst enemies can accuse him of bad motives. Those he has gathered round him he has striven to teach the virtue of pure and holy lives, and for a reward is treated as if he had committed some of those sins against which he wars. Surely, if only in the interests of civilisation, those who would better the condition of our people, and, by example as well as precept, teach them to lead nobler lives and embue them with higher tastes, should be the last to be attacked and imprisoned.

Madam, as a wife and a mother, I appeal to you.

LIFE OF THOMAS PELHAM DALE

Only one who knows as I do the thoughts and life of my husband can appreciate the purity of his motives and the unselfishness of his devotion. And oh! Madam, certainly only one who has suffered as I now suffer can thoroughly understand the misery and sorrow that will fall on our land if husbands are to be taken from wives and fathers from children for religious opinions, and if a conscientious and right-minded man has to choose between the welfare of his family and his duty to his God.

Madam, I feel that in appealing to you my efforts will not be in vain, for I am assured by your life and by your actions that you love England and liberty too well to permit the dark cloud of persecution to obscure your hitherto free and happy country.

I subscribe myself, Madam, with all due reverence, your Majesty's loyal and faithful subject,

MARY DALE.

This was duly delivered to the Queen, and received this answer :—

BALMORAL, *Nov.* 13*th*, 1886.

MADAM,—I am commanded by the Queen to acknowledge the receipt of your letter of the 10th instant, in which you appeal to her Majesty "to right a grievous wrong" committed in the case of the Reverend Thomas Pelham Dale, now incarcerated in Holloway Prison.

In reply, I beg leave to inform you that such a petition can only be submitted to her Majesty by one of the responsible advisers of the Crown, and I would therefore suggest that any communication you desire

to make upon this subject should be forwarded to the
Secretary of State for the Home Department, for the
purpose of being laid before the Queen.

I have the honour to be, Madam, your obedient
servant, HENRY PONSONBY.

On this advice Mrs. Pelham Dale wrote once more :—

MADAM,—Your Majesty has graciously vouchsafed
to acknowledge, through General Ponsonby, a letter
which I took the liberty of addressing to your Majesty,
begging that your Majesty would use your royal prerogative to right a grievous wrong.

Your Majesty, through your Majesty's secretary,
informs me that my appeal must take the form of a
memorial. I venture on this encouragement to once
again bring my case before your Majesty, and beg of
your Majesty to consider whether you will allow my
husband to remain a prisoner in Holloway Gaol. My
husband has for thirty years laboured in the Church,
he is a scholar, was a Fellow of his college, one not to
take up a matter lightly, or to compromise himself by
rash enthusiasm. It cannot be in such an age as this,
with such a sovereign as your Majesty, any one, least
of all one like my husband, is to be imprisoned for
conscience-sake.

I feel I am right in petitioning your Majesty for justice. Your Majesty's loyal subjects know that their
gracious Queen loves liberty and truth ; and this persecution is not liberty, and to force a man to act against
his conscience is not truth.

I appeal to your Majesty as a wife and a mother to

take pity on me and on my children. We love and reverence my husband; we know most certainly the truth of his convictions, the purity of his devotion, and knowing this, what must we suffer when we see him a prisoner for conscience-sake, driven to choose between us and what he most solemnly believes to be his duty to his God.

Oh, Madam! let me not appeal in vain.—Your Majesty's most loyal and respectful subject,

MARY DALE.

This was sent to the proper quarter, and received the following unsatisfactory answer:—

MADAM,—I am directed to acquaint you that your application in behalf of your husband, the Rev. T. Pelham Dale, having been referred by the Queen to the Secretary of State, he regrets that he is unable to advise her Majesty to interfere with the process of the law in this case.—I am, madam, your obedient servant, A. F. O. LIDDELL.

So it was evident that Mr. Tooth's liberation, supposed to come from the Queen, was rather due to Lord Beaconsfield's diplomacy. But the Liberals, not feeling the same responsibility for the Bill, were inclined to encourage a law that seemed to lead to disestablishment.

Once again the hopes reckoned upon so certainly failed, and the prison doors were as firmly closed as ever.

It did not seem likely that the Church Association would willingly set its victim free, for at the first meeting after Mr. Pelham Dale's arrest, when his imprisonment was announced, the statement was received with cheers, and cries of " Let him rot ! "

The following letter to the chairman of the Church Association was written by one present at the meeting :—

SIR,—I am no Ritualist, for I am a Nonconformist, although brought up amongst the Evangelical party in the Church of England. Yesterday, chiefly out of curiosity, I attended a meeting of the Church Association, and I regret that I cannot congratulate you on the present spirit and temper of the Association. The "devil" of Ritualism (as you call it) cannot be cast out by the "devil" of religious spite and intolerance such as I witnessed yesterday. I purpose to make as public as possible my impressions of your meeting. I watched the countenances of many of your speakers and hearers, and I shall not readily forget the shade of malignity which was depicted thereon. Born in another age and under another sun, many of you would be worthy members of the Romish Inquisition ; you have all the fiendish rage and spite of Dominican friars. Fortunately the folly and ignorance of most of your supporters is limited by their obscurity. The *fiendish delight* with which the imprisonment of poor Mr. Dale was received made a painful impression upon me, and I overheard from all sides "Let him rot in prison!" from lips that had been professedly joining in prayer to God! Some of you would stop at nothing—you would gladly rekindle the fires at Smithfield, provided only they were for Romanists and Ritualists! Your pretended Association is a great humbug and a sham. You have in all cases singled out for opposition the needier men, and you have left the rich men in full possession of their "liberties." You have ignored the gross manner in which Evangelicals defy the law; but you seek by the most unworthy means to crush the weak. You are doing more harm to religion than you can ever do good to Protestantism. You mistake religious passion and religious hate for divine grace! Your whole wisdom is "earthly, sensual, devilish," and the liberties of Englishmen are unsafe in your hands.

After this meeting, of which the writer of the above letter gives his impressions, those, and they were not a few, who had believed that imprisonment would fail as a punishment, being as painful to those who inflict it as to those on whom it is inflicted, found their mistake.

Imprisonment for contempt was to last until the prisoner would purge his contempt, which, put into plain English, meant that he was to be kept in prison until he acknowledged Lord Penzance's right to be considered his spiritual superior.

There was in this position a tyranny of force that aroused the indignation of many men. A great number joined the English Church Union, and vestments were introduced into several churches on Advent Sunday. Where they had refrained for the sake of peace hitherto, they would not refrain from fear.

Meanwhile meetings were being held all over the country, both by the English Church Union and the working-men. The large London meeting of the former was announced for the 18th of November. It had been intended to take the Hall at Cannon Street for that, but the directors refused to let it on the ground of its inadequate size for the former meeting and consequent inconvenience.

In many churches Mr. Pelham Dale was prayed for by name, most of the letters from clergy and congregations promised him their prayers, and especially to remember him at the Celebrations of the Holy Eucharist.

The Church of England Home Mission Society printed the following prayer for daily use :—

A Prayer for the Rev. T. Pelham Dale, a prisoner for conscience-sake.

O God, without whom nothing is just, nothing is holy, in Thy pity, in Thy love, look down upon Thy Church, defend and bless it in this time of trouble, forgive all who, through ignorance or malice, are offending Thee in persecuting Thy faithful servants.

And most earnestly we pray that Thy Holy Spirit may support and comfort Thomas Pelham Dale, now a prisoner for conscience-sake. Grant, O Lord, that all shame and suffering patiently borne for Thy glory and the good of Thy Church, may be sanctified by Thee now, and rewarded and blessed to him for evermore.

Grant this, O God, for the sake of Thy Son Jesus Christ our Lord. Amen.

Arthur Dale made an effort to see the Bishop of London, but was refused an interview; and, as has been said, the second Sunday of the imprisonment passed without an answer to the letter written as follows from her Majesty's Prison, Holloway, November 6th :—

MY LORD,—I am advised it is my duty to nominate a clergyman to take my duty during my enforced absence. I beg to nominate the Rev. Arthur Murray Dale, now acting as curate of Sausthorpe, under the permit of the Bishop of Lincoln. Should your Lordship prefer my nominating a beneficed clergyman in your diocese, the Rev. R. T. West, Vicar of St. Mary Magdalene, Paddington, will undertake the charge.— Your faithful servant, T. PELHAM DALE.

P.S.—I regret that the bandage which I am obliged to wear on my right hand for the present compels me to employ an amanuensis.

As on Sunday the church was in possession of the churchwardens, the absence of reply did not cause the collision that the Rector feared. On November 11th came the following answer :—

MY DEAR SIR,—I beg to acknowledge your letter (which did not reach me till the 8th), in which you nominate the Rev. Arthur Murray Dale to take your duty during your enforced absence. I am unable to accept such nomination.

I need not remind you that, upon the publication of your inhibition by the Arches Court, I proceeded to make due provision for the services of your church and the cure of souls, and that I appointed and licensed the Rev. Charles Tabor Ackland to the charge of your parish during the continuance of your inhibition. Mr. Ackland has always been and is prepared to act under the license, and will consequently take charge of the duties of the church. I may add that it would not be possible for me to allow any clergyman to officiate in your church who would not be prepared to certify that he would perform the services of your church without those ornaments and practices which you have been monitioned to discontinue.

I am, my dear sir, faithfully yours,

J. LONDON.

The *Times* prints this letter, with the remark that the friends of Mr. Pelham Dale were much disappointed by the absence of any reference on the Bishop's part to Mr. Dale's present unfortunate position.

The members of the congregation of St. Vedast signed the following letter to their Rector :—

REVEREND AND DEAR SIR,—We, the undersigned members of your congregation and communicants of the Church of England, desire to express to you our sincere sympathy at your incarceration for conscience-sake in Holloway Gaol, to record our strong disapproval at your arrest, and to pledge ourselves to use every constitutional effort in our power to secure your unconditional release.

We must add that we shall recognise no clergyman officiating at St. Vedast unless he is duly authorised by you, and shall protest against any intrusion on or usurpation of your rectorial rights, should such be offered.

In conclusion, dear sir, you have our entire good wishes and prayers, believing that the battle you are fighting will help much to win back to our beloved Church that religious liberty which a State Church has done much to rob it of.

We are, reverend and dear sir, yours very faithfully in Christ.

They also held a meeting of protest in the Aldersgate Street Rooms, and made arrangements for such weekly meetings and services as should keep them together until a better time should come.

They met often for service in a chapel belonging to a mission-house of St. Alban's, Holborn. Once when the writer of these pages was going to one of these services with her sister, the cab stopped and the driver came to the window. "You'll excuse me, ladies," he said, "but the address you've given me must be a mistake; it ain't a fit street to take ladies to." He was thanked for his kindness, and it was explained to him that it was a mission-room, upon which he expressed himself satisfied, and drove to the address.

There, in this little oratory, the members of the choir and guilds connected with St. Vedast met for prayer, and to hear the few words of affection and greeting written to them from Holloway prison.

At first all deputations were refused admittance to the prisoner, but later the members of his choir were admitted, filling his room to overflowing, so that when he gave them his blessing at the end of the interview, some were kneeling in the passage outside. The organist of St. Mary Magdalene's, Paddington, Mr. Redhead, and his choir, got permission also to see Mr. Pelham Dale. He had taught for a time in the choir-school, so the boys knew him well. Mr. Mackonochie he had chosen as his spiritual director, and the visiting justices, unable to refuse pastoral visits amongst others, were at first disturbed at the selection. The perpetual curate of St. Alban's, Holborn, himself always more or less monitioned and inhibited by the new courts, brought the comfort of the Blessed Sacrament to his fellow-priest in his prison-cell. Such a scene hardly seems to belong to the present century. There was nothing sensational or hysterical in manner or mind of either of

these two. Mr. Mackonochie, a tall, thin, angular Scotch-
man, quiet, even repressive in manner, going his own way
with a stern determination to swerve neither to the right
hand or the left, refusing to acknowledge the worry and
anxiety of his position, being steadily resolved to go his
own way, do his best, and leave the issue altogether in
God's hands. Mr. Pelham Dale, a scholar, a scientist, and
a theologian, happiest when alone with his books and
studies, able for a while to forget his troubles in the
mysteries of logarithms or Hebrew roots, but hating the
publicity and the endless disputes that embittered his
resistance. Only the conviction that the liberties of the
Church were intrusted to him, and that to give up his
post would have meant yielding them, gave him strength to
stand firm. Those behind the scenes knew that these men,
each in their own way, suffered considerably under their
persecution. Mr. Mackonochie's ill-health and his touching death were the outcome of his stoically-borne anxieties.
Mr. Pelham Dale, retiring from his much-loved London
with shattered health, died of the weakness that first declared itself in prison.

END OF VOL. I.

PRINTED BY BALLANTYNE, HANSON AND CO.
EDINBURGH AND LONDON.